'The magic of silent cinema…is bro
of characters, some of them almost
eccentricities, make for engaging co
you'd expect from an author who is ;
The York Press

'It's not often I say so, but this novel is ripe for television. There is a
mixture of emotions: humour, poignancy, heartache and remorse – all
part of life's rich tapestry which deserves to be given some glorious
technicolour.'
Yorkshire Times

'A highly enjoyable novel, cunningly plotted and often moving - a sort
of Cinema Paradiso of York.'
Andrew Martin, author of bestselling *Railway Detective* series

'Fascinating…the ending was a lovely surprise – romantic but in a
completely unexpected way.'
Clare Chambers, author of bestseller *Small Pleasures*

'The Electric is an evocative, almost poetic, love letter to 1920's York
and the silent movie era. Poignant, charming, and wryly funny, with a
cast of beautifully drawn and unforgettable characters. Not to be
missed.'
Emma Haughton, bestselling author of *The Dark*

'Evocative, compulsive and beautifully researched, albeit that research
wasn't over-egged at any point. Fascinating characters, detail and good
twisty narrative. Bravo.'
Neil Brand, internationally renowned film composer and silent cinema
accompanist

'Like a restored film print, Tim Murgatroyd brings York cinema's golden
age vividly back to life. A beautiful story that reminds us that movies
were never silent, and nor is the human heart.'
Tom Harper, bestselling thriller writer, and collaborator with Wilbur
Smith on *Tiger's Prey* and *Storm Tide*

The Electric

a novel

by

Tim Murgatroyd

Stairwell Books //

Published by Stairwell Books
161 Lowther Street
York, YO31 7LZ

www.stairwellbooks.co.uk
@stairwellbooks

Layout design: Alan Gillott
Cover design: Elliot Harrison

Paperback ISBN: 978-1-913432-43-0
eBook ISBN: 978-1-913432-53-9
p10

For William Lea

A thing of beauty is a joy for ever:
Its loveliness increases; it will never
Pass into nothingness; but still will keep
A bower quiet for us, and a sleep
Full of sweet dreams, and health, and quiet breathing.

John Keats

Summer, 1969

Clifton jumps up onto the rail of the balcony. With a sharp intake of breath, I imagine his little body tumbling four storeys to the basement flagstones below. Or impaling himself on the iron railings. A puff of ginger fur, outstretched legs. He'd need more than nine lives to survive that crash.

I sidle over to where he licks an insouciant leg, defying the void, and scoop him in my arms. There. Safe for now. Stupid cat.

Don't ask why we called him Clifton. Another long story. At my age, you burst with stories like an overstuffed cushion.

The view from the balcony halts me. I stand with him in my arms, looking up the Thames towards Chelsea Bridge. A haze of fumes and summer twilight lies sleepy across London. Only a few cars and buses pass along Chelsea Embankment, directly below our balcony. The day is fading into something else, always something new. Even as I watch, the streetlamps glow in anticipation of a warm, breathless night.

A young couple walk by on the riverside pavement. She wears a flowery skirt so short it might pass for a tea towel; the flares of his purple and orange trousers are wide as a Mexican bandit's chaps. Her head rests on his shoulder: they are draping one another with desire. An unworthy rush of envy and hot grief for the past troubles my heart.

The low wall of the embankment leads to the slow Thames, running full tonight. It must be high tide on the coast. Across its boat-littered waters the trees of Battersea Park are in full leaf. Perhaps the young lovers will walk there tomorrow. Their story lies all before them, flowing away to unimaginable seas.

Despite my quickened heartbeat, I sense rightness in the world. All the elements are present and correct. Always have been, world without end. Air and water, earth and fire. Plus a fifth, sparking through living veins. I think of it as the electric.

What does the old fool mean, you probably ask, suspecting a half full whisky bottle. Only that he, too, once was young. That he, too, played youth's game for the highest stakes. That he faced scrambles to gain a niche: home and a steady income, children to reward and mock parental genes. Above all, to be vivified by that current like lightning or blue static. The St Elmo's Fire of loving. And being loved in return.

The heart has its own truths. Like music. Which is why I wish to sail back up the river of my memories, while I still can. Back to the source of my best shot at life, a miraculous chance I never anticipated, or perhaps deserved.

Clifton flows like quicksilver out of my arms and mooches to the sofa. I hover on the thick burgundy carpet before a Victorian marble fireplace carved with grapes on the vine. Its shape reminds me of the Electric's proscenium arch, the glowing silver screen it framed.

I dare myself to ignore the easy chair where drowsing is seductive, where the newspaper headline calls me, predicting Apollo 11's landing on the moon. I dare myself to switch off the television's gabble and offstage laughter, to settle at the table with its prospect of the river, the lights of the glimmering city.

I dare myself to uncap my old green, lacquered fountain pen, veteran of many a musical score and composition. Then the Electric might glow for me, one last time.

Winter, 1919

One

Bitter winds chased us inland and pursued us up the Ouse, from Goole to Selby, through a landscape grey with frost and fog. A long, slow haul. The steam barge's flat belly was laden with cocoa beans for Rowntree's chocolate factory in York.

The skipper and his crew ignored me, other than to indicate I should 'mash us some tea, lad'. Tea was necessary for a little warmth, even when the wind dropped and the sky darkened, charged with that expectant inner light you get before snow.

As dusk thickened, we turned a bend in the river. It began to snow. Heavy, soft, delicate flakes floating down like a cloud of airy white seeds.

The chug and huff of the barge's pistons faded from my ears. All fatigue of body and heart left me. I experienced a strange feeling. That amidst our steady advance up the river and the flickering, constant motion of the snow, I had found a doorway.

People on the riverbank seemed ghostly as the flakes drifting down. Street lamps and the headlights of a motor truck lent glamour to the snow.

My reverie was broken by the skipper at his tiller.

'It won't last,' he predicted, indicating the sky with an upraised palm like Jesus. 'Wet snow this. Not the settlin' kind.'

I blinked at him, crystals melting on my eyelashes. The spell broke. Again we were in winter, entering a city of smoky, stinking factories, shops and narrow terrace streets. Many were little better than slums. Again I was poor and hungry, lost in the world. But that snow, wet or dry, had washed a tiny corner of war from my soul. I sensed it. What began with a small corner might spread across the whole room.

The skipper offered me a berth in the barge's tiny cabin with the other lads – it was late, after all – but I asked him to drop me off. We bumped to a halt beside a cobbled quay.

'Thanks for the lift,' I said.

He examined me frankly. At once, my hand twitched up, covering my left cheek. Ashamed of weakness, I lowered it.

His own fingers as we shook were black with soot and oil, a mass of calluses.

'Tha's got soft hands, I reckon, for my way o' life,' he said, not maliciously. 'And mine are too rough for yours. Good luck to you, lad.'

I did not tell him those same soft hands – though wearing lambskin gloves to keep out the cold at five thousand feet – had cut short as many lives as I possessed years. And not in a pleasant manner. Oh no. A count haunting my dreams. Well, I was not alone in that. It wasn't done to talk about such things. Hide them away in secret pockets of your memory like filthy rags, and hope time would launder them.

'Thanks,' I repeated lamely.

Then I made my way into the town, guided by two words on a torn slip of paper in my pocket: *The Electric.*

When you are young, you feel beyond history. The future is unresolved like dough yet to rise. Mostly, that winter twilight, I felt wretched and numb.

All your own fault, I could hear my stepfather's pedantic tones assuring me. Like bread and history, some voices get chewed into a sour pap. His was my inner voice of nagging reproach. A dry sniff, a sigh. *Next time try the train.*

Except that, even Third Class costs money. Even so short a journey as Hull to York required a few shillings. As I possessed barely enough capital to patronise the cheapest tearoom, I naturally leapt at the offer of a free ride.

There is an old beggar's saying: 'From Hell, Hull and Halifax may Heaven preserve us.' After the war acquainted me with the first location on the list, I had reasoned Hull must be *some* kind of improvement.

Besides, an old comrade-in-arms from the squadron had written – a brief, offhand reply to an enquiry of my own – about 'cast-iron' vacancies in my particular line of work. Driven by unemployment and daily, sometimes hourly, probing from my stepfather as to job prospects, I spent what remained of my money on a ticket from West Ealing to Hull. Mother (bless her, ever the great handwringer) had confined her maternal affections to mournfully comparing me with my dead father as I carried my suitcase out of the door.

Once in Hull, my old comrade seemed mightily surprised to see me, violin in hand, and not best pleased.

It soon became clear the 'cast-iron' vacancies were scrap. If they ever existed. Nothing much was in the offing apart from depping – and as any professional musician will tell you, man cannot live by depping alone.

Luckily, my pal recollected rumours of another 'cast-iron' vacancy. This time in York. He was also blessed with an uncle skippering a steam barge to that ancient city on the plains. As one ex-Navy man to another, he made a large occasion of 'doing me a favour'.

There are few more dispiriting positions than being superfluous. I was among hundreds of thousands, recently demobbed, returning changed and baffled, forbidden to speak of all they had seen and perpetrated. Home felt stranger and colder than the moon.

An hour later, fortified by tea and a buttered slice that consumed a disturbing proportion of my assets, I loitered outside the Electric Cinema for reconnaissance. Was this what I shivered the length of the Humber and Ouse to find? The Electric's glory days had peaked even before Kaiser Bill donned his spiked helmet and invaded Belgium.

The exterior consisted of a ticket office and double doors, flanked by pillars and plaster friezes in a style between Tutankhamun's Tomb, the Palace of Versailles and your neighbourhood bordello. Fresh paint would not have gone amiss.

A wooden sign on hooks read, *Come right on in! It's warmer inside!* I later found out that in summer the same sign was reversed to read, *It's cooler inside!* Another notice assured customers, *These Premises are Regularly Treated with DDT.*

One of the Electric's employees returned my scrutiny. A barrel-chested man in his fifties, his face fleshy, nose bulbous and veined. He wore a burgundy uniform with canary yellow epaulets and a peaked cap. His buttons and shoes glinted with pride. The commissionaire folded his arms.

'Tonight's last showing is half done,' he advised. 'There's another tomorrow.' He added dryly, 'And there's usually one the day after that an' all.'

'I was hoping to see the manager about a job.'

I raised my instrument case. His manner softened.

'Fiddle, is it?'

'Violin.'

The commissionaire nodded sagely and waved to a thin, faded lady behind the ticket office window. Dressed in widow's black, apart from a white maid's hat, she was counting halfpennies, pennies and sixpences. She slid open a glass panel.

'This young chap's brought his fiddle, Esther,' the doorman advised. 'Best tell *Him Indoors*.'

Her glance danced round my face. Women were the worst for that, especially when pretending not to stare. First, at the dusky complexion inherited from a great grandmother who Father – my real father – had dubbed in a droll mood, 'Nefertiti, the African Queen'. Then, inevitably, at my neck and left cheek. Well, it wasn't as if I could expect anything else.

'You wait 'ere, love,' said Esther. She had a quiet, woebegone way of talking, like the rustle of autumn leaves. 'I shan't be long. Mr Ackerley will keep you company, won't you, Ambrose?'

'I most certainly shall,' declared the commissionaire.

She vanished in search of *Him Indoors*.

I felt for a cigarette, realised I was out. Ambrose regarded me regally. His jaunty peaked cap and yellow braid epaulets brought to mind cockatoos.

'Not from round 'ere, lad, are you?'

4

'No.'

He nodded at his own perspicacity. We left it at that.

A moment later, the front doors swung open and a head popped out. It belonged to the founder, manager and sole proprietor of the Electric Cinema: Horatio Gladstone Laverelli.

🎬

The name Laverelli conjures up sun-drenched olive groves in the Apennines, rather than a drizzly Pennine mill town like Halifax. But no, Halifax it was. Laverelli's accent and manner were West Riding as oatcakes, high teas, flat caps and ginnels.

I had done Hell. Then Hull. Now, embodied in the dapper little man before me came the third location on the beggar's list.

Laverelli's moist brown eyes weighed me from hat to scuffed boots. He was in his mid-forties, twice my age. The customary cinema manager's uniform of black dinner jacket and bow tie was enhanced by shiny lapels and patent leather shoes. A mauve, perfectly folded polka dot handkerchief rose from his breast pocket. When he grinned, pearly dentures caught the electric light. His eyes crinkled at the corners.

'Come right on in! Esther says you're looking for a job. I reckon me and you need a powwow. Violin, is it?'

'Fiddle,' Ambrose the commissionaire corrected.

Mr Laverelli ignored this sally and waved me into the foyer. It was decorated in the same style as the entrance, a potpourri of pastiche. Over a long and well-travelled career, I have observed that, unlike people, you can judge a theatre or cinema by its front of house. The carpet of the Electric, worn by tramping feet and scarred by cigarette burns, told its own tale. As did a faint but lingering aroma of blocked drains.

Laverelli pointed at my violin case. 'Experienced kind of fellah in this line?'

I nodded. He seemed to expect more, so I added, 'Orchestra, light music and dance band mainly. Some cinema.'

'I see.' He looked boldly at my cheek. 'And I can see you was *out there*.'

My left hand started to rise. I jerked it back down. He added smoothly, 'Only reason I ask is you have a military bearing. A chap who's seen his share.'

I glanced at the exit. 'A bit.'

'Thought so.'

He launched into a long story how his last violinist had been seduced by the fleshpots of Scarborough, leaving a sudden vacancy, and that there might, just might, be an opening at the Electric. I wasn't really listening. Ever since the hospital I'd developed a habit of drifting into dense clouds. I suspect his question about the war triggered this episode. Nor am I really sure how long it lasted. One second, I was listening to the piano and cello seeping from the auditorium and wondering why they were playing Fletcher's *Woodland Pictures* so, well, woodenly, the tempo more sedate waltz than gambolling forest sprite or pixie, then I was high over a grey sea, flak opening flowers of black smoke as we circled a German destroyer far below, and it was unnaturally quiet up there, the silence of bad dreams, no engine noise or wind or explosions from the flak, none of the world's clashing music, just Hell, Hull and Halifax with little hope of Heaven to preserve us… '

'So there you have it,' concluded Laverelli. His voice faltered. I shook my head to clear the clouds.

'I'll listen to the orchestra,' I suggested, hurriedly. 'See if I fit in.'

Laverelli clapped my shoulder. 'Aye, lad, you do just that. You'll find we're all friendly here. Nothing to worry about here. And I'll send Gladys to bring you some nuts.' He winked. 'You'll like Gladys. All the chaps do.'

Leaving my suitcase with Esther in the ticket kiosk, I approached the heavy black doors to the auditorium. No doubt Laverelli and Esther exchanged curious looks behind my back. His thick, dark eyebrows might even have waggled. Laverelli was a big eyebrow waggler.

Behind me, I heard Ambrose mutter in a tone of wonder, 'Told yer he's not from round 'ere.'

A black cat sat before the swing doors of the auditorium, scratching its white bib with a white paw. It examined me coldly. I made a *psshing* noise to get past. The big cat yawned, did not budge.

6

Stepping round it, I pushed open the swing doors, entering a world where make believe is refreshingly real. Everyday reality the burden you trade for a handful of coins: the best flickering dream you can afford.

Two

The auditorium of the Electric was a one hall, six hundred-seater. Even in 1919 it was starting to look quaint. That's how fast things moved in the picture trade back then.

It boasted a fair-sized stage with a small pit for the band. A proscenium arch with chamfered corners and plaster mouldings of grapes and fleur-de-lys surrounded the silver nitrate screen. Tiers of seats sloped down, heavily padded near the foyer, spartan close to the front. With the logic common to all superstitions, especially snobbery, seats near the front were considered 'common'.

The air was dense with cigarette smoke. A fair-sized audience for a Wednesday evening. Well, you needed something to get you through a sixty hour week at the local factory or laundry or shop counter. Something to take your mind off husband and errant kids – every cinema's regulars being mostly married women. That something happened to be a Western I'd watched in London two months earlier. Like the foyer, such a main feature told tales about the Electric. The print had seen several runs in plumper establishments before reaching York. You could tell from occasional flickers of light made by scratches on the delicate nitrate film.

I found a seat close to the orchestra. Ignoring the action above their heads, I assessed my potential colleagues.

In the smouldering afterglow of the War to End Wars, female cinema musicians were rare birds, so I watched with interest the young lady behind the piano – and she was a lady, you could always tell. Subtleties of class distinction were dyed into our marrows from childhood.

It soon became clear she served as 'leader' of the orchestra, though more like a lance corporal than captain. Her forces consisted of a single cellist of advanced years.

An extended cowboy and saloon girl love scene flashed across the screen as they performed *In a Monastery Garden*. The old cellist gamely blew a bird whistle stuck in his mouth while sawing away. The lower half of the girl's face and neck were up-lit by a dim lamp illuminating the music. She sat very straight, staring too fixedly at the score for the leader of a decent cinema band, even a paltry duo. You see, the trick was to glance up every few seconds to check your music fitted the drama. It didn't do to play a dark misterioso meant for a villain if the scene had shifted to two squealing flappers. You had to switch moods in an eye's blink.

She pursed her lower lip. A few tresses of long hair – pinned and piled decorously – had come loose. Not for her one of those daring bobs you were beginning to see round Piccadilly. From the intent way she peered through thick spectacles, I could tell she was sweating hard for her pay.

Unexpectedly, I felt sorry for her. Then the lights went up. I became conscious of my burned, mulberry, mottled left cheek and upper neck. My droopy squint like a leering sinner from a Victorian morality play. Definitely Mr Hyde rather than Dr Jekyll. There was much to be said for hiding in the dark, for pretending to be invisible. I had lived that way ever since they invalided me out of the Senior Service.

The last of the audience drifted out, pursued by a dispersing fug of smoke. Horatio Laverelli bustled down an aisle littered with cigarette butts, sweet wrappers and orange peel. The little orchestra was packing away music and instruments. Neither the girl nor old cellist noticed me.

I became aware others were gathering at the back of the auditorium. Ambrose Ackerley, the commissionaire, and the woebegone ticket dolly, Esther, in her maid's hat. A young chap wiping his hands on a rag, who I guessed to be the projectionist. Finally, an usherette in the same style of outfit as Esther, only far curvier. I recalled Laverelli winking about a certain Gladys. The long-legged girl with wide green eyes was worth a wink or two. Nor, from her arch way of standing, one leg crossed before the other, was she averse to displaying a flash of ankle. She held the black and white cat I had met in the foyer to her bosom, stroking the top of its head. Its contented purrs were oddly magnified by the silence.

It seemed the entire staff of the Electric, animal and human, had assembled for my audition.

After a brief introduction from Laverelli, the girl pianist obliged me with a grudging middle A. I tuned up.

All were eyes upon me. But what to play? Having heard the pianist, I didn't trust her with a furioso or gallop that would really showcase my skill.

'Well, lad,' said Laverelli.

It was obvious he considered me an oddity. As I was to learn, anyone with a whiff of the curious interested him.

I glanced down at the girl, who happened to be facing my left hand side. She stared up at me with polite revulsion. Realising I had noticed, she pretended to fiddle with her music. A sense of observing myself from the outside came over me. Who was this young man without a home, violin in hand, face burned and blistered, needing the approval of strangers? A certain tragic wistfulness touched me.

That feeling determined my choice. I leafed through the small stock of standbys I'd brought, passing some sheet music to her: Elgar's *Chanson de Matin*.

'Sorry, I haven't a cello part,' I told the old timer.

He replied by taking out a pocket watch the size of a carriage clock. The only bar that interested him served pints of bitter and the only finale last orders.

The girl was busy scanning the score for nasty bits and transitions.

'We'll take it steady,' I reassured her.

'Any tempo will be fine,' she replied, with a proud flash of eyes.

I indicated the tempo with my bow. Then she was off, the arpeggios of the introduction leading me into music's dappled world of shadows and light.

What inspired me that winter night? Something bigger than myself. The music of the spheres never stops singing. Maybe it was a hunger for beauty, the ever-pressing need of the lonely and forsaken. Hurt lover or soldier back from the war, widow or grieving parent, their faith in life wounded. Maybe I sensed the tens of thousands settling for bed in York, before another weary day of labour to make rich men richer. Perhaps I gathered my own bleak frustration into an earnest voice of romance, charged with yearning.

From nowhere, in my mind, the piano was replaced by a full orchestra. I heard strings and gentle harmonies of woodwind, the murmur of flutes. The undertow of the brass section floated me upon soft currents and eddies. The girl at the piano responded, followed, did not falter. I sensed her flare. As we reached the climax, my violin sang out a swooning cry, before pirouetting into a whimsy of longing, then silence.

People always said my face took on a far off expression when I played. An expression banished by the war. Well, it was back, I could feel it.

For a moment, absolute hush. The girl-pianist gazed up at me in wonder. Even the old cellist had woken sufficiently to shuffle his feet, the musicians' version of applause. The little audience at the back was clapping, too, and enthusiastically.

'Thank you,' I said to my accompanist.

'Oooh, that were lovely!' exclaimed Esther in her faded voice. 'We'll have to hand out hankies at the door if you play like that.'

'What's your name, lad?' asked Laverelli.

'Young,' I said, 'David Young.'

'And do you play any other instruments?'

I shrugged. No one likes a bragger. 'Some.'

'And what might they be?'

He grinned with a twinkle of encouragement; the gap between his shiny upper and lower dentures widened.

I looked round, aware everyone was listening. 'Well, clarinet and piano, principally.'

'As good as the violin?'

'Yes. I mean, pretty much so.'

'Any others?'

11

'Well, ukulele and banjo – just for fun, you understand.'

Laverelli nodded. 'Oh, we like a bit of that at the Electric.'

'And viola, if pushed, of course.'

'Of course.'

I laughed apologetically. 'And basic tuned percussion rather than drums. I once stood in for a pal. Oh, and treble recorder, though there's not much call for that except in…' I hesitated.

'In what, lad?'

'You know, to accompany historical films. Elizabethan dances, that kind of thing.'

'Oh yes.'

Seeing he was so interested, I added, 'Of course, playing the clarinet I dabbled with those new saxophones when I could borrow one. They're quite fun, actually. And I used to sing a bit. Choirs, mainly, the odd solo part. But I haven't done that since…   You know.'

'Very good,' he said. 'Say no more. We're all among pals here. College man, I'm guessing?'

'Royal College,' I conceded. 'Of Music, that is.'

'Oh, I've heard of it. Well, that seems in order.' He turned to the girl. 'Miss Mountjoy, I'm assuming you are, err, satisfied with Mr Young here?'

She evidently was not. I sensed how precarious her position as leader must be in a world of more qualified and competent musicians. Also, that she needed this job very badly. Which seemed strange for such a well-spoken girl. Perhaps her family had 'come down', as people used to say.

'If you are quite happy, Mr Laverelli,' she said, 'then so am I.'

The sole proprietor of the Electric nodded to the leader of his little orchestra. Louisa Mountjoy crimsoned. An exchange I found hard to read.

'Come to my office, Mr Young,' he said, sphinx-like in his affability once more. 'We need to discuss terms, I reckon.'

If the audition had been a triumph, I showed no sign. I was exhausted, hungry and speculating whether I could cadge a cigarette from Laverelli without looking a tramp. Besides, the position of violinist at the Electric was no great prize, just a modest wage. Maybe that was all I deserved.

12

I shall spare you the details of our negotiations, conducted in a broom cupboard office heavily scented by eau de cologne and Turkish tobacco. The simple fact was, Laverelli needed me, and I needed a temporary job. Above all, I needed a place to sleep that night, other than York Railway Station.

'Come on then, lad,' said Laverelli. We'd shaken on thirty shillings a week with digs thrown in, minus board. 'I'll show you the amenities.'

Back in the auditorium, everyone had gone, including my new boss and leader of the orchestra, Miss Louisa Mountjoy. Likewise, the old bugger of a cellist, who Laverelli had introduced as Maurice Skelton. Only the cat remained, as though waiting for us, its tail swishing.

The lights in the main hall were off. As we paused by the open swing doors, a vast cave of darkness greeted us.

'The gas generator will be shut down soon, lad,' said Laverelli, 'so you'll be needing this.' He handed me an army surplus torch and produced a pocket version of his own. 'We're connected to the mains, of course, but I find it cheaper to keep the old generator going.'

Laverelli led the way through silent rows of tip-up seats, somehow desolate without a crowd. It was a veritable soup of blackness in that auditorium. Groping a way out in the dark would be no fun at all.

'I suppose we don't seem much compared to your fancy London cinemas,' he said. 'But beauty's in the eye of the beholder. And there's many a tear of laughter and joy and every feeling beside in folk's eyes at the Electric.'

'Well, they say size isn't everything,' I replied, diplomatically.

He seemed to consider this. 'Oh, I don't know. One thing's for sure, you'll make a few tears flow round here with your playing, Mr Young. Now won't that be something?'

His voice was bright.

'There are good and bad tears,' I said.

He halted, turning the torch on my face, so I blinked.

'Now that's the truth. I call what we do here a service to the public. We spread a little hope and happiness where it's often needed. Never more so than these days.'

His torch beam picked out a thick velvet curtain beside the silver screen. Parting it, revealed a backstage area, cluttered with damaged seats.

'We put on variety sometimes,' said Laverelli. 'Now yon door leads to a toilet and sink you can use. There's also a small dressing room over there.'

I assumed my new digs would be in the dressing room, but Laverelli took me to another door, giving onto steep, unvarnished wooden stairs. It had a bolt on the inside, preventing entry from the auditorium.

'This way,' he said.

I struggled after him with my suitcase and violin case. The black and white cat followed us curiously, ears bent. We both ignored it.

A landing led to a long attic room with a low ceiling and thick beams holding up the cinema's roof slates. Up here, it was bitterly cold; dusty, musty and dark, as though unvisited for a long while.

The amenities consisted of a small sink and cold tap (fed, I was to discover later, by a water tank on the roof popular with dead pigeons) and a card table with two chairs. Cupboard space comprised a few shelves and nails driven into the brickwork. Oddly out of place, was a double bed set well away from the window. A bed roomy enough for a married couple. The only way it could have got there was through the window, winched up in bits then assembled. A pile of blankets lay on the bare mattress.

Laverelli looked round. 'A right little hideaway, don't you think?' he said. 'A man as wanted a bit of privacy could be happy as a canary up here.'

Oh, he was a shrewd one, Horatio Laverelli. No digs could have suited me better. Here I need not contend with a landlady's potential mothering or disapproval.

'Nice bed,' I remarked.

'Aye, aye.' His face was in shadow but something suggested... I didn't know quite what. Not then. 'I'll get a bit of carpet put down tomorrow. And we've a grand paraffin heater in the store. We'll find you a couple of oil lamps, too. You can use the electric lights downstairs when the generator's off but keep it to a minimum. The bloomin' Corporation take a fortune off me as it is. You'll be snug as a bug in a rug up here.'

God knows I'd slept in worse places during the war. But the attic room had one more attraction Laverelli failed to mention.

A tall dormer window projected six feet out. When I pulled open the heavy drapes, I almost gasped.

This high, the ancient rooftops of York were a tide of chimney pots and gables and ridges flowing in jumbled waves. Specks of glimmering snow filled the sky with motion. The closeness of the Minster startled me. Its arched windows and square towers, the sheer massive bulk of faith and folly pointing at Heaven. In between, just behind the Electric, medieval city walls rested upon earthen ramparts, complete with fairy tale crenulations and walkways.

'Like a postcard,' said Laverelli, as I gazed. 'It's so bloody old round here, you can't help feeling young. As soon as I saw that view, I told myself, "Horatio, this is exactly where the Electric belongs".'

'Yes,' I could find no more eloquent word. 'Yes.'

Three

Back then people spoke of their local picture palace as *sixpenn'orth o'
dark*. And warmth, of course. For many, a good fire was a luxury.
With winter settling in hard, Laverelli kept the radiators blazing.

That first week at the Electric my life simplified into two places:
the auditorium and attic room. Until payday, I told myself, I couldn't
afford to explore the city properly. In truth, I wasn't much inclined to
wander, except to seek bread buns, tea and tins of cheap food.

Places are like people, they deepen with acquaintance. That week I
grew at home in the freezing attic – no radiators up there, just
Laverelli's 'grand' paraffin heater. But the oil lamps cast a golden
glow, perfect light for reading treasured books in my suitcase, *Sherlock
Holmes* and *Great Expectations*. I could warm up with a brew from the
camp kettle boiled on a tiny kerosene stove, so smoky it spotted the
ceiling with soot smuts. Besides, I had been given a prodigious
quantity of thick, horsehair blankets, as well as an army surplus
sleeping bag. As Laverelli promised, I was snug as a bug in a rug.

The cinema cat – I learned his name was Clifton – adopted me early
on. Most nights, he padded up the steep wooden stairs to my
hideaway on his white paws, in search of happy hunting grounds. The
scurry of mice serenading my first night soon dwindled to a cautious
rustle. His tyranny against rodents in the auditorium was terrible.
Little wonder Clifton sauntered round like a lion king patrolling his
patch of veldt. Nor was he averse to his human subjects flattering him
with a stroke of the head, ears back, eyes narrow, purring like an
engine at full throttle.

At night, rain rattled on the slates above my head as I lay on the wide double bed, cocooned in blankets. Those were the worst hours, the long watches of the night, haunted by dreams of the war and before, everything twisted and hot with fear, so I awoke sweating, gut twisted. Sometimes I had a distinct sense of someone else in the room, watching silently. My torch beam revealed nothing but cobwebs.

One person truly did haunt the Electric, of course, its guardian spirit and ringmaster, Horatio Laverelli. Although he didn't live on the premises, Laverelli arrived early and left late. His business was usually conducted in the tiny office; sometimes the basement or projection room.

After a few days, Laverelli buttonholed me. I was smoking in the silent auditorium, waiting for my two new musical colleagues. I must have been daydreaming. He seemed to pop up out of the very earth.

'Mr Young,' he announced. 'I thought a little powwow wouldn't go amiss. Just to see how you're settling in.'

I examined him, cigarette in hand.

'Not too bad.'

'And how are we finding Miss Mountjoy and Mr Skelton? You're certainly knocking up a grand old sound together. A proper musical love match, if you'll excuse my French. The three of you hard at it every night.'

I fumbled for a diplomatic reply. Miss Mountjoy and Old Maurice did make quite a concert party. You couldn't call them positively bad; neither positively good. Nor would I have likened our collective efforts to a love match. More like mismatch.

Back then film accompaniment was a distinct musical art. One killed off by the arrival of the talkies just ten years later. We cinema musicians were only a rustle of leaves on humanity's tree.

To be clear, there was never such a thing as silent cinema. Films were always shown with music, right from the early days. By 1919, solo pianists were rare, trios the bare minimum for a respectable cinema orchestra. Every showing was a concert, serenading patterns of light and movement and emotion on the glowing screen. And audiences knew the difference between a good and bad orchestra.

Like magicians, we breathed feeling and significance into the two-dimensional dumb show. It was we who made the film live or die.

One old chap even came to the Electric for the music alone. Which didn't say much for his musical appreciation. How did I know this? Gladys would lead him hobbling to a seat near the front, showering him with smiles he could not see. There he would sit, head bowed, white stick in hand, while the beam of the projected film passed over his head. He was, of course, quite blind.

'Well, Mr Laverelli,' I began.

'Yes, lad?'

'I fear, Miss Mountjoy... '

How to say it nicely? The leader of our orchestra, the person charged with choosing a range of contrasting, appropriate pieces to suit every manner of scene, seemed to know only a dozen. At least, with confidence. But it was not for me to show her up. She clearly needed the money. I was merely blowing through the Electric on my way back to London, soon as I'd worked up enough for train fare and digs at the other end.

'Although she plays very well,' I lied, for it takes an excellent amateur to make a poor professional, 'she does seem to prefer, well, quite a narrow selection of pieces.'

So small, in fact, I knew them by heart after two days on the job, no longer needing to consult the sheet music. When Louisa Mountjoy realised this, an anxious expression settled on her proud yet subdued face. She kept glancing up the aisle to see if Laverelli had noticed too. Out of pity, I pretended to need the scores, after all.

'Aye,' he said. 'Miss Mountjoy likes what she knows. And she knows what she likes. Especially that one, you know... '

'Hearts and Flowers,' I offered, helpfully.

'Aye, that's the one. Very popular.'

I made a neutral noise.

'And Mr Skelton?' he asked. 'All fine there, as well?'

Old Maurice's lack of spark stemmed from sheer indifference. He only stirred for sound effects. A bucket of old tins and bottles kicked over for a train crash. Special clappers for horse's hooves. A long-barrelled, cap-firing revolver for gunshots. Bird whistles: cuckoo, nightingale, honking geese, duck call, he was a one man aviary, a human flock. Maurice seemed especially fond of a rain machine devised from a coffee jar full of dried peas. This he agitated by cranking a handle.

I attempted a smile. 'He's fine. I'm fine. We're all fine.'

Laverelli's shiny dentures reappeared.

'Thought so. If there's one thing I pride me self on, it's happy, friendly staff. Napoleon's army might have marched on its stomach. At the Electric, we march on willing hearts. A friendly greeting for one and all! That's our motto. There's nowt quite like it.'

On cue, Louisa Mountjoy hurried down the aisle to join us. She had a pale, delicate complexion, an English rose flush. I could tell she didn't like me in private conversation with Laverelli. Also, that she would spend the show worrying whether we had been talking about her.

Early on that evening I made a couple of small, deliberate mistakes. It seemed to set her mind at ease.

My first pay packet offered an opportunity to get to know York better, before I returned to the capital.

Some are drawn to nature as their well of truth. My younger self gravitated towards crowds and where they gather. I was a natural observer, though an aloof one. A wounded face and heart saw to that. Yet I moved through the packed market on Parliament Street or the bustle of Coney Street, watching curiously. People's clothes and mannerisms, their endless variety. Here were factory workers and North Riding farmers in town to sell their eggs and vegetables. Housewives after a knockdown bargain, kids in tow. What did I hope to detect? Connection, perhaps. The comfort of belonging where so often I felt ignored and unloved.

Without brother or sister for company, mine had been a solitary childhood in the West London suburbs. A loneliness reinforced by my bumptious, scornful stepfather and cowed, nervous mother. Which is why, perhaps, I filled the silence of home with music, following in my father's footsteps. He had been a successful clarinettist before blood poisoning hastened his farewell concert.

York offered much to see – and eat. A sensible traveller combines the two pleasures.

Whenever there wasn't a matinee performance, I donned overcoat and trilby, setting out into the city at random. It is a fine thing to be a tourist where you live. That, surely, is the wisest state.

Soon I was lost in mazes of narrow streets little changed since the Middle Ages. High gables and wooden beams leaned between plastered brick walls. Everywhere, Gothic churches worth a thoughtful half hour, not least the Minster. City walls and gatehouses felt like the set of a historical epic, except in real life. And the present soon becomes history.

Best of all, after a year of bland hospital rations, strong flavours of every kind. Wonderfully fresh fish and chips wrapped in copies of the Yorkshire Herald, tart with vinegar and salt, the batter crisp to the bite, haddock or moist cod swimming across the tongue. Much, I imagine, as the poor blighters swum off Scarborough or Whitby a few hours earlier. Frying in beef dripping made for crispy, crunchy chips worthy of a meal in themselves.

I also discovered a pie shop specialising in faggots – known to Yorkies as 'ducks'. The minced pork offal in each meatball was flavoured with a subtle, peppery, scented blend of fresh green English herbs, parsley, sage, rosemary and thyme. Served on paper plates, they came with thick onion gravy, and a fresh-baked bread roll thrown in for mopping up the sauce. Common folk's fare, you might say. One helping never seemed enough.

Yet the city had its share of dark slums and factories. Indeed, poverty was normal inside the quaint, historic walls. The winter air was dank, acrid with coal fires, even when a change of wind carried cocoa scents into town from the chocolate factories along the River Ouse.

York was also notable for its asylums. Sensitive souls favoured the term 'hospital'; many preferred 'loony bin'. Old cruelties die hard. Only a few generations earlier, respectable folk paid good money to laugh and stare at the lunatics.

In 1919, there was a whole new breed of madmen: shell-shocked and war-mangled young men. It was that accident of history that led to a reunion I never expected, or wished for.

One Sunday morning, I left the Electric for an aimless stroll. River fog swirled round the broad avenue of Bootham. Visibility was restricted to fifteen or twenty feet. The thick fog reminded me of desperate occasions 'navigating' our flying boat at three thousand feet through billowing clouds and sea mists, conscious the petrol gauge quivered on red.

I had just drawn parallel to the tall iron railings of Bootham Park Lunatic Asylum. A procession of nurses in blue uniforms and starched white caps emerged from the murk, each supporting a man in a military greatcoat. They were guiding their patients into the elm-lined avenue that led back to the main hospital building. I realised they must have attended a memorial service of some kind at the Minster, and were on their way home.

Naturally, I stepped aside, removing my hat. These were terribly wounded men. You could tell from the shuffling steps and sticks, missing limbs, crushed grey faces. A full year after the Armistice, the war wasn't over for these poor devils. It never would be.

A few moaned and muttered, staring fixedly at nothing. A variety of nervous tics twitched. The crocodile passed through the tall iron gates and down the mist-obscured avenue.

Then it was my turn to stare.

At the end of the procession I recognised a face. Yes, it must be him! Never mind the rearranged features and crooked nose. The burns not unlike my own. Except the extent of his shrivelled skin covered his entire upper torso. Deep, deep burns and scars on hands and arms and face and chest.

He didn't see me. Busy peering nowhere.

It was Fitz alright. In the flesh. Or what remained of it. Right Honourable Archibald 'Fitz' Fitzclarence, VC, DSC, DFC, and numerous other bits of tin.

Then he, too, vanished into the fog. My heart beat painfully. Palms felt clammy with sweat. Why hadn't I greeted him? At the very least, saluted? Surely I owed him that little courtesy. Yet I felt profound relief he hadn't noticed me. I was done with the war. If only it would be done with me. Somehow I could not leave it behind, neither in my thoughts or heart.

And now, against all expectation, Fitz! Still, I reasoned his presence in York made sense. There had been talk in the officer's mess of his family's ancestral pile in the North Riding, a vast estate with lands and stables and servants.

Though I was glad he had passed by blindly, somehow I felt cheated. Yet I never cared for the man. And he had never cared for me.

A pal of mine in the squadron, a Scots Canadian who vanished along with his bus somewhere over the Dogger Bank, warned me when I was assigned fresh from Naval College to Archie 'Fitz' Fitzclarence's crew:

'So, Young, you're to be Archie's new Navigator Observer?'

He was deep into a third whisky and soda, thawing his frozen bones after a patrol.

'Yes, I am.'

'Know how his last observer copped it?'

'No.'

'Our *Fitz* got a bit too close to *Fritz*, if you see what I mean. Archie wanted his first kill very badly. Chased a Brandenburg too near for its gunner to miss.'

'I see.'

'You know where the *Fitz* in Fitzclarence comes from, don't you?'

'No.'

'It means his ancestors were royal bastards.' He raised his glass and laughed, chinking the ice. 'Right royal bastards.'

Back in the deserted cinema, I sat at the piano in the big, cold darkness of the auditorium. A paraffin lamp cast a globe of illumination. My sole audience was Clifton, who rubbed up against my shins then hopped onto my warm lap, where he accompanied the sad, minor chords I played with a loud, contented purr.

Four

The day before Christmas Eve, I wandered to the foyer and heard a whisper.

'Over 'ere, lad.'

A meaty hand and yellow braid cuff beckoned from the entrance to the Gents. Next emerged Ambrose Ackerley's florid face, minus peaked cap. Slick-backed, brilliantine hair had been combed to vainly conceal his bald patch. A trick learned, perhaps, from the urbane heartthrobs on dog-eared publicity posters adorning the foyer. The pursuit of glamour can be a catching disease.

Ambrose's usual manner combined affability with strict no nonsense. A difficult balance to strike, but essential given his job. Keeping a queue four hundred long in order whilst maintaining a friendly face took presence. An off-putting commissionaire could badly damage a picture house's profits. Luckily for Laverelli, Ambrose knew how to manage a crowd. I always got the sense he was trying hard to make a strong impression, as though to redeem himself for something. What I never guessed was who he wanted to impress.

Today the confident front had slipped. You might even call him nervous.

'In here!'

I followed him into the Gents. Before shutting the door, he craned out his head to check for spies.

'Now you're a discreet sort of chap, Mr Young,' he said, straight off. 'As likes to keep himself to himself. I can trust you to save your breath to cool your porridge. Besides, you're not from round 'ere.'

He could rely on me for that.

'Well, I've a favour to ask. Not a big one, mind, but a favour.'

I made a non-committal noise at the back of my throat.

'It's like this, there's a certain *lady* in this establishment, who I would like to give a special Christmas present. 'Nonymous, like.'

''Nonymous?'

'Aye.'

Cherchez la femme. I ran through the possibilities. Miss Mountjoy? He was not remotely in her class. That left the usherette, Gladys Bannering. Could Ambrose, in his late fifties, paunch and all, really fancy his chances of lifting her usherette's frilly pinny? They say there's no fool like an old fool.

Gladys had no shortage of admirers, most a good three decades younger than Ambrose. Despite her smiley, plump-cheeked Irish colleen's face, there was something decidedly appraising when she looked a man over, a hand draped loosely on her hip. Something provocative I didn't quite trust. In short, something rather common, as though she had watched too many vamps flounce across the screen and decided to model herself upon them. I should add her hemline was invariably a few inches above her shapely ankles.

'Sure?' I said, feeling sorry for him. December chasing May seldom ends well.

'Aye. We're agreed then.' He ran a finger round his collar. 'Man to man, like.'

He produced a sizable flat rectangular box wrapped in dark blue paper.

'Why not just give it to her yourself?' I suggested. 'I'm really not sure I'm the right person.'

Ambrose Ackerley shook his head solemnly.

'Nay, lad, that would never do.'

'Why not?'

'I tried to give her a present before – in a friendly way, you understand – and she took it right bad. Said it would be disloyal to her former husband. She's a widow, you see. If I offered it again, p'raps she'd say the same thing. That's why she mustn't get told it's from me. Not official, like.'

Youthful Gladys Bannering, a widow! What with the war, such tragedies were all too common. It made her flirty ways even less appealing. I could not help wondering how the poor chap would feel to see her in action now.

'She won't know it's from you,' I countered.

Ambrose tapped the side of his fleshy nose with a thick forefinger. 'You've a lot to learn about the ladies, son. She'll know.'

With that, he thrust the box into my hands, and donned his peaked hat for the queue front-of-house.

'Remember, man to man,' he cautioned. 'And do it tonight. Slip it into the ticket office while her back's turned. She'd see me if I tried. Softly, softly, catchee monkey.'

Then I realised which widow the present was meant for. Not Gladys, at all, who was the opposite of widowhood. I had to suppress a smile.

Incredible as it seemed, burly, brazen Ambrose Ackerley was fluttering after plain old Esther Jones. The same dolorous lady who perched each night like a bony sparrow behind the pay desk.

Somehow it didn't seem natural. Shouldn't they know better at their age? Ah, the vanity – and naivety – of youth to claim a monopoly on romance. Love is hope, and hope belongs to every age.

Esther was already at her station, black uniform prim and square. White cap starched and stiff on her grey hair. She could hardly fail to spot me sidling up with a large gift-wrapped box.

I tucked the present under my arm and joined the band. Louisa Mountjoy frowned slightly at the wrapping paper then adopted her standard policy of ignoring my existence. She had dressed with particular care that evening. I wondered if there was someone in the audience she hoped to impress.

*

Three hours later the auditorium lights went up. The box still lay by my feet as the audience rose. A few people talked excitedly; most were dazed by the flickering world they had shared. Leaving a cinema can feel like surfacing from a dream. In those days, moving images were still so new, the illusion undiluted by familiarity.

Maurice leaned forward and pointed down. His smile made me uncomfortable.

'For anyone we know, lad?' he asked.

'Oh, you know.'

Louisa Mountjoy was earwigging hard. She seemed a little nervous, and even took off her reading spectacles.

Gripped by the absurdity of the situation, and to escape further probing, I packed away my violin and marched up the aisle with the gift box.

Enough of this demeaning subterfuge, I told myself. Was I not once an officer and a gentleman in His Majesty's Royal Naval Air Service? Sub-lieutenant Young, no less. A commissioned Navigator Observer charged with defending the realm from aerial assault. People had saluted me on a regular basis.

I would just hand the box to Esther. Tell her an anonymous friend of hers – yes, friend was safer than admirer – had entrusted it to me and that I was honour-bound to reveal no more. Just my name, rank and serial number. So help me God. And if Ambrose Ackerley didn't like it, he could stuff it up the backside of his commissionaire's uniform.

It seemed a straightforward enough plan at the time.

At the ticket office, I found quite a gathering. Laverelli was handing out Christmas bonuses in brown envelopes. The entire staff of the Electric was there: Ambrose, Gladys Bannering, Esther, even the projectionist, Victor. I marched over, holding up the box in its fancy wrapping paper like one of the Three Wise Men approaching Jesus's crib. All five stared.

Laverelli's eyes twinkled.

'You shouldn't have bothered, lad!' he quipped.

The misery on Ambrose Ackerley's face pulled me up short. Only then did I understand the depth of his passion for Esther.

'It's not for you, Mr Laverelli,' I said, awkwardly.

Silence followed. Five pairs of eyes upon me. I became aware they had been joined by two more pairs. Louisa Mountjoy and Maurice had followed me into the foyer.

Laverelli's grin broadened to reveal his dentures.

'Perhaps you'll tell us who it *is* for? It's Christmas and we all love a present at the Electric.'

I found Ambrose Ackerley's eye. He was mortified alright. No, I could not betray this man's higher feelings, not with decency. Even if those feelings were ridiculous. If I passed the damn box to Esther his whole scheme would come out.

Desperate, I looked round the circle for a plausible recipient. Ignorance what the box contained did not help. Why hadn't I asked? There could be anything in there, from confectionary to saucy ladies' underwear. Laverelli and Ambrose were out of the question. Likewise, Victor and Maurice. It would look queer indeed if I gave it to Miss Mountjoy, and so publicly, having kept it by my music stand all night. That left one alternative.

My head swam. I sensed the inevitability of humiliation. And when you are young, acute embarrassment is a deeply felt wound. What a noodle they would think me! What an awkward fool I considered myself.

Again I sought Ambrose's eye. He had gone a shade of puce. A beefy finger was in his collar as though it choked him. That settled it.

'Here you are,' I mumbled, thrusting the present into Gladys Bannering's hands.

By now Laverelli's grin was set to split his face.

'Good for you, lad!' he said. His mouth twitched. 'Still, as they say, stay out of the water till you learn how to swim.'

He turned to Esther. 'Right folks, show's over for one night. Let's cash up and clock out. It's been quite an evening!'

With that, the small crowd dispersed. Not before I was treated to a look of lofty disdain from Louisa Mountjoy. She sailed out into the dark.

Maurice merely shook his head, pausing on his way past to murmur, 'I can see tha's no judge of women, lad. I'd watch that hussy, if I was you.'

Ambrose Ackerley looked solemn as a hanging judge. Was he grateful for my sacrifice? I felt past caring.

Only Gladys was happy. Her handsome face grew dimples as she smiled at me. She flushed ripe as a young peach; and, I suspected, she was as bright as one.

27

'Oooh, that's right nice of you, Mr Young,' she cried, clutching the box to her pert bosom. 'What a lovely surprise!'

I didn't hang around for more. With the few shreds of dignity left to me, I retreated to my garret. After several stiff rums, followed by several more until the bottle was empty, I could laugh at the absurdity of it all. In those days I wasn't a big drinker. That came later in life. So when Clifton slipped into the attic, he was treated to me leaning out of the dormer window, the Minster having doubled in size and acquired four towers instead of two, the sky swirling, while I croaked out the melody of *Chanson de Matin* between deep lungfuls of air as a way of avoiding being sick.

Five

When I entered the auditorium next morning for the Saturday matinee, my forehead throbbed and stomach churned. I was keen to avoid the accusing eye of Ambrose Ackerley.

Actually, I was pretty eager to avoid just about everyone.

Inevitable then to find Gladys Bannering hanging round the orchestra pit. Louisa Mountjoy was already at the piano, examining the scores.

Gladys flashed me a bobby-dazzler as I shambled over, cradling my violin case. I must have made a grim prospect, huge bags beneath my eyes, scented with cigarette smoke and last night's rum. Shaving had gone badly; two cuts on my neck clogged with soap.

'Right lovely chocolates, Mr Young,' she cooed. 'I just wanted to say thanks again!'

'Good, good.'

A faint snort indicated Louisa Mountjoy overheard the exchange.

Gladys glanced nervously her way. But she was not discouraged. She began talking six to the dozen. Her strong York accent bore a hint of mellifluous Irish brogue – no doubt acquired from a parent – but it reminded me, especially with well-spoken Louisa listening in, how *common* she sounded. It should be remembered those were the days of elocution lessons. And dreadful snobbery. The way you talked proclaimed your status as loudly as your hat.

'All of us are right enjoying your, you know.' She mimicked a bow scraping air. 'Not just Esther and me. Quite a few of me friends have started coming just to hear you play. That's lovely, isn't it! Even me

Mam – and she's got a cloth ear like a dish rag – she said you brought a tear to her eye the other day.'

'Oh, good.'

She shot another nervous glance Louisa's way.

'Do you like it here at the Electric, Mr Young? It's the best job I've ever had. You get to see all the new pictures for free and every day is a bit different, don't you think? You wouldn't believe how lucky I was to land this job! I were working over at Armstrong's making fuses for shells, when I had to leave because of... Well, you don't want to hear about all that, I'm sure. If someone hasn't told you already. The gossip in this town is a shocker. But Mr Laverelli offered me the job here, even though it cost him a few customers.' She tittered. 'I've had right bad luck with jobs, come to think of it. I even got sacked from the packing department at Rowntrees. I were only fourteen! The overlooker caught me pretending to waltz with a broom instead of working.' She put on a deep, stern voice. '"We'll 'ave none of that in *my* section, lass. It's like 'avin' a bloomin' Hottentot on the line."'

My jaundiced eye rose to her hot face. I have already mentioned my great grandmother, Nefertiti the African Queen, from whom my dusky complexion derived. When in a jeering mood, Stepfather sometimes called me 'The Young Hottentot'.

'Good, good.'

I stepped round her and headed for the stand.

'Mister Young!'

Gladys Bannering's hands flew to her hips.

'Yes?'

The hangover beat in my forehead like a steam hammer.

'Why exactly did you give me them chocolates? Me Mam thought they must have cost a fortune. She said I should give them back.'

I considered for a moment.

'Because someone had to have them,' I said. 'And why not you?'

Which was merely the truth.

There came another snort from the piano.

'Excuse me,' I mumbled. 'I really do need to get ready for the show.'

Saturday morning matinees were dedicated to a tribe of savages. As soon as Ambrose threw open the doors a stampede commenced. Hundreds of kids jostled and fought with Darwinian vigour for the best seats at the front. Their racket shamed the Tower of Babel. That morning they were particularly excited, it being Christmas Eve.

Maurice, who distrusted kids as much as he did 'the ladies', ducked out of Saturday matinees. This left Miss Mountjoy and the resident fiddle player to satisfy the most demanding audience of the week.

Where are they now, those ruffle-haired lads and lasses born a few years before the Great War? They would stare up, eyes wide with wonder then, a moment later, roar with glee that shook their thin frames. Too many were thin, dragged up by families weighing every shilling like gold.

But poor of pocket didn't mean poor of spirit. Pranks involving water pistols, elaborate hair-pulling, catapults or improvised missiles of monkey nut shells were common. Mr Laverelli, Ambrose and Gladys patrolled the aisles like circling vultures, ready to seize offenders by the ear and eject them through the fire doors with a loud clank of the push bar and a rush of cold air. It would have distressed the usherette's admirers to witness her unladylike enthusiasm for this work.

What followed perhaps does me no credit.

After the newsreel and Felix the Cat, we were well into the main feature – a piratical tale – when the worst of all cinema musicians' bad dreams unrolled.

Miss Mountjoy's role as leader not only involved selecting which pieces matched the moods on the screen. Just as crucial was signalling the exact instant to change piece.

That Saturday morning, the day before Christmas, she was out of sorts from her first chord. Discordant notes grew more common as the film progressed. Then it happened.

She was bashing out an agitato in line with her handwritten cue sheet, peering through thick spectacles at the score. I felt a sudden unease. Wasn't she aware the full scale sea fight on the poop deck had given way to the World's Sweetheart, Mary Pickford, petting a faithful hound?

Catcalls went up. Promptly she ploughed into a cloying rendition of *Hearts and Flowers*. But by now the villain was grappling with another heroine desperate to free herself from his unlawful embrace. An intertitle flashed:

> # Ha! I shall possess this
> ## virgin as my own!!

Hundreds of the kids had cottoned on. Jeering intensified to braying and hoots. One scamp literally rolled round the floor to indicate his mirth, all the while pointing at the unfortunate pianist. A moment later the first missiles landed in the orchestra pit. Still she persisted, accompanying a moment of pathos with the sinister arpeggios usually reserved for arch-villains and child-beaters. By this time I had stopped playing myself.

'You're out of sequence!' I hissed.

Peanut shells and sweet wrappers rained down.

She ignored me womanfully, banging away at the keys. Did she not hear the laughter? I am quite sure she wished simply to cling to her dignity. And keep me in my place.

Then I did a bad thing. Oh, blame it on my hangover. Or the soggy piece of orange peel that hit me in the eye. I reached across to the keyboard and stopped her playing.

So raucous was the audience by this time, they probably didn't notice. She went rigid with shock.

'Play *Pomp and Circumstance* now!' I commanded in my best Observer Sub-lieutenant's bark. I pointed fiercely at the screen.

And she did. *Old Pomp* was one of her better standbys. Within a minute she was back in control. The kids subsided as Douglas Fairbanks swung to safety across the deck, cutlass between his teeth.

As the children charged for the exits, Louisa slammed down the piano lid. The crash reverberated.

'How dare you!'

'I'm sorry, Miss Mountjoy, but... '

'You call yourself a *gentleman*? And an *officer*? How dare you touch a lady's hand. And... and without permission.'

'You wouldn't stop.'

'I did not need to stop.'

'You jolly well did, Miss Mountjoy... '

'And you reek of stale spirits! You have been *toping*, Mr Young, haven't you? I will not stand for it. I shall complain to Mr Laverelli.'

I'd had enough. Was this ticking off why I had suffered such pain and fear in the war? Was this amateurish mishmash of music why I practised my youth away?

'Oh, complain as much as you like,' I said. 'If you were more of a *trained* musician you might understand my frustration. Perhaps you should consider going to college, Miss Mountjoy.'

That got to her. Bang on the target. Her chest positively heaved. Only later did I discover why it cut so deep.

'Did you know, Mr Young, that you already have a nickname? I mean among the locals.' Her voice assumed a parody of a coarse York accent. Somehow it reminded me of Gladys Bannering. 'A *sobriquet*, no less. *The Phantom of the Opera*.'

We froze. My hand shot up to cover the left half of my face.

Just as moods on the screen changed in a moment, her anger vanished. She blinked tearfully, her own hand rising to cover her mouth. Perhaps she saw how I flinched.

'I really didn't mean... ' she began. 'I'm most awfully sorry.'

Self-disgust forced me to my feet. The Phantom of the Opera. Well, well. What else could I expect? Yes, until the day I died.

Taking up my violin, I went to the velvet curtain concealing the staircase to my garret, my little redoubt. Hadn't the Phantom of the Opera hidden from humanity because of his hideousness? Except his sanctuary had been catacombs beneath Paris. York didn't offer the same subterranean facilities.

Six

I stood by the attic window, cigarette in hand. Fortunately, it being Christmas Eve, only the one showing had been scheduled for that day. I was free to retreat and not emerge until the cinema re-opened. And then? I looked no further than a train ticket to London.

Oddly, I bore no ill will towards Louisa Mountjoy. We all have levers and buttons. She had found mine when lashing out. Just as I had, somehow, pressed hers by mentioning college. The best of me didn't blame her. I had behaved like a cad. Such things as stopping a colleague in mid-performance – especially one's leader, however incompetent – were simply not done.

My gaze lingered over the rooftops of York and the Minster. Christmas Day tomorrow, a Sunday. The cinema would be closed until after Boxing Day. Two days of solitude while the world busied itself with conviviality, family, affection.

I had laid in extra rations, including liquid ones, to last me until the cheaper sort of cafes reopened. But there it was. Christmas 1919 in the Land Fit for Heroes.

Perhaps my eyes were moist. Perhaps they were. Here's a thing: back then the salt in tears used to make the burned half of my face sting. That faded over the years. Time toughens your shell.

A discreet tap on the door. I hastily rubbed my eyes, sucking hard at the cigarette to loosen a lump in my throat.

'Come in.'

Laverelli, naturally. He had a concerned expression, his head set slightly to one side. In his hands was a cardboard grocery box.

'Any chance of a little powwow, lad?'

I sighed. 'Don't bother, Mr Laverelli. I'll take a train back to London on Boxing Day. If it's alright for me to stay here until then.'

'Ah.'

He looked wistfully round the attic.

'I used to like it up here,' he said. 'It's cosier in spring and summer. You can't imagine that in winter.'

I wondered what on earth Laverelli found to do up there. But I was too absorbed by my own troubles to give it much thought.

I stubbed out my cigarette, lit another. The match rasped and flared. The first sulphurous drag scorched my throat.

'She's really not a bad lass,' he said. 'You might even get to respect her a great deal.' He frowned, as though afraid of betraying a confidence. 'Things haven't been easy for her. Nor are they set to get much better, I reckon. She needs this job very bad. I'd like to help her grow into it, if I can. Everyone deserves a chance. Don't you think?'

The neglected cigarette smoked between my fingers.

'She asked me to tell you,' he said. 'She's right sorry for her remarks.'

I smiled. 'I can't imagine her saying *right* sorry.'

'I think she used the word *ve-ry*.'

He did a good job at Louisa's posh vowels. Neither of us spoke. He cleared his throat.

'I know you've seen things that can choke a chap.' His face grew still. 'I had a friend who went out there, too. I tried to persuade him not to. And he never came back.'

'It's alright,' I repeated.

'No, hear me out. We'd all be happier if you stayed, Mr Young. You're damn good for business, take my word for it. Takings are up twenty per cent the last few weeks.'

Laverelli looked round the attic again as though remembering.

'You get good days and bad days,' he said. 'My point is, each day is a gift. Never you mind what folk round here say.' He coughed delicately. 'They say a few choice things about me, I can tell you. And Miss Mountjoy, come to think of it. Not pretty things either. Even our Gladys gets her share of stick. But you're very welcome at the

Electric. I'd like to offer you this here box. As a Christmas bonus. You've earned it.'

With that, Laverelli thrust the box in my hand. It was surprisingly heavy. He left me to open it as the bells of York Minster chimed out the hour.

Inside, I found a feast. A miniature fruit cake topped with glazed almonds. Pork pie with egg in the middle. Thick slices of York ham. A jar of homemade piccalilli – possibly received in part-payment for a ticket. A loaf of crusty bread. Fresh butter. Tea. Ground coffee. Tinned salmon and ox tongue. A pungent triangle of Wensleydale cheese. Brandy snaps and a pot of whipped cream to fill them. A box of dates and rose-scented Turkish Delight. York being famous for its chocolates, there was a doorstep slab of milk chocolate. In addition, there were packets of cigarettes – my favourite brand.

As darkness fell, I laid out a grand Yorkshire Christmas Eve supper on the old card table. With a pot of coffee and slice of fruit cake, I settled beside the paraffin heater in a tent of blankets to read *Great Expectations* by the soft light of the oil lamp. Outside, sleet fell diagonally and wind moaned round chimney pots.

When Clifton appeared on his nightly hunting safari, he took a breather from slaying rodents. Licking his white paws, he sat before the paraffin heater. I felt snug and safe. For the first time, I wondered if there might be something for me in York. A chance, a hope, I did not know what.

Perhaps – we are creatures of contradiction – that frail sense of hope freed me to dream of the war more vividly than I had for months. Seeing Fitz led like a broken child into Bootham Park Lunatic Asylum had lit a flare that fell slowly through the dark pit of my mind. Its descent filled the whole night until dawn...

First the juddering, shuddering of our two-engined seaplane, its long wings ruffled by air pockets, boat-like hull vibrating. In the distance, lightning flashes against black cloud, the sea running high beneath us, dark save for lines of wave crests. On the struts and double wings, the bright blue flash and dance of St Elmo's Fire...

Then circling over the beach at Felixstowe, waiting for the rest of the squadron to get airborne and join us. Below, streets of holiday villas and old fishermen's cottages. Our station: several huge hangars beside the beach with slipways for the seaplanes to be rolled down and pushed out into the surf by ratings in rubber waders. Behind the hangars, communal huts for the non-commissioned ranks. We officers sleep and mess in huts all our own.

At two thousand feet, I can see for miles: a clear winter's morning. Harwich to the south, to the east slate waves speckled by breakers, the smoke plumes of a Royal Navy convoy on the horizon...

Next I am in the officer's mess. Right down the bottom end of the long dining table with the other Sub-lieutenants. A mere Navigator Observer. Oh, you must learn your place in His Majesty's Navy. In my dream, I feel myself sweat. Further up the table, I can see Archie 'Fitz' Fitzclarence holding forth to his fellow Flight Lieutenants.

One thought grips me. I don't want him to shame me. Don't want to hear his patrician drawl mocking me while he downs a few more ports. He has nicknamed me Baby, a play on the surname Young, and it has stuck. (*Did you know, Mr Young, that you already have a sobriquet among the locals? The Phantom of the Zeppelins*).

Our C.O. is on his feet, glass in hand. A toast to the ladies! A toast to His Majesty the King! Chairs scrape. Young men in dress suits brushed by diligent batmen rise. But I cannot. Must not. If I stand everyone will see. Everyone will laugh at me, or worse. Because I have no trousers on. Not even underpants.

Fitz's face is ugly, angry. 'On your feet, Baby! You're letting me down. My damn navigator, letting me down... '

Now there is no land, nothing but sea and air. No safety in either. We're in loose formation. Four F.2s bristling with machine guns. In each bus, four young men scanning the quarters of sky assigned by their position. Me, front of house in the nose cockpit, observer and navigator. Behind me, Fitz, our skipper, the leader, wedged between two Rolls Royce Eagle engines roaring fit to burst your eardrums. A constant vibrating racket to drown out words and sea and wind. Every noise, in fact, save the scream of diving Hun fighters – you always hear those – the crump of flak and archie, the pop-pop of machine guns...

Fitz's face hidden by mask and goggles, scarf and helmet, like all our faces. Our engineer, Flight Sergeant Gus, who we call the old man because he is twenty-seven and married with kids. Flight Sergeant Smittie, manning his double Lewis guns, and the new-fangled Morse wireless behind the pilot's cockpit. When I look back, their eyes are dark discs of goggles. Inhuman, lifeless...

I gasp in my dream, heart pounding like our engines – all around us German seaplanes buzzing and spinning, monoplanes, biplanes, smaller and more nimble than our burly F.2s. I follow a Hansa-Brandenburg biplane with my gun sights while he banks. *Tat tat tat tat* as the twin Lewis guns spit tracer and incendiary.

Now we're banking, too, Fitz crazy for his first medal, his first big kill, leaving the cover of the formation. At once, we're surrounded. They are all around us. Whirling Hun seaplane fighters.

Gus and Smittie and me firing wildly, burning through drums of ammunition. A hole tears through the fabric beside me. Tracer flashes at the corner of my eye. Then Fitz is twisting our kite into a hard curve, risking a stall, shaking off a Hun so Smittie and Gus can pour it out.

When I search the sky again, our pursuer's on fire. Hit his fuel tank! Smoke trails as the Hansa struggles to keep airborne. With a howl of engines it rushes down at the sea. Two German airmen struggling to get out. Smoke hides them. A moment later, a splash, spout of water. In my dream I share their final terror.

Then another Hun fighter dives for us. Another. Another. Another... All night until dawn.

The bells of the Minster clanged and pealed. It was Christmas Day. I let myself out of the small backdoor at the rear of the Electric and wandered into York.

Another dank morning, as though spring would never reawaken. Wet snow flurried down.

I could not help contemplating ghosts of Christmas past. Father presiding at a laden table, warm from a sherry or two before we sat down to dinner. He was a natural gentleman, except for his bank account. I always admired his easy knack for setting everyone at ease. A talent I entirely lacked. Mother would clap and cry out in her decorous way when the brandy on the pudding blazed blue. Back then we still had a maid-of-all-work. Before Father died. Before Mother became my stepfather's nervous, obedient skivvy. Before her rushed marriage to mollify fears of 'coming down'. She would have sold – did sell – her soul for respectability. At least my stepfather offered that.

It was a relief to be two hundred miles from their festive dinner salted with dry sniffs and Mother's sighs. Still, I felt the unique loneliness of a solitary Christmas Day.

My walk took me past the front porch of York Minster, just as crowds were streaming out of the morning service, everyone wearing their best clothes.

Amidst the laughing, talking mass of worshippers, I spotted Louisa Mountjoy. Clean and prim, she walked with the stately grace of a young lady's deportment lessons. Head and shoulders back, a light, pleasant smile fixed on her lips. A boy held her hand, perhaps four years old, chattering excitedly.

Then she relaxed a little as the crowd thinned, talking brightly to the child. He hopped and pulled at her hand. I hesitated. Here was my chance to match her apology with my own.

On instinct, I followed, joining the flow of people heading towards the ancient gatehouse in the city walls at Monk Bar. Snow continued to flutter, melting to slush on the pavement.

Who, I wondered, was the boy's father? Unless, of course, the little chap was her much younger brother. Hence the facial resemblance. If so, where were her parents? Perhaps they were dead. Working in a fleapit like the Electric – in fact, working at anything other than a well-heeled marriage – was a serious descent for a girl like her.

Having passed under the city walls through Monk Bar, she headed for an alley laced with cinders and broken beer bottles. My pace slowed. Now I was curious. Snooty Miss Mountjoy, toddler in hand, taking a filthy shortcut into the Groves.

Every city is many cities; every house many homes. York back then was not all picture postcard views. Within half a mile of mansions adjoining the Minster, spread districts of narrow, back-to-back terraces, two-ups, two-downs, their brick walls stained by damp and soot. Some slum dwellings dated back to the eighteenth century or earlier, lightless courtyards with a single communal standpipe for water. Bodily waste was catered for by brick earth closets built above cesspits. Whole families crammed into a couple of rooms, paying half their measly earnings to the landlord.

The Groves was a notch above the very worst slums. A marginal notch. It stank of smoke, over-boiled greens, sewers, mud and something sweet and faecal I can only call the perfume of poverty.

As Louisa Mountjoy entered the snickleway her pace quickened. I hurried down the alley after her, just in time to see her emerge onto a cobbled street.

Shoeless urchins with little prospect of a solid Christmas dinner stared as she passed. A few men smoking cigarettes hung round the street or outside dingy corner pubs. One shouted something at her. What I could not hear. She ploughed on, quickening her pace to enter a narrow, muddy yard between rows of tiny terrace houses. A filthy sign hung at the entrance: *Princess Street*.

She did not look back, did not notice me. But a familiar figure was sweeping a doorstep a little way along the terrace.

The older woman with the broom was none other than the cinema's daily cleaner, Mrs Bertha Kettlewell. The little boy ran forward into fat old Bertha's embrace. A moment later, all three vanished inside the small terrace house.

At last I understood. Louisa lived there. Probably as Bertha's lodger. And I saw why the job at the Electric meant so much to her. There's no place like home if you're afraid of not having one. Particularly with a kid in tow. Next step down the ladder would be going on the game. What people used to call 'going gay'. Or signing up at the workhouse for oakum-picking and laundry work. Sensible folk considered the former fate preferable.

Seven

A new year commenced. How to use it? Many a drudge trapped in factory or office, domestic service or loveless marriage, would have envied my freedom. True freedom always belongs somewhere else.

Early in January came a chance meeting. Nothing much compared to what had been considered normal during the war years. A lingering symptom from a wounded time.

One lunch I drifted into the Cricketers Arms. Seats were scarce, so I approached a man alone at a table with his back turned towards the other drinkers. A broad-brimmed hat concealed his face.

Holding my pint, I sidled round him with a grunt of apology to take a seat. Now I could see his face for the first time, across a crowded ashtray and empty glasses. My pint of bitter hovered beside my mouth.

Though his kind were everywhere after the war, many fresh out of hospital or convalescent home, few could compete with this poor fellow.

Something – shrapnel, I guessed – had punched a hole in the lower portion of his face, rupturing chin and bottom lip. Where a mouth should have been, there was a moist, pink, gummy hole the size of a fat plum.

The face above the hole was entirely normal. It belonged to a handsome chap around my own age. In fact, the upper lip and teeth were perfectly intact. It was the lower jaw that had been torn apart. Jagged stitches of wire bound it to the rest of his head. A few chipped, bright white teeth dotted the rim of the pulpy hole.

His tongue poked out to lick a lower lip no longer there. He had cultivated a bushy moustache as camouflage. My nose twitched involuntarily at the ammoniac stink of antiseptic Dakin's Solution, a scent taking me straight back to my own time in hospital.

A long, awkward pause while I settled.

'Afternoon,' I said.

He grimaced. Red-rimmed eyes scanned my face; assessed my burned cheek and squinting eye. We both wore badges of war.

'Haff-ter-noon,' he muttered.

His voice was thick from a swollen, clumsy tongue.

I lit a cigarette. Opened the Yorkshire Herald I'd brought along to hide behind: it felt fake, somehow ridiculous, a theatrical prop.

He coughed, his eyes still on me. 'Fouldn't haff let me out, fould they?'

'Wouldn't say that, old chap. Not at all.'

He took up a glass of whisky.

'I diff-charged myfelf from the hoffpital,' he said. 'Nothing more they could do.'

I nodded. Didn't know what to say.

He gestured at his face. 'I wanted them to fee me back home. Juft fee me.'

He grinned obscenely. It might well have been intended as a sad, rueful smile. All subtlety of expression had been taken from him. The lightning quick transformations of face we imagine uniquely our own.

The pub was hazy with cigarette smoke. A small crowd round the bar roared with laughter.

'Know what you mean,' I said.

His eyes widened. He had blue, sensitive eyes.

'Do you?' He chuckled. A breathy, phlegmy laugh. 'Went to fee my fianfée thif morning. Ex-fianfée. Threw me over a while back… ' He waved again at his face. 'Poor girl burft into tearf.'

He lifted his glass. Sipped the whisky. A delicate procedure. Some of it dribbled onto the raw flesh round his mouth. It must have stung like hell. I waited, frozen.

'D'you know,' he demanded, suddenly loud, 'd'you know? Emily kept on at me to enlift. On and on. "I expect my beft boy to be a man." Must haff heard it somewhere, like they do. *Bitch.*'

42

'Steady on,' I cautioned.

'Told me fee'd just got engaged to a fellow who couldn't go out to France. Failed the medical. Flat feet.' His chuckle was oddly monkey-like. 'Turns out he'f a travelling falesman. A falesman! Can walk well enough for *that*.'

He examined my face again. Then I realised he was jealous of me. Horribly jealous of my disfigurement. To him it was a graze, a shaving cut, a pimple, nothing.

With a scrape of his chair, he rose. Swayed drunkenly.

'I juft wanted her to fee me,' he said.

Once he had gone, I pretended to read the Herald. The wounded man's grotesque presence lingered at the table.

Some meetings are offered to us by fate. Chances to pick out an outline of the truth through fogbanks of ego – and, in my case, self-pity. Poor, poor wretch. What did I have to complain about?

Yet behind his maimed face the man inside had burned bright, conscious that love and children and an equal place in the world were irrevocably lost to him. However hard he tried to resist, he would be hidden away like something shameful.

How much better to be the Phantom of the Opera, respected for my music, than dependent on charity and forbearance? I was lucky. Damn lucky. It amazed me I had not comprehended it before. The realisation blew open a closed doorway of self with an echoing bang. A door I had deliberately held shut, perhaps because it felt safer that way. Beyond that gateway, lay futures I had forgotten were possible. If only I could find the courage to walk through. Out, out into the world.

I thought of Archie Fitzclarence. I had glimpsed him entering Bootham Park Asylum at the end of a crocodile of lost souls. Fitz was quite as pretty a picture as the young chap in the Cricketers. Except, on top of physical wounds, he must be half-crazy, his mind shot to hell. Why else lock him in a lunatic asylum? Thinking of Fitz led me back to Gus and Smittie, how all our wars ended.

Out of our crew in the bus, I alone survived relatively intact. Did that impose an obligation upon me? Even then I knew what that duty entailed. But I shrank from it. Lacked the nerve. Or kindness. Maybe I was just too damned small.

I wandered back to the Electric in time for the afternoon showing. Laverelli was in the foyer, putting up posters of starlets and male stars. I paused at the display, looking from face to face. So much soft-focus beauty, gay, sophisticated insouciance. The glass case in which they hung reflected back my own face as a blur.

'Everything alright, Mr Young?' asked Laverelli. 'You look like you've seen a ghost.'

How could I explain that I teemed with ghosts?

'I'm fine. Just fine.'

I waved at the perfect faces on the wall.

'Do you think they're freer than us?' I asked. 'For being beautiful and rich?'

He pursed his lips. Scrumpled up last week's posters depicting last week's stars. He popped them in the waste bin.

'Do you know what I think, lad?'

'No.'

'You're as free as you feel.'

With that, he withdrew to his cubbyhole office.

I wonder how many millions, in those years, sought escape in anonymous darkness. In the imagination's flickering cave. That theatre with glowing walls where enormous faces filled mind and heart. Where impossible situations became real for a few hours. All through a simple act of faith: the acceptance of illusion.

Most nights the queue outside the Electric stretched halfway down Gillygate, patient and disciplined. Oh, we were that all right, our generation. We who obeyed insane orders to walk – not run – into hails of machine gun bullets. But we were hungry for a better world, too. There was independence of spirit in that, perhaps even rebellion. No power or dominion yet devised has managed to suppress young dreams.

Being young myself, I naturally noticed those in the audience of my own age – and especially the opposite sex. Cinema's cargo of fantasy drew us. Women outnumbered young men, in any case, with so many squandered in the trenches. We all longed to put horror behind us. Hope and sex danced their eternal tango in our blood. Films were the mirrors of the age; and, inevitably, so much lucrative trade provoked intense competition.

One evening, I stepped outside for fresh air. Ambrose Ackerley was marshalling the six-thirty queue when I noticed something odd.

Two men in evening dress and overcoats were walking along the line, distributing flyers. Ambrose hurried over to me.

'Quick lad! Go get *Him Indoors*. Tell him, Ernie Precious is handing out these buggers.'

Ambrose thrust one of the leaflets into my hand. It was the first time he had properly spoken to me since the chocolates affair.

'You mean, fetch Mr Laverelli?'

'Who else? The Pope? Sharp now, go get him!'

Laverelli emerged in his dinner jacket. By now the interlopers had covered nearly the entire queue. People were reading and talking excitedly.

'Shall I put a boot up Precious's backside?' offered Ambrose.

I wouldn't have put it past him. There were dark sides to the commissionaire. Laverelli placed a restraining hand on the burly man's arm.

'No point, Ambrose,' he said. 'I knew Precious would try something clever. This means war.'

I stooped for one of the flyers blowing down the street.

WHY PATRONISE AN *INFERIOR*, OUT OF DATE CINEMA?

HAVE A **GRAND** TIME INSTEAD AT THE NEW **GRAND PICTURE HOUSE, CAFÉ AND BALLROOM!**
SETTLE ONLY FOR THE LATEST IN *QUALITY*.

GRAND OPENING CEREMONY AND CHARITY PERFORMANCE *NEXT MONDAY*!

45

I seemed to remember talk of a spanking new cinema half a mile away on Clarence Street. The Grand could seat one and a half thousand paying backsides, not to mention the attractions of a decent café and dancing, a craze rivalling films in popularity. No wonder Laverelli was concerned. All empires rise and fall.

I resumed my place in the pit.

Next day, Laverelli summoned me to his office. He was staring at a framed photograph of a young man in a dapper suit.

'Mr Young,' he said, slipping the picture face down into a small closet where he kept his account books. He closed the door. 'How does an evening off sound? On the house.'

I waited for the catch.

'Now, I wouldn't offer that to just anyone. But I recollect you mentioning that you was an observer in them *airplanes* during the war.'

I lit up while he talked. I'm sure the word *reconnaissance* featured. My thoughts drifted back over the North Sea.

'I was never the pilot,' I announced, suddenly. 'Only the navigator.'

Laverelli fell silent.

'You've lost me there, lad. I'm not asking you to fly to Clarence Street. It's just down the road.' His eyes brightened. 'But if you need a *pilot* to navigate, I've just the ticket.'

'What do you mean?'

'Like I was saying. They're having a gala opening at the Grand and you just agreed to go.' He cleared his throat. 'As a sort of representative of the Electric.'

'I agreed?'

'Oh, aye. But if you want a *pilot*... ' His voice took on a decidedly blue tone. 'I'll give Gladys the evening off. She can check out the ladies' lavs and report back.'

He conducted me to the door.

'Well done, lad. No one will notice you. Keep your eyes and ears open. See how it compares to them fancy London cinemas. No need to dress up, just blend in.'

'Why not go yourself?'

He looked appalled. 'And give Mr Ernest-bloody-Precious the satisfaction of gloating over me? For all York to see? I'd sooner... By God!'

What he'd sooner do was clearly answerable in a court of law.

When Louisa Mountjoy heard about my evening off, she laughed. I should explain an uneasy truce had been established between us after the kids' matinee.

'Oh, golly! Mr Laverelli asked you to *spy*? And with Gladys Bannering?'

'I think reconnaissance was the word he used.'

Her voice lowered to a conspiratorial whisper. 'Without wishing to be unkind, *our Gladys* is, well, awfully... you know.'

She meant common. I shrugged unhappily. Promenading with Gladys Bannering at so public an event might earn me a new nickname. Not just *Phantom of the Opera*, but *Beauty and the Beast*.

━

'Ooh, I'm a bundle of nerves!' declared Gladys Bannering.

Six o'clock found us in a queue stretching from the entrance of the Grand Picture House.

She wore a red cloche hat with a home-stitched burgundy jacket and gown. Cheap versions of designs flaunted on the screen and in fan magazines. Hollywood and its stars were educating us all. How to dress, smoke, walk, smile, even how to kiss. And *our Gladys*, as Louisa Mountjoy called her, was top of the class.

Everything about the usherette's get up suggested sex. The daringly short hemline, liberal make-up – allurements no respectable woman in provincial York would consider.

And me? I was out of the game. My face alone reduced me to the role of perpetual observer, not pilot.

Two older women behind us in more decorous finery (including fox furs with hungry little glass eyes), indulged in a stage whisper.

'It's that Bannering girl. What a nerve some people have.'

'Hussy,' agreed her pal, even less discreetly.

I felt a movement beside me; Gladys's arm slipped through my own.

'You wouldn't believe how parky I am.' Her light, nervous laugh revealed a slightly crooked front tooth. 'I never thought it'd be this cold out.'

It's quite possible my character was in decline. But in one regard I retained a little pride: I was a snob. Being seen arm-in-arm with Gladys Bannering reduced me to her level. Somehow I dreaded Louisa seeing us together. After the chocolates episode, it would be easy to get the wrong idea.

At the same time, the warmth of her arm seeking mine – and she was definitely cold, I could feel her shaking in her thin, home-sewn jacket that lacked a lining to save expense – set off strange sensations. As did her scent, natural rather than from a bottle.

In a movement brusquer than I intended, my arm extricated itself. A decorous distance was restored between us.

'Yes, it is rather cold,' I said, stiffly.

The queue edged forward to a printed sign on a wooden easel proclaiming: **TONIGHT ONLY! SPECIAL CHARITY PERFORMANCE. ALL PROCEEDS TO YORK COUNTY HOSPITAL.**

Gladys occupied herself with the posters of upcoming features.

'I do love the pictures,' she sighed. 'There's no harm imagining you're someplace else. Or that you are someone else.' She paused. 'Or even that you're *with* someone else. '

I glanced her way; then resumed my dogged interest in the queue ahead.

'There's nowt like imagining,' she added, with a faint, far away smile.

'Except when you wake up to reality,' I replied.

For another minute we were silent.

'I hear you was a flyer in the war, Mr Young,' she said. 'How did a musician get into that?'

This I really did not want to discuss.

'Bad luck, mainly.'

'No, go on.'

I pointed at my eyes. 'Twenty-twenty vision.'

'Ooh! What's that?'

I scanned round slowly. Then indicated a house a good hundred feet way. 'See that window,' I said. 'The one with the open curtain and light on.' She leant against me to follow my upraised arm. 'No, look closer, that window in the middle. See him now?'

A very fat, bald, middle-aged man in an unbuttoned shirt and whalebone corset could be seen pacing to and fro. He was clutching his enlarged stomach.

'Too much pie for dinner,' I said. 'Not that I'm against pies.'

Perhaps he had the bellyache. Or was mourning a lost athletic physique. To wear a corset at his age suggested more than vanity, maybe sadness at what he had become, what time had done to him. Suddenly I felt ashamed to spy on him unseen. Quite unreasonably, I blamed Gladys for the fact I had pointed him out as a figure of fun.

Her hand slipped to her hip. 'I can see one thing, Mr Young. Nothing gets past you. We'll have to be careful where you're looking.'

At last we entered the foyer. Staff in evening dress or natty uniforms hung round the high-ceilinged vestibule. Everything glossy as the chocolate and white paintwork. I produced the tickets Laverelli had given me, manfully ignoring Gladys by my side. We were shown to the best section of numbered, tip-up seats, the back stalls.

Here my suspicions ripened. Was this why Laverelli had advised me not to 'dress up'?

Eight

Again Gladys clutched my arm. Again I extricated myself.

'Blimey, that's the Lord Mayor,' she whispered, stifling a giggle. 'He's in the same row as us. Only two seats along. Wait till I tell me Mam.'

Our seats were among gentlemen in immaculate evening dress, complete with patent leather shoes and the odd top hat. Councillors and aldermen and their fur-coated ladies. Even the Sheriff of York, wearing his ceremonial red robe and chain of office.

I detected a continuous shiver beside me. Gladys was either scared witless or hilariously amused. I suspected the latter.

The manager of the Grand, Mr Precious, sidled over as we sat down. Gladys had told me while we waited in the queue that Ernest Precious fell out with Laverelli when both were travelling showmen. Why exactly, she did not know. This was in the early years of biograph shows, around the time of the Boer War.

We certainly diminished the dignity of Mr Precious's opening night. Which no doubt explained why Laverelli had bought us the most expensive seats, slap bang among the charitable bigwigs. My battered demob suit smelt of sweat and cigarette smoke. My collar was a little frayed. Gladys had dolled up as though ready to turn a trick for a few shillings. All very amusing for Mr Laverelli. Our neighbours examined us, less than pleased. I could see Precious hovering, deciding how to eject us while avoiding a fuss.

Before he could, we were cast into darkness. The ten-piece orchestra struck up.

As the overture played, a sudden panic swept me. Back then I was bitterly ashamed of my occasional panic attacks. The sweating palms and wildly beating heart. The certainty of inadequacy.

A single thought made me wretched as I watched the conductor. How far I had fallen musically. After the Royal College of Music, so many doors lay open to me: symphony orchestras, successful dance bands, trios and quartets. Particularly as a soloist. Then I had enlisted for the Royal Naval Air Service on a whim.

Too often life makes your choices. In that dark cinema I acknowledged for the first time that I might be deliberately punishing myself by lingering in York. Because the war... the war... I did not feel a hero. I had done things in the war. And not done things. Too easy to blame someone else, anyone else. The Germans. My stepfather for goading me to enlist. Even poor Archie Fitzclarence. Too easy to find excuses for what happened to Gus and Smittie. What happened when we bombed Cuxhaven. What was done was done without repeal. York had summoned me via Hell, Hull and Halifax to see it played out.

The main feature that evening was *Comradeship*, advertised as 'A Tale of the Great War'. Two soldiers from different classes, high and low, brought together on the battlefield. Wildly popular for a while, no one has heard of *Comradeship* now or its stars, Lily Elsie, Guy Newall, Gerard Ames. I doubt even a single reel survives.

Yet half a century later my inner eye fills with flickering scenes, emotions, none in black and white, more glowing sepia, serenaded by the orchestra.

All over the packed auditorium stray sobs. Sniffles, gasps, raw outpourings, fiercely repressed. Wounded, grieving hearts granted a slight release. White hankies appeared like dove wings.

Even Gladys Bannering got in on the act, conforming to the general mood. When a minor heroine got pregnant out of wedlock with a soldier who never came back, then suffered a miscarriage upon receiving the fateful telegram (why the War Ministry sent it to his former mistress was unexplained), I heard her choke and sob.

In a rush, her cheap emotion disgusted me. It was common for those of us who had 'been away' to resent civilians. Despise them, even. Ironic, of course, seeing our sacrifice was supposedly for their sake.

At last, the final credits played. I rose. I'd had enough. Bugger espionage for sodding Laverelli, I was off. The Cricketers' Arms my natural destination.

Was it ungallant to leave Gladys gawping at my receding back without a word? Probably.

The lights were bright as I left the auditorium, fumbling for a cigarette and pushing past people to the street. My feet led me where they would. Straight past the Electric, on past Exhibition Square, down Museum Street to Lendal Bridge. There my heartbeat slowed. I leaned dangerously far out over the low parapet, casting my cigarette butt into the dark waters of the River Ouse. Street lights revealed slow eddies in the murky water. Dive in and you'd be sucked under, dragged beneath the arch. A minute of terrified struggle then blackness…

A hand touched my arm. I started. Nearly unbalanced over into the river below.

'What the . . !'

'You alright, Mr Young?'

There was no escaping her. I rubbed my forehead. Glared suspiciously.

'Just a migraine. That's a special type of headache.'

Gladys frowned down at the swirling Ouse.

'Weren't thinking about jumping, was you?'

'No, I was not.'

'Good. You'd make a right splash. And I can't swim.'

Again the nervous little laugh. The bad teeth. I wearily reached for a cigarette. The packet was empty.

'Weren't it a grand film?' she breathed. 'That bit about… Well, all of it were grand. Though I don't suppose Mr Laverelli would like to hear *that* word when we tell him!'

Was Gladys making a pun? It seemed unlikely.

'No.'

'The part about the orphan boy was very sad, don't you think? I could have cried.'

I recollected Louisa Mountjoy's little boy being led through the slums on Christmas Day.

On impulse, I asked, 'Does Miss Mountjoy have a young son?'

It was not a gentlemanly question. One might easily call it gossip. Though I immediately regretted it, Gladys had no such scruples.

'Didn't you know? You see, just like in the film, she met a soldier – an officer, they say – and before they could marry he was called away to France. And killed. Later, well, she had little Freddy.'

I looked at her with something worse than surprise. Louisa Mountjoy was *fallen*. The world had much nastier names for such women back then. Likewise, a nasty name would haunt her poor son all his life. A name of shame and secrecy.

My voice took on a pompous edge. 'That's quite enough, Gladys. I find gossip about a lady unpleasant.'

'But you're the one who asked... '

'I think you have said enough.'

Women can be the cruellest judges of their own sex. I was certain the usherette felt superior to Louisa. An unfortunate girl from a far better class than her own, a girl twice her worth in education, intelligence, deportment, elocution, everything but that swiftly passing grace, youthful beauty.

'But Mr Young... '

'Goodnight.'

My voice was magnificently icy. I marched back to the Cricketers. There, the prospect of meeting Louisa Mountjoy by accident as I returned to my attic room kept me in the bar until chucking out time.

Next morning, Laverelli asked about the Grand. I grunted he should try Gladys. As for the usherette, after my rebuke on the bridge she grew stand-offish. Thank goodness, I had been struck off her list of admirers.

The new cinema's opening brought smaller audiences to the Electric. Laverelli took to loitering in the foyer for oily salutations with customers; his fixed grin acquired an uneasy edge.

After these initial skirmishes, the war between the rival picture houses intensified. Ernie Precious even attempted a poaching raid.

One Sunday evening, I was in my private corner of the Cricketers. This was a table tucked away near the fire, half-hidden from view by a small screen of varnished wood and stained glass projecting from the wall. A quiet place to sit, read a newspaper or book, or simply stare at the glowing coals in the grate.

No one bothered me and I bothered no one. A reasonable enough proposition. Around nine o'clock a throat cleared. I lowered my library book to discover a ruddy face with a potato-shaped nose and handlebar moustache.

'Recognise me, son?' he began, affably enough. He had a distinct London accent. It was pleasant to hear familiar tones.

'Yes.'

The last time we met was at the opening night of the Grand. He had been looking to expel me and Gladys from our seats among the local big bugs.

Ernest Precious made a tipping gesture with his hand. 'Drink?'

Actually, I was trying hard to cut back on the alcohol. For a moment, I wavered.

'I've got a little proposition to make,' he said. 'If you can spare the time.'

'Thank you then. Just a very small rum.'

I watched him at the bar. He wore a loud checked suit and seemed to know several of the regulars by their first name.

When he returned, it was with a double. I'd barely taken a sip before he made his pitch.

'Like it at the Electric?'

This was a charged question. 'It's easy enough.'

'Too easy, eh?'

'Since you ask, sometimes.'

Precious offered me a cigarette.

'Well, the thing is, son, I've heard good things about you. The director of my orchestra, Mr Cooper, popped into the Electric to sound you out. Ve-ry impressed, he was. Ve-ry impressed.'

I took another sip.

'Mr Cooper said you'd make a top notch first violin. And I'm the kind of chap who knows a tip-top man never comes cheap. That's why I want to make you an offer. Fifty shillings a week. In your hand.

How does that sound? I'll bet it's more than that cheapskate Laverelli pays.'

It was considerably more.

'Yes,' I said.

'So what do you say?'

I nodded as though mulling the matter.

'Thank you, Mr Precious, I'll need to think about it.'

He rose and thrust out his hand.

'Don't think too long. Remember, top billing beneath Mr Cooper. You won't regret it.'

He considered me in the bag. With that, Precious left. As he pushed through the cigarette smoke fogging the place I spotted Ambrose Ackerley leaning on the bar, in earnest conversation with the landlord. Instead of a proper drink he had a bottle of lemonade in front of him.

Next day, Laverelli buttonholed me. His black bow tie hung a little askew. I smelt spirits on his breath.

'Mr Young, a powwow before the six o'clock?'

I was led into his tiny office.

'Now I don't want you to imagine anyone's been *spying* on you,' he began. 'That's not our way at the Electric. Not our way at all.'

I took the cigarette he offered.

'Do you remember the first time you came here, lad,' he reminisced. 'In a snowstorm? Like Mary and Joseph wanting refuge at the inn. Shocking weather. Parky as a snowman's trousers. You needed an urgent job. No one can deny we provided a sheltering wing.'

I supposed not.

'So let's be straight. If someone happened to mention you'd been seen with Ernest Precious, that's no doing of mine. A chap cannot help what he hears. And I believe this is a free country. At least, the last time I looked.'

I shrugged. 'He offered me fifty shillings a week. *In your hand*, were his exact words.'

'Did he now?' Laverelli grew still. 'It's that way, is it?'

His turn to light a fag. A strong tang of sulphur rose from his match.

'I should tell you, me and Mr Precious go back a long way. Aye, before you was born. We were pals at one time, business partners. It didn't end the way he liked and he's been waiting for his chance to even the score ever since.'

I listened.

'Somehow, he swung himself a job as manager at the Grand.' Laverelli shook his head sadly. 'They'll regret that. Unless they have a damn sharp book keeper.'

'Fly, is he?' I ventured.

Laverelli nodded. 'It's not my habit to malign any man on God's earth. But with Ernie Precious, I make an exception. He'll stop at nothing to get at me, Mr Young. And use any willing pawn that's daft enough to fall for his snares.'

'He sounds a bit like Professor Moriarty,' I could not help saying.

'Aye. So what did you tell him?'

'That I'd think about it.'

'And what are your thoughts, Mr Young, if I might make so bold as to ask?'

'I could use fifty bob a week.'

'Well, I'm afraid even the leader at the Electric gets far less than fifty,' said Laverelli. 'Some of us aren't bankrolled by Alderman Pulleyn. Or his moneybag pals. Unlike Ernie-bloody-Precious.'

The Grand had important backers among York's leading businessmen and civic luminaries. Whereas Laverelli was defiantly his own man.

A weary, resigned sigh escaped his lips. Along with wisps of cigarette smoke.

'How about I pay you forty. And you get to keep your room in the attic?'

I shrugged. But he was onto something. The attic held unique charms.

'I know,' he said, 'you're bored, aren't you? Playing the same old music every night?'

'Yes.'

I spoke from the surest part of my soul. What pride we musicians took in our craft! Hand us a difficult score? Sight reading to deliver a faultless performance was a given. Yet here I was, recycling the same twenty or so pieces in different combinations. I had begun to indulge in impromptu variations while Louisa ploughed on. And Maurice's bird whistles were starting to trouble me deeply. Even the attractions of the attic could not quite compensate for his duck calls.

Another sigh from Laverelli. 'How about if you was leader of the orchestra?'

His offer took me by surprise. I studied his face. But he meant it.

As it happens, I did not feel flattered. A trio is a very small orchestra indeed. Taking on the role would mean delaying my return to London, burying myself in a provincial fleapit. Then I remembered the blind man who came to appreciate our performances several times a week, as one would a concert. Maybe he deserved a more stimulating programme.

'You know, lad,' said Laverelli, as though reading my mind, 'York could be good for you. And you could be good for York. And it's not a life sentence. You can quit any time you please.'

'What about Miss Mountjoy?'

A memory of the tiny terrace house on Princess Street made me reluctant to accept. Not to mention the bonny little boy dependant on his mother's position. It seemed doubtful she would have sufficient savings to tide herself over until another job came her way.

'She'll come on board,' said Laverelli. 'Only, if you become leader, she stays on. That's not in question. Agreed?'

'Agreed. Very much agreed.' I hesitated. 'Perhaps I could show her a few tricks.'

Laverelli's eyebrows shot up.

'You know, how to fit up a film properly. That kind of thing. Without relying on *Hearts and Flowers*.'

His smile was all shiny dentures.

'I'm sure she'd appreciate it,' he said. 'Though there's a lot to be said for both hearts and flowers. Not a word to the lady, please, until I've had a little powwow.'

So I played out my swansong as first (and only) violin in the Electric's orchestra. Every time I looked Louisa's way I felt guilty. She had begun to confide in me a little. A tentative, fragile trust, that Laverelli's little powwow would end forever. It seemed inevitable she must hate me. Perhaps even fear that, after stealing her job, I would seek to replace her at the piano.

On the way over to the Cricketers after the show, I was treated to the spectacle of Louisa Mountjoy emerging from Laverelli's office. She was rubbing furiously at her eyes with a lacy handkerchief salvaged from the shipwreck of better days. Hastily, I crossed the road and ordered a double whisky to toast my elevation in the musical world of York. It tasted distinctly sour.

Nine

A hunchback, the left half of his face twisted, hideous, gazing down from the bell tower of Notre Dame Cathedral at the Festival of Fools capering in the cobbled square below...

D eaf – half-blind – shut off from
his fellow-men by his deformities,
the bells were the only voice of his groping soul!!

A lone violin sobs through a slow, fateful toll of tubular bells, purchased second hand in Selby at the new leader of the orchestra's insistence and played by the cellist.

Onward the scenes rush! King and cunning courtier. . . soldier and poet. . . whore and nun. . . thief and saint. With each change the musicians shuffle sheet music hired that Monday from the New Century Picture Company, Leeds, thence borne to York in a battered demob suitcase on the 12:05 express. Choice musical delicacies selected with utmost taste by the Electric Cinema's new orchestral conductor, Mr David Young (BA Mus., Royal College of Music).

See! The poor creature skulks in his attic, hurling bitter scorn at an indifferent world!

But hark, the mood shifts. Beauty enters the square of fools and frantic revellers. Expertly performed appassionato strains from the leader's violin fill the darkness of the cinema.

Esmeralda, a child of mystery,
whom the King of the Beggars
had bought from gipsies as a helpless babe
and raised as his own.

How her loveliness is transfigured by the violin's yearning voice. She whirls in a dance of grace and joy and flawless youth. With what hungry longing the hunchback dotes upon her, an angelic creature forever beyond reach.

The tale unfolds and sheet music is swapped upon the stands using an efficient system of numbered and colour-coded pegs devised by the new leader of the orchestra until, at last, a tragic end...

See how Esmeralda beseeches Quasimodo's aid to spare her, a fallen woman, from the vengeance of the mob. He finds impossible strength, hurling down masonry blocks upon her enemies from his lofty sanctuary in Notre Dame Cathedral. With each crushing stone the cellist crashes two cymbals.

The deformed creature wrestles with an older man who would ravish Esmeralda! He seizes the would-be defiler, carrying him to the bell tower ramparts. See! The villain's knife plunges into the hunchback's hump, time and time again. With each murderous blow, the piano plays a heavy, thumping discord – all in accordance with strict instructions from the orchestra's new leader.

At last, the poor hunchback, forgotten and despised, must behold his beloved in another man's embrace. It is not he – her saviour – she adores. The violin throbs a tragic love theme. As the fatally wounded, twisted, vile creature crawls away, lurch by lurch, to perish alone, piano and cello and violin utter single, fateful chords, each more discordant than the last, until the hunchback expires, his sufferings stilled for eternity. All for love...

Stunned silence in the auditorium. A lone man's voice, exclaims, 'By 'eck! That were worth the full shilling!'

$$\text{\huge F}\text{inis.}$$

Winter melted washes of waxy light over York as I gazed from my attic window. Rooftops, church spires, industrial chimneys. Dark, upraised fingers trailing smoke. There was usually a tang of ash in the air, often scented with cocoa from the chocolate factories.

One morning, I was daydreaming with a mug of strong tea when the door shook in its frame. A knocking fit to wake whatever ghosts haunted that dusty room with its capacious double bed.

Without waiting for permission, a florid pumpkin head poked inside.

'Mr Ackerley,' I said, weakly.

'Now then lad,' he huffed. The steep stairwell had taken its toll. 'I were hoping to catch you alone.'

My usual state, especially when surrounded by people. I reached nervously for a packet of fags.

'I've a favour to ask,' he said. 'Though I'll be first to admit, I were right disappointed when you gave them chocolates to Gladys Bannering. Ten shillings they cost! Not counting the wrapping paper.'

I made a neutral noise. Lit up.

'I want you to understand,' he carried on, 'there's no hard feelings between pals. That's why I'd like to ask that favour.'

His voice took on a troubled urgency. 'You know, lad, me and that *certain lady* go back a long, long way. Nigh on fifty year. We were at the same school and all set to be engaged when I landed a respectable

61

job at Rowntrees.' He sighed. 'Now I know I can rely on this staying between ourselves, but she broke off from me because of a certain weakness of mine.' He made an upward tippling gesture. 'And she married another fellah, a Primitive Methodist. Nor do I believe that marriage went happily. He were over fond of using the back of his hand.'

I picked a shred of tobacco from my teeth.

'She's been a widow these eighteen months with hardly a penny coming in. Her son's a skinflint, nowt better than his dad. And I'd like her to know I'm still fond, if you follow my drift.'

How could I not? If there was one thing the Electric's nightly fare nourished, it was an appetite for improbable romance.

'I'm not sure how I can help.'

His old assurance returned. 'Leave that wi' me, son. The point is, you're not from round 'ere. And I can tell you're discreet.'

Ambrose described his 'favour' conspiratorially, as though Esther Jones might overhear.

'You're joking,' I said.

'I'm dead serious. Nobody'll guess a thing.'

'I really think this time… '

Suffice to say he wore me down. Perhaps I just wanted to get rid of him.

'I'll look it over,' I conceded.

He produced a very fancy Valentine card and envelope. A sizable investment for a working man on a below average wage in 1919. This specimen was a whopper. Say what you liked about Ambrose Ackerley, pinchpenny didn't apply when it came to wooing Esther Jones.

The card depicted a circular alarm clock with hands like Cupid's arrows. Clinging to the top of the clock was a cherub in shorts with curly hair and round, long-lashed eyes. In front of the clock, on a low stool, a little girl in a red party dress, a red ribbon in her hair. Hands on chubby little knees, she simpered up demurely at him. What she made of the little blighter hanging on the clock was anyone's guess. Above them ran the legend, **Now's the time – To be my VALENTINE.**

Ambrose was leaning over, his grizzled face eager, anxious.

A terrible sadness at the human condition flowed through me. How many decades had ticked emptily by since Esther threw him over? Yet still he hoped for one last flare of time. Like a burning match that glows bright before it goes out.

I made a final, feeble attempt to put him off.

'I've only got violet ink up here.'

'Even better. Now this is what I want you to say… '

He took out a piece of paper and dictated: *Though time has been unkind, please think fondly of one who loved you of yore and would win most gladly thy heart again.*

I wrote in my best copperplate handwriting, a style I used for the cue sheets listing accompaniments to films.

'That's very strong,' I pointed out.

'Aye, I copied it from a title in one of that Italian fellah's films. You know the chap, Rudolph Valentino. I know she likes him.'

He gathered up his precious Valentine card, leaving me to finish my tea, muddy and cold. Doubts stirred. But what could go wrong with copying out his little message?

In the war, I grew accustomed to cold invading my marrow. Perhaps that is why February's bitter frosts did not trouble me too badly in my shadowy attic. Far worse were the dreams. I often woke, curled beneath layers of coarse blankets, sweating, gasping.

Almost always it was the war, even when the dream masqueraded as something else.

Flying machines fascinated me as a young man, which partly explained why I volunteered for the Royal Naval Air Service. That, and a desire to pre-empt the meat-grinder of conscription. By autumn 1916, when I took the shilling fresh out of music college, rumours were everywhere about the hellish abattoir of the Western Front. Wallowing then drowning in mud held little appeal. Better to soar above the fray on glamorous wings. So I reasoned at the time.

As an educated young man, fit, active, with a musician's quick reactions and a talent for mathematics, I was channelled into the flight navigators' training at Wormwood Scrubs. Of course, Observer Navigators got in a few hours basic flying time, in case they had to take over in an emergency. But mainly it was maps and gunnery and the imperfect art of bombing.

Within a few months, I was transferred to the flying boat squadron at Felixstowe for patrolling the North Sea to intercept U-boats and Zeppelins.

Here isn't the place to write about those remarkable flying machines – marvels of design for the time – or how the flying-boat station operated, its rules and routines.

In fact, I dreamt more often of the people I met there. Many of whom perished, one way or another.

As the skipper of our bus, Fitz was fond of telling me: 'Your little job, Young, is to get us there and back. My billet is to fly this crate like billy-o, so Herr Fritz doesn't know what's hit him.'

Most young officers of 'the best sort' affected such devil-may-care banter. One of many reasons I felt uncomfortable in the officer's mess. Fitz's 'little job' also included taking complete credit for our successes. He craved a Victoria Cross, the most prestigious medal on the rack. I suspected a compulsion to impress Ma and Pa 'like billy-o' lay behind it.

Even at his most infuriating (behaviour he jokily dismissed as *just me being beastly, ha ha!*), I sensed something hapless, even a trifle scared about Fitz. It lurked behind his arrogance. A boy trying too hard to be the best. A boy never quite good enough in his own eyes. It rendered him human. Weakness can make anyone worthy of sympathy. Even those who might not deserve it.

Oddly, the film, *Comradeship*, spurred me to do my reluctant duty by Fitz. I came to know the picture well. First, watching it at the opening night of the Grand, and later when it had a ten day run at the Electric. Its tale of two very different personalities, from contrasting backgrounds, forced together by the perils of war was obviously relevant. So I polished my shoes, took a deep breath, and decided to visit him once, just once, to appease my conscience.

A clear, icy morning found me walking up the avenue to Bootham Park Lunatic Asylum. Crows cawed in trees. I paused to watch a long goods train clank and huff along the adjoining railway line. Steam billowed in the cold air.

64

My throat tightened as I approached the steps leading up to the asylum. It resembled a gloomy country mansion, or would have done, if not for a few patients in pyjamas and overcoats taking the fresh air, accompanied by nurses.

A small office with a porter led to a stern matron. Then, after a ten minute wait on a long bench in the corridor, to a short, bespectacled man. He wore a white coat over his tweed suit. I rose hastily, knocking my trilby to the floor.

Offering a firm handshake, he examined my burned face with cool, professional interest.

'How do you do? The name's Middleton. Dr Middleton. I hear you wish to call upon a patient of mine.'

I explained my connection to Archibald Fitzclarence. Part of me hoped he'd declare his patient unfit for visitors.

'Of course, one never knows,' he mused, 'in cases like his, whether the mental associations stimulated by an old comrade-in-arms will be beneficial.' He shot me a swift glance. 'It depends on their prior relationship, among other factors.'

I looked at the floor shiftily. A long pause followed.

'Well, given the circumstances, why not,' he said. 'This way, please.'

He led me through corridors smelling of carbolic soap and bleach. Past nurses who acknowledged him with a bobbing little curtsy. Up a winding flight of stairs. All the while, he talked briskly: 'Flight Lieutenant Fitzclarence is a private patient, naturally, coming as he does from an awfully good family. We've got him in with a dozen other officers. The ward is dedicated to men with both severe physical and mental scars. We believe the two to be interconnected. I should warn you at once, he may not recognise you. Poor fellow does not even recognise his own parents. Very sad all round.'

We passed a ward where a small group of female lunatics slumped in easy chairs, unattended knitting on their laps. One began to utter queer, rhythmical little cries. Her moans were oddly sexual. None of her companions noticed.

'Don't expect too much,' he concluded. 'Ah, here we are.'

A long ward, its tall windows over-looking the park at the front of the asylum. A dozen beds lined the walls. Each had plenty of space for an easy chair and bedside table. My eye immediately fell on the upright piano. The patients were dotted round the room. Only a couple lacked visible wounds. Several lacked limbs; in one case, a nose. Some twitched silently. Others muttered an unceasing threnody to themselves.

There he sat, the Right Honourable Flight Lieutenant Archibald 'Fitz' Fitzclarence. A hooked hand lay lifeless on his lap.

I was suddenly nervous. Should I salute? He always liked lots of saluting. I pulled up a chair.

Fitz peered at me. No sign of recognition. Scarcely a reaction to my presence.

'Ah, Archie!' said Dr Middleton, laying a hand on his shoulder. 'Look who I've brought. An old comrade. Come specially to say hello.'

Fitz's breath rasped as he exhaled slowly.

'I'm sure you have lots to catch up on,' beamed Dr Middleton.

Inspecting his fob watch, he left us to it.

'How are you, sir? They seem awfully nice here.'

Nothing. Not even a change in the rhythm of his breathing.

'I'm living in York now. Just a temporary thing. Playing my old fiddle for a living! Do you remember, sir? You always liked me to play the piano in the mess.' I ploughed on desperately. 'Perhaps I could play something here. There's a piano in the corner. *Keep the Home Fires Burning* was your favourite.'

My voice trailed. References to fires were unwise. Third degree burns stained his face crimson as a demon's. An ear was melted away. His mouth twisted into a hideous sneer. One eyeball was gone. His blonde hair had failed to grow back except in thick tufts. His face had always been plump, ruddy with health and confidence. Now the skin bubbled like melted cheese – I can think of no other way to describe it. It must have stung and itched unbearably. That was just his head. I knew the whole upper half of his body had suffered a similar fate. Not least, the right hand reduced to a useless claw.

We sat mostly in silence for half an hour. I ventured a few remarks he may or may not have heard. He did not reply. At last, duty was done. I rose to leave.

Then a miracle occurred. Fitz lifted his head like a tortoise poking out of its protective shell.

'Carry on, Young,' he croaked.

I stared down at him.

He seemed to chuckle. A painful gasp. 'Carry on, Baby.'

Seconds later, a nurse appeared by my side.

'It's the first time he's spoken in months,' she whispered. 'Ask him a question!'

I bent down to his level, touched his shoulder. Unintentionally, I spoke too loud, as you might to a foreigner or old person, someone deaf or stupid.

'Would you like me to visit you again, sir?'

The remaining eye goggled. Our faces were just a couple of feet apart.

'Carry on, Young.'

I straightened and met the nurse's eye.

'Let's take that as a most definite *yes*,' she said. 'Dr Middleton will be very pleased.'

I wished I could say the same.

Ten

The following afternoon, Laverelli summoned his staff to a meeting in the auditorium.

The announcement stirred predictable flutters. We all knew audiences were down since the opening of the Grand. Maybe he needed to let someone go. As for me, I felt merely curious. Under my bed was hidden a tobacco tin containing enough cash for a one way ticket back to London and a week's digs when I got there. Ample time for me to secure another position.

Louisa Mountjoy was already seated when I arrived. She wore a stylish but plain dress and jacket that flattered her figure. Her hands rested modestly on her lap.

As usual, she avoided my eye. I scared her a little since her demotion – and disliked myself thoroughly for it. Here was a chance to set her mind at rest.

'Miss Mountjoy,' I said, sitting next to her. 'How are you?'

A quick glance sideways at me.

'Very well, thank you.'

'And your – everyone at home?'

'All very well, thank you.'

I resisted a temptation to reach for a cigarette. She did not smoke and sniffed when others did.

'I'm glad we've got a chance to talk,' I said.

Again the sideways flicker. 'Oh?'

'You see, I wanted to thank you for your excellent work since I varied the repertoire.'

'After you replaced me as leader?' she asked, rather too sweetly.

Her question confused me. 'Yes, that's it. Anyway, thank you. Well done.'

For a moment I feared a tart reply building. But she touched the corner of her eye. And sighed.

'I didn't expect... Thank you, Mr Young.'

'No, thank *you*, Miss Mountjoy,' I replied, ever the idiot.

Before we could exchange another round of gratitude, Victor the projectionist joined us. He was a young lad, not long out of school. We rarely saw him. Mostly, he skulked up in *t'box*, fiddling with his reels. I should explain every cinema was obliged by law to keep its projector and film stock in a fireproof iron box. Nor was this an unnecessary precaution. Fires broke out regularly when nitrate film spontaneously combusted. A few years later, seventy-one kids were crushed to death in Glasgow after smoke started a stampede.

We waited in silence until Gladys arrived.

She surveyed us, and smiled. 'Ooh, you look just like the three wise monkeys sat there. All in a row.'

She sat down, crossing her long legs. Louisa's thin smile and raised eyebrow would have withered green corn.

Maurice joined us, less than pleased at clocking in early.

'You know why we're here, don't you?' he said, darkly.

'No.'

'*Him Indoors* is worried about 't'Bench.''

'T'Bench?'

'Magistrates bench, of course.'

He took great pleasure in explaining how every cinema was legally obliged to apply annually to the local magistrates for an operating licence. I sensed Victor listening carefully.

'That wa'n't a problem when the Electric were the biggest in town,' said Maurice with gloomy relish. 'This place was the only one worth talking about during the war. What with t'war over, and the Grand opening up on Clarence Street, and half its backers being aldermen and magistrates and the like... '

He broke off to blow his nose in a grubby grey hankie, as if to say, *even you can work it out, lad.*

Maurice considered me, at best, an unworldly noodle. At worst, a drunk with a suspect libido. The only thing he gave me the slightest credit for was my ability as a musician.

He leaned forward. 'An' Laverelli may well sweat about t'Bench and his precious licence. Given how many *oo-ers* hang around the place.'

Oo-ers was Maurice's pronunciation of *whores.*

'Steady on,' I cautioned. 'There are ladies present.'

Beside me, Louisa Mountjoy adjusted uncomfortably her demure posture.

Gladys Bannering rolled her eyes. 'You'd know better than most about *that*, Maurice Skelton,' she said.

Although I didn't take Maurice's warnings seriously, my mother's infallible sixth sense when it came to respectability did detect whiffs of seediness about the Electric. Aromas that might affect its licence.

Take Louisa Mountjoy, a fallen woman, and word did get around a small place like York. Then there was the musky allure of the apprentice tart about Gladys Bannering. The commissionaire, Ambrose Ackerley, was by his own admission a former alcoholic and possibly jailbird. As for Maurice, there was something about Maurice... I only discovered what later. And then came Laverelli himself. He had mentioned folk whispering a few choice things about his reputation.

Only Esther was entirely respectable. But no one, apart from Ambrose, paid her the least notice.

Once we were all assembled, Laverelli leant against the piano, as though about to launch into a sentimental Victorian parlour song.

'Thanks for coming, folks.'

'Didn't realise I had a blinkin' choice,' muttered Maurice.

'I won't take too much of your time. But I do need everyone on board.' Laverelli fixed Maurice with a baleful eye. He unfolded a sheet of paper. 'Now then, I've been sent this by the Chairman of the York and District Magistrates' Bench himself, Alderman Pulleyn. It seems every cinema in York is receiving the same.' He grinned mirthlessly. 'Including, let us hope, the Grand on Clarence Street.'

Laverelli raised the letter. 'In the light of this, we're dropping from the schedule *The Bigamist* and *Afraid of Love*.' The latter concerned itself less with shyness than a husband's failure to consummate 'the deed of love' and his younger wife's 'illicit consolations'.

'Why should we do that, Mr Laverelli?' piped up Victor the projectionist.

His was a dreamy, drowsy, fluty voice for a strapping, broad-shouldered lad.

Laverelli shook the paper like a hellfire preacher. 'It's all in here, Victor, plain as your nose. "The Bench",' he read aloud, '"is minded to condemn as an affront to public morality any exhibition of an indecorous or indecent nature." There's a whole list of it. "Actors divesting themselves of clothing at the slightest provocation" and "white men in a state of degradation amidst native surroundings". Oh, and "the pernicious glorification of free love." There's a lot more like that, I can assure you.'

Gladys Bannering perked up at "the gratuitous, prurient, lewd and sensuous exposure of girls' legs for the purposes of titillation".

All the while, Maurice nodded approvingly.

Laverelli returned the letter to his jacket pocket. 'I hope for his sake Alderman Pulleyn doesn't wander into Walmgate or the Groves on a Saturday night,' he said. 'He'd have the shock of his life. Nevertheless, we'll be squeaky clean from now on until the hearing. Apart from tomorrow night, of course. Seeing it's our Valentine's Day special, *Sex* stays on.'

I should explain *Sex* was one of those Hollywood movies masquerading as a strict morality fable while showing plenty of sin – in close up.

Sex turned out hot enough by the standards of the time. Louise Glaum vamped it up in a sinuous 'spider dance' as Broadway starlet out to entrap a rich male 'fly'. Alderman Pulleyn would have mopped his brow and loosened his collar. Drunken debauchery, bared flesh, illicit seduction outside of wedlock, enough bare leg work to make a centipede feel at home. Stage-door Johnnies canoodling and kissing

71

'loose' chorus girls while wetting their whistles with fountains of champagne.

I should confess here that I was, apart from a few relatively innocent late night encounters at the Royal College, less experienced in the film's subject than I desired. Too much time fiddling with the violin instead of playing other strings, you might say. It struck me as a paradox that despite having seen – and done – too many acts I would rather not, the one act my body urged me to pursue eluded me.

Maurice's face took on a grim cast as he sawed away at his cello, furtively glancing up at the screen every few bars. As for Louisa Mountjoy, she played more false notes than usual when Louise Glaum got her comeuppance and a wronged, long-suffering wife claimed back her lawful spouse from the actress's clutches.

At last, the final title flashed up:

The standards of
morality eternally
demand that the
naked soul of SEX
be stripped of its falsehoods –
which can only be
atoned for through
bitter tears.

I had packed away and was heading into the foyer to reach the Cricketers' Arms for last orders when I discovered a huddle round the ticket kiosk: Laverelli, Ambrose Ackerley, Gladys and my colleagues in the orchestra. The centre of attention, for once, was none other than Esther Jones. The grey haired lady clutched a large rectangle of cardboard.

Such a look of astonished pleasure on her thin, careworn face!

'I found it here this evening,' she explained breathlessly, 'with me name on the outside. I never got one of these in forty years of marriage to our Alfred.'

Ambrose's expression was worthy of a mooning calf.

'It's got such a lovely message inside,' sniffed Esther.

'What does it say?' asked Gladys.

'I don't know if I should... '

'Oh, go on! I know, just let me read it. No one else.'

Esther allowed Gladys a quick peek. Then it was the usherette's turn to *ooh*.

'That *is* lovely!' she chimed.

Gladys had almost certainly received a sack load of Valentines, and could afford to be magnanimous.

I felt rather pleased with myself. By lending my penmanship to Ambrose, I had added a dab of romance to his obsession with the old gal. In short, I'd done a good deed.

I was almost at the street door when Maurice thrust his head between the conspiring ladies.

'Hang on!' he cried. 'Blow me if I don't recognise that handwriting! And that fancy ink.'

Why did I hesitate? I should have kept on walking. Just like Felix the Cat traversing all obstacles life threw at him. Straight through those swing doors to the safety of the Cricketers' saloon bar.

Maurice guffawed. 'By 'eck! That's Mr Young's writing. Or I'm a Dutchman.'

All heads swivelled in my direction. Staring, accusing eyes surrounded me. My right hand rose to cover my left cheek.

'I... I should explain,' I began, turning desperately to Ambrose Ackerley for support.

But the big man's face was a hard blank, though his glance darted miserably at his beloved.

Esther's excitement deflated like a punctured barrage balloon. It wasn't hard to read her thoughts. She'd been the victim of a cruel joke, a heartless hoax. She, a widow of less than eighteen months. And the perpetrator? *Him again*, the lad not 'from round 'ere' who drank like a fish, half his face a hideous little devil's.

For a long moment no one spoke. Moistness gathered in poor old Esther's eyes.

'That joke was in very poor taste, Mr Young,' said Laverelli, trying to sound stern. He probably considered this a worthy sequel to the chocolate box episode. 'Very poor taste indeed.'

'Aye,' echoed Ambrose, feebly.

The rat! Why didn't I expose him there and then? Explain whose shillings had been lavished on that vulgar card. And yes, expose the origin of the sodding chocolates while I was at it. Somehow I couldn't. Joy at the effect of his Valentine on the woman he loved, and had longed for all his life, had turned in a flash to bleak despair.

A familiar, jaded weariness washed over me. I lowered the hand that had partially covered my cheek.

Gladys put her arm round Esther's hunched shoulders and shot me a barbed look.

'I'm sure Mrs Jones didn't deserve *your* pranks,' she said. 'I'm right disappointed.'

That made quite a few of us. Still I said nothing. How paralysed by embarrassment you can be when young. At precisely the moment I should have explained my innocence I was tongue-tied.

Louisa Mountjoy departed without noticing me. Maurice followed with the verdict, 'Daft as a brush.'

Then it was too late to straighten things out without looking even more of a fool. I shambled off to the Cricketers. I could feel Gladys Bannering's eyes on my back.

That night I dreamt again of the raid on Cuxhaven. A nightmare I had rehearsed a hundred times over...

We're coming in fast at just under a thousand feet. Lower better for a true aim. Daybreak, we departed in near darkness to cross the North Sea, hoping for surprise and luck. Fitz is eager to bag a U-boat. He's heard of a chap who got the Distinguished Flying Cross for his first sub.

Cold, always so cold, especially at dawn. The eastern horizon catches fire, beams of light peek over the curve of sea. I take bearings from the sun's angle and position, catch Fitz's attention and point north-north-east.

'We're for it this time,' I think in my dream.

I think the same each time we sight the German coast. It's coming, you see, always coming closer...

Cuxhaven, concrete harbour walls dotted with anti-aircraft. Misty and murky on the coast. Then the storm begins... *Flash*. Flares rise and crack open the sky with blinding white magnesium. Searchlights stab through the fog, pursued by red dots of flak that burst with dull, rolling crumps. They're reaching out for us, finding our distance.

Crash. Metal shell fragments scatter round the plane, tearing a gash in the upper wing. A shard of metal bounces off one of my twin Lewis guns. I dare not fire it now in case the barrel is slightly bent, and explodes.

My God, we're low. Fitz revving too fast for accurate aiming. Perhaps he's seen a sub. We're weaving side to side, confusing the archie, but I can see only destroyers and patrol craft in the harbour. All firing up at us, machine guns, tracer, Hell, Hull, Halifax... the docks and town rush towards us through the mist. I'm crouched over the bombsight, my brain juggling height, wind speed, airspeed from the dials of the dual controls. I spot a warehouse ahead. Damn it, why not. I wave to Fitz and he holds her steady. Nearly, nearly then *boom* – a shell blast rolls us out over the rooftops of the town. Fitz revving like mad to avoid a stall, my finger on the bomb release squeezing involuntarily. Jesus! Explosions fall behind us, smoke rising. I've hit the town. Bombed the civilians.

We tear off inland to escape the ack ack. Flat country beneath, farm country, oddly like Essex...

That's the moment I often wake, remembering how our Squadron C.O., Tiny Thomas, shows us an intelligence report a few days later. One of my bombs hit a small nunnery. Four nuns buried alive with a couple of orphans for good measure. Another bomb hit a bakery, killing the baker, his wife, and their young daughter. The German newspapers are full of it.

'Do try to hit the target next time, Young,' says Tiny. 'Bad luck though, old chap, could happen to any of us.'

Fitz gives me the cold eye for letting down the side – worse, letting *him* down.

'Damn bad show,' he says, gruffly.

There are no medals for blowing to pieces four nuns and two kids. A harmless working man plus his missus and their little girl. None at all.

Still half-dreaming, I realise what has awoken me. And I'm grateful for the disturbance. Sometimes I can dream the Cuxhaven raid several times in a single night. The next morning I always feel exhausted, nervous, hollow of heart. Not tonight, because a pal has come to call.

The scratching continues at the door, along with a faint mewing. I throw aside heavy blankets, pad over on stockinged feet.

'Come on then, Clifton. Welcome to the party.'

He purrs and rubs my legs when he's let in. I pour him a saucer of condensed milk and watch, cigarette in hand, by the light of a torch as he laps it up.

But I know he won't hang around. A few licks of his white bib then he's back on patrol. After he's gone, I linger in the armchair in an igloo of blankets. There I fall asleep. The next time I wake the dormer window is grey, not black, and I can just make out the silhouette of the Minster against an incipient winter dawn.

Eleven

Then it was March. Sunday morning. Clarions of bells from the Minster summoned the faithful and woke the poor in their crowded slums. I rose with a clear head, having neglected my usual medicine at the Cricketers' Arms.

Birds sang arias and scuttled their claws on the slates above my head, a symphony for spring. A haze of dappling light softened the ancient city's hard corners.

As I stood by the open dormer window, mug of tea in hand, anticipation flowed through me like green sap. I was young and growing. All life lay ahead. At any time a chance meeting could change my life forever. Like the daffodils poking up on the grass banks round the city walls I felt a buried confidence stir. My months as leader of the Electric's orchestra had let me glimpse a genuine talent in that line. Audiences were drifting back, despite the attractions of the Grand on Clarence Street. And my music was a large part of the allure.

I took a walk beside the Ouse, the path guarded by budding willows and alders. Near the high walls of a country house, I reached a lane climbing steeply away from the river. The muddy track led to the cast-iron gates of a public park.

Two cherry trees dense with half-opened buds of pink blossom framed the entrance, along with bare flower beds awaiting blooms. The soil smelt moist and rich. Small birds were about their business: squabbling, feeding, breeding, nesting. The essential business of all mankind, all creatures.

Inside the park, families in Sunday best strolled amidst trees and shrubbery. The excited cries of children reached the gate where I stood alone. I often avoided such public places, aware of too many eyes. A paradox, you might think, seeing my living came from sitting in the dark before a crowd every night. But there is a profound separateness to being a musician on stage. And the mind is never quite one thing or the other. Contradictions grow through us like tangled roots.

I followed the gravel path into the park, until I came upon a building of white-washed bricks with a mossy, red-tiled roof. Wire mesh covered its open front.

It was an aviary for parrots, as well as a monkey house. Half a dozen apes lolled upon bare logs around a scum-covered little pool in the centre of the concrete floor. There was a strong tang of urine and dung. On either side were enclosures, filled with tropical shrubs and small trees. Here parakeets and parrots were visible, red, yellow, brilliant blue among the leaves.

I was watching a monkey yawn and masturbate when a treble voice piped up.

'You got funny face!' cried a little boy who had appeared beside my knees. He was no more than three or four. He giggled, hiding his mouth with a hand. 'I like monkey!'

Home Counties and Yorkshire vowels met, not unpleasantly, in his accent. I recognised him at once from Christmas Day.

Obligingly, I made a low monkey noise. He was delighted by my performance.

'You got funny face!' he repeated,

I looked round for his mother. He must have run on ahead of her.

Crouching down, I touched my scorched, mottled left cheek and neck. 'Ever seen a robin? Robin Red Breast?'

He nodded. Though I doubted they had many robins in the backstreets of the Groves.

'Well, my name's not Robin Red Breast. Guess what it is.'

The boy shook his head. 'Rob-ing?'

'No.' I paused dramatically. 'Davy McPurple Face.'

His chortle was full of glee. 'I want mac-people face!' he cried.

'Oh, it's not easy to get a purple face,' I said. 'You have to play the stupidest game in the whole world.'

Pray to God this little boy would not endure another war. Yet twenty years later we had learned no better. I ruffled his curls. He had the same thick, nut-brown hair as his mother.

'You're Freddy, aren't you?'

Gladys had mentioned the boy's name on the night we reconnoitred the Grand.

He pushed forward to the cage and stared intently, almost forensically, at the monkeys. Freddy was that kind of boy, I could see. My heart went out to him. Poor little blighter. Without a father, it wouldn't be long before he heard the taunt of *bastard*.

'Freddy! Don't bother Mr Young, dear!'

Louisa wore a long blue skirt and jacket with a rather old fashioned, broad-brimmed hat. Her face wore a new expression. Or new when it came to me. Curiosity, cautious amusement. Guarded sympathy, too, maybe. She must have overheard my joke about Davy McPurple Face.

She laughed. 'It was strange hearing you talk with Freddy like that, Mr Young. I... I never imagined you talking that way.'

I wasn't sure how to take that.

'Just fooling around, you know. Hope you don't mind.'

'I don't mind at all.'

She hesitated. 'Actually, people really don't just see... ' She waved to indicate her own face. 'They soon stop noticing.'

I stood, hat in hand, resisting the urge to reach for a cigarette.

'People see someone far worthier than you imagine,' she said, softly.

A blush found her cheekbones. She had rather fine, delicate cheekbones.

'And I can assure you – a little enviously, I must confess – they love to hear you play. You're awfully good.'

'Thank you for saying so.'

Louisa leaned forward. 'Freddy! Don't put your fingers in the cage, dear! It's dirty!'

'And a naughty parrot might nip you,' I added with a smile.

From nowhere, we both laughed. After all, what were we? Two young people who had made a hash of everything we once hoped to be. Why shouldn't we laugh before a cage of languid, masturbating monkeys in a park charged with the electricity of spring? A park choired by flocks of busy, chirruping birds, the very earth warming hidden seeds. Why shouldn't we share a laugh?

'What a lovely place,' I said. 'I had no idea it was out here.'

'Yes,' she said, 'it was built by Mr Rowntree. For poor children to have somewhere healthy to play. Awfully generous of him, don't you think?'

It would have been awfully bad form to point out the chocolate millionaire could afford to be generous. Or that, seeing he was the local MP, you might even call it bribing the electorate.

'Do you come here often?' I asked.

'It is rather a favourite place of Freddy's. And the flowerbeds are very colourful in summer.'

No mention of escaping the stinking Groves for a gasp of clean air. The two-up two-down on Princess Street lacked any garden save a tiny backyard.

Suddenly we were awkward with each other again. We both watched Freddy try to communicate in monkey language with the apes in their cage.

'Well, it was very nice to bump into you,' I said.

Louisa nodded gracefully. However empty her purse, she was rich in middle class niceties and manners, what used to be called *polish*.

'Yes, it was jolly nice. Say bye-bye to Mr Young, Freddy.'

The little boy was too fascinated by a squawking parrot to notice. I crouched at his level. He pointed up at it and laughed.

'That's the spirit,' I said.

On impulse, I fumbled in my pocket for a shilling.

'Please buy little Freddy a treat from me,' I said, offering it to Louise.

'Oh, I really couldn't!'

'Some might think it better spent that way than in the Cricketers Arms,' I said, with a wry smile.

Before she could argue, I had popped the coin in her gloved hand.

'That's awfully kind of you. Say thank you to Mr Young, Freddy.'

Sensing his mother's confusion, the boy went shy and embraced her skirt. Raising my hat in farewell, I left them still pressed together. Had I once clung to my own mother that way? Before the years piled distrust and incomprehension between us? The thought brought a knot of sadness. It crossed my mind that dear old Mother would approve of Louisa Mountjoy. Her faultless manners and refined vowels, her determination to cling to a little *niceness*. Apart from the bastard son, of course – the vicar and neighbours would definitely not approve of *that*.

Despite my best intentions, I fell into the habit of visiting Archie Fitzclarence each Tuesday. With no matinee that day, time could drag until the five-thirty show. I suppose I pitied what he had become. Besides, strolling over to Bootham Park gave me an excuse to escape my bare attic.

Mostly, I felt a curious compulsion, one I could not explain. As though he might – I had no rational idea why or how – help me fly free of the war. Things lay between us, unspoken things.

Dr Middleton and the nurses grew accustomed to me on Tuesday afternoons. Not so Fitz. I'd sit by his armchair-throne while he glowered at the world. There I would try to draw him out a little. A hopeless task. The first few visits he barely acknowledged my presence. Perhaps that came as a mutual relief.

Once he glared straight at me, grumbling, 'This is the *officer's* wardroom and mess, Young. It is for *gentlemen*. You'd do well to live up to it. Damn fools let anyone in.'

His opinion of my place on the social ladder had not changed. Despite all he owed me. Not by a single rung.

Another time, after I complained about the griping weather, he grasped the knob of his walking stick in exasperation, muttering: 'Baby's cold, eh? Good lord!'

Then he began to complain on his own behalf, rarely meeting my eye. So and so on the ward was as common as a tinker. Dr Middleton had a suspicious air. He growled the doctors were little better than Boche spies. As for the nurses, they were eating his personal supply of ginger biscuits. Actually, that was me. There had to be some compensation for his rot.

Nor were the other patients congenial. Disturbing laughter and cries often broke the silence of the ward. A particular chap – the one lacking a nose – wept pitifully at the approach of twilight. The dusk carried him straight back to his own version of Hell, Hull and Halifax. It could take a long while for the nurses to calm him, his sobs echoing round the carpetless room. Fitz would peer through his one eye at the poor sod. You could almost hear his thoughts: *Bad show, jolly bad show.*

One time, a subaltern with severe shell shock had a fit. He'd grown thin as a whippet. Up he rose from his bed in underpants, socks, string vest. Buttocks pushed back, chest out, he staggered towards the exit, staring sightlessly. Then he was tottering on his heels, shaking, quaking, arms flailing for balance.

With a convulsion, he fell to the linoleum floor. He lay on his back unable to rise. Arms, legs, buttocks scrabbled wildly for purchase like a pinned spider.

The nurses rushed over and helped him back to bed. Fitz watched with infinite scorn.

'Does it every few days for a little bally attention,' he muttered.

Why did I return each Tuesday? A part of me belonged with those lost souls, drawn to them by instinct.

Matron, an Irish lady with a capacious bosom, once buttonholed me on the way out: 'You *are* doing him a power of good, Mr Young,' she assured me. 'Don't you be getting discouraged on us now.'

Several of the younger nurses were pretending not to listen. They watched us from the corner of their eyes. I had seen a couple of them in the front row of the Electric, near the orchestra. I blushed. Fled.

If I was hoping for excuses to stop visiting the ward (and I surely was), Fitz obliged the following Tuesday.

He took one look at my face then pointedly refused to acknowledge my existence. Something childish and desperate lurked in the way he sat with folded arms, gazing at raindrops beading the windows.

What are you doing here? I asked myself. *He doesn't want you here. He never respected you. He just used you to navigate his damn bus to glory. No one wants you here. You don't belong anywhere except on sufferance.*

82

I wandered over to the Robert Morley upright near the nurse's station. After testing a few minor chords, I began to play from memory a popular standby for tender love scenes or moments of special pathos, Debussy's *Claire de Lune*.

Music and the feel of my fingers on the keyboard revived the best of me. The side I seemed always to mislay. Waves of arpeggios, chords and melody immersed me in deeper currents of feeling, far beyond the petty tides of my stupid existence, this spoiled world, like the moon reflected gloriously on the sea as a long, shining road, a sight glimpsed often as we flew high above the waves...

I barely registered how one of the patients had risen, the one with no nose. He commenced a solitary dance, eyes and arms thrown open. The nurses and Dr Middleton watched in silent wonder.

My fingers danced with him over the keys. An outpouring matched by the lone, lost soul in the central aisle of the ward. The Matron was dabbing her eyes with a strip of surgical bandage.

A burly, clumsy figure appeared at my side. Fitz.

'Dammit, Young. Stop showing off. We've work to do!'

His shaking hand reached out for the piano lid. It swung down, almost crushing my fingers. I snatched them back just in time. For a long, discordant moment the piano reverberated.

'Dammit!' he repeated. 'Stop acting like a pansy. Letting the side down *again*. Just like that damn crash!'

Horrified, I stared up at him from the piano stool. Then I rose with as much dignity as I could muster. It didn't feel much.

'It is clear my visits are doing you no good, sir,' I said, with growing anger. The swine had nearly broken my fingers. Was this his revenge because I had escaped the crash relatively unscathed? Or was it spite that I possessed a talent he did not share, let alone appreciate? I struggled to keep a steady voice. 'For my part, I tried. Despite your... Well, I tried. Good luck, sir.'

With that, I swept over to the door where my overcoat and hat waited on a peg. My footsteps echoed down the grand staircase.

'Mr Young!'

Dr Middleton called from the landing above me. I ignored him.

Twelve

There was a camera technique in silent films you never see nowadays. The iris shot. An initially black screen opens out from a pinpoint of light until the full picture shows. That spring offered me an iris shot. A chance to reopen, inch by inch.

Every so often, I told myself it was high time to reclaim my London existence. Then reasons to linger in York occurred, none compelling, but enough. I woke and ate and played and drank and slept and took solitary walks, repeating that modest fugue through March and April.

As the weather warmed, so did Laverelli's rivalry with the Grand on Clarence Street. Especially with his old foe Ernie Precious.

Drumming up custom for any business was a fairly primitive art in 1920. When it came to the cinema trade, two standbys existed: puffs and stunts.

Puffs relied on the local press. Every column inch came at a cost. There Precious had the upper hand. His backers were not just wealthy, their names often appeared in the Yorkshire Herald and Evening Press for political reasons. What could be more natural than dropping a word in a local hack's ear? Or slipping over a few free tickets – for review purposes, naturally.

'Seen this?' Laverelli fumed as I trudged through the foyer on a quest for fags. 'Look what it says in the blinkin' Herald this time. Ernie-bloody-Precious must be the editor's love child.'

Laverelli shook his head at the perfidy of the world. 'Avoid newspapers like a bad dose, lad, that's my advice. There's always more upset in 'em than truth.' He waggled his eyebrows. 'Aye, I've known a few *newsmen* in my time. *Personally.* Believe me they're worse than ladies on the game.'

After such a build-up I couldn't help asking, 'What does it say in the Herald?'

He cleared his throat to read aloud. '"The Last of the Mohicans is truly a modern masterpiece. A cinematic production worthy of the inspiring décor and architecture of York's new premier entertainment venue, The Grand Cinema and Ballroom. Readers of the Herald are advised to test out the Grand's amusements for themselves." That's an abuse of press freedom, that is.'

I left him to wring the Herald's neck then bury the corpse in the waste bin.

Apart from puffs there were stunts. Even here, Ernie Precious proved nimbler than Laverelli. He hired costumes from a fancy dress shop matching the theme of the week's main feature. His staff could be seen patrolling Coney Street in sandwich boards. Cowboy outfits advertised the latest Western. Robin Hood and Maid Marian outfits a medieval romance. Once, he made them black up and wear grass skirts over black tights.

Laverelli brooded until the final provocation.

We had just released a torrent of rampaging kids from the Saturday matinee. A breathless Esther Jones appeared, deserting her post at the pay desk.

'Mr Laverelli!' she gasped. 'You 'ave to see this!'

I followed her out into Gillygate. A familiar sound made me crane my neck.

'By the blazes!' declared Laverelli. 'What's the bugger done now?'

It sounded like the raspy engine of a B.E.2c to me. I'd heard about a flying circus coming to York. No doubt they were using ex-military machines sold cheap. A single engine biplane approached the Minster – definitely a B.E.2c – trailing a long white banner: **THE GRAND CLARENCE STREET FOR *SOARING* CINEMA**.

It came in low enough for me to see the pilot's helmeted, goggled head. He waved at the people below then circled the crowded market on Parliament Street with a touch of throttle.

At the engine noise, people rushed from shops or houses onto the street. Kids jumped up and down.

I felt my heart quicken. How glorious the ancient city must look from up there. How revealed. The churches and serpentine maze of courtyards, the river lined with factories and warehouses, the city walls and castle. It was a long time since I had imagined flying with anything other than fear or dismay. The old excitement rushed back. Like a dolphin pushing up from the depths towards the sunlit surface. Yes, once flying had felt as exhilarating as music. The moment of lift off when the earth fell away and you were free. That had been another me, of course. A dead me. A young man unafraid.

By coincidence, I had earned my pilot's wings in a good old B.E.2c. I could picture exactly the controls and instruments up there, the tension of the joystick as the pilot banked. His was another kind of performance, the whole earthbound world his audience. Yet I knew only too well that daring to take an aeroplane up lay beyond me now. My wings were thoroughly clipped. The best I could do was watch from below.

For half an hour the aeroplane circled York before heading north. Laverelli followed its progress through narrowed eyes, arms folded across his chest.

'If he wants blood then blood it is,' he muttered.

With that, he stalked into his cubbyhole office.

Chance encounters can turn you into a reluctant witness. Of course, in the stories I accompanied each night coincidental meetings were *de rigeur*. A kind of scripted random destiny neither character nor audience could avoid. When Charlie Chaplin stepped onto the street, twirling his cane, bowler hat askew, it would have been implausible for him not to encounter a performing dog or lost orphan or winsome sweetheart or blustering villain. Fantasy is never truly free; it imposes its own rules.

Perhaps I was touched with a little Hollywood magic. Because there were a couple of odd meetings round that time that forced me into the role of extra.

First, I was wandering down Clarence Street when a girl exited the Grand's double doors. She was being shown out by none other than Ernie Precious, his podgy hand under her elbow.

Gladys Bannering! I watched him squeeze her arm. A tram rattled to a halt on my side of the street, hiding her from view. When it lurched away, Gladys was dwindling in the distance. She walked fast, her head lowered, as though something was wrong. Or she wanted to get away. I suspected she'd seen me watch Precious handling her like fruit you squeeze before buying. Then she turned a corner in the direction of the Groves and was out of sight.

Her little game with Precious was none of my business. If she wanted another job, good luck to her. The Grand was a far more fashionable establishment than the Electric and tolerated higher hemlines.

But for no justifiable reason I felt disappointed. By her own account she'd been damn lucky to secure the position of usherette at the Electric. Deserting Laverelli for a rival he openly hated seemed a strange kind of gratitude. Perhaps she knew something about the Electric I didn't. Rats leaving a sinking ship came to mind. Not that it mattered to me. Except somehow it did. You swiftly develop strong loyalties when you are young. I'd come to want the best for Laverelli.

The next queer event also concerned the usherette – at least, indirectly.

I was safe in my corner of the Cricketers Arms one Sunday evening. Rain speckled the frosted windows, adding damp to the scent of ingrained tobacco smoke and hoppy beer.

The pub was quiet; I looked up when two men entered. From their clothes both were identifiable as members of the respectable working class. Perhaps because of my own father's early death – and his sorry replacement – I've always paid close attention to fathers and sons. The family resemblance here was striking.

The son, around my age, seemed nervous. I had a sudden intuition he'd been crying, though no tears were visible. I sensed his father wanted to stiffen him up with a drink.

They reached the bar. Alf, the landlord, looked them over. His attention flickered round the pub to assess who was present. It fell instantly on me. Ascended to my cheek. He assumed a dogged air.

'Evening, Sid,' he said to the older man, affably enough.

'Evenin', Alf.'

'I should warn you now,' said the landlord, 'we're not serving.'

A long silence filled the area round the bar. The click of dominoes ceased. The lad's father bristled. By contrast, his son shrank a little further into himself.

'You're always welcome, Sid, you know that. But we don't serve conchies.' Alf nodded at the young man.

In those early years after the war, most folk hated conscientious objectors more fiercely than Germans. And hating Huns was as popular as football and sex combined.

'Sorry to hear that, Alf,' said the Father. His accent had a touch of Irish. 'Good night to you.'

The pair stepped back out into the rain. Although the elder wore his dignity grimly, his boy was shaken.

Not long afterwards I went to the bar. Alf stopped polishing a glass with a wet rag. I could tell he was put out.

'Sorry about the earlier unpleasantness,' he said. 'That young feller is not long out of Richmond Gaol for being a conchie. His old man's alright, as it happens. A good union man on the railways. He stuck his neck out in the railway strike last autumn. There's plenty of folk round here as respect Sid Bannering. In fact, I consider him a decent man myself. He's a red, of course, like all them Bannerings. Red as Moscow.'

I grew more interested.

'Bannering, you say? Unusual name.'

'Not round 'ere. There's a load of 'em over in the Groves.' Alf sighed. 'It's a shame all round. Sid Bannering has been coming 'ere as long as I had the licence. But his son and daughter have run right wild. A proper shame, as I say. Have this one on the house, Mr Young.'

He pulled at the pump.

'You'll know his oldest daughter right enough. She's the usherette at the Electric. A little too fond of the lads, so they say. Or one in particular.'

I considered his information over my free drink. Laverelli had dropped hints people said harsh things about Gladys Bannering. I wandered over to the pub piano and played a slow, melancholy version of *Keep the Home Fires Burning*. That song had been Archie Fitzclarence's favourite. When I finished, rain still beaded and trickled down the frosted windows like redundant tears.

The next day we learned the nature of Laverelli's riposte to the Grand's aerial stunt.

When he tried to rope me in, I folded my arms, shook my head. Some musical drainpipes should never be crawled down. Not as a graduate of the Royal College of Music. Nor did he have the right to press the matter. Louisa Mountjoy, however, was in a different position.

Even as she agreed to Laverelli's request, she showed signs of distress.

The film in question was a popular, romantic tale, *Way Down East*. It starred the doyenne actress of *Broken Blossoms*, Lillian Gish. Renting it didn't come cheap, and Laverelli was taking a risk with such a first run feature. He needed full houses for the majority of showings.

Advertisements appeared in the Evening Press and Herald. But his stunt was something new for the Electric.

Once he was safely in his office I cleared my throat.

'Louisa... I mean, Miss Mountjoy.'

Her head shot up proudly.

'I really don't mind if you call me Louisa.'

'Good. Fine. Louisa. He really can't *insist* you do it, you know. If you'd rather not.'

'I would rather not. The whole prospect is demeaning. And beastly.'

'Then don't. I will explain your scruples to him. You are... ' I didn't know quite what she was in the musical department, so I settled for, 'A lady, not a common busker to be gawped at. On the street, I mean.'

Laverelli had slipped ten shillings to a pub in return for pushing their piano out onto Parliament Street. His scheme was for Louisa to play the theme tune of *Way Down East* over and over. Meanwhile,

Ambrose and Gladys would hand out flyers in York Market. A vulgar, exposed position for any respectable lady – even a fallen one.

Louisa took off her reading spectacles. She regarded me frankly.

'Mr Laverelli has been jolly good to me. I owe him more than you know. In a way, he saved my life by giving me a job here during the war. Otherwise I would have had to find work in a munitions factory. Or worse.'

We both knew what *worse* meant. I could not help contrasting her loyalty to Laverelli with Gladys Bannering. Not that Gladys had jumped ship to the Grand just yet. She was still there each night with her tray of confectionary and torch.

'I simply feel he deserves my support, David.'

She produced a lacy handkerchief. Fiddled with it.

'I was once at a college for ladies, you know,' she said. 'I never expected any of this.'

'Was that in York?'

'No.' There was pride in the way she straightened her neck. 'In Oxford, actually. My college was part of the Association for Promoting the Higher Education of Women. St Hilda's. I'm really not at all stupid.'

I recalled the officer-fiancé who copped it in France.

'Would you feel better if I took your place?' I said, on impulse.

'I… Would you do that, really?'

'Yes, I would.'

Emotion touched Louisa's face. It was striking for someone so guarded. You see, life was teaching her an air of habitual disappointment, even distrust. You could see it in her eyes, the way she talked, her arms folded to cover her chest. Now layers of settled cloud parted. She brightened. Like an iris shot starting from a dark screen and unfolding to reveal a quiver of surprise and pleasure. She blushed quite becomingly. I could not help smiling, even as the first doubts set in.

Thirteen

That's how I found myself outside the Clock Inn on a busy market day, a bustling Saturday lunchtime. Busking for a few bob to the customers of a stall selling cabbages and turnips. Every so often, the cry went up, 'Penny a pound! Lovely spuds, penny a pound!'

Is this all you're worth? Is this what your precious college scholarships have come to? Penny a pound? Is this why you practised hour upon hour and dreamt of glorious symphonies? The sublime music of the spheres? My stepfather's contemptuous sniff hissed like the stuck needle of a wind-up gramophone.

York Market was noise and babble. A motor lorry chugged behind a clip-clopping dray, making the carthorses snort. Earthy scents of vegetables mingled with the stink of fish. There were piles of cheap army surplus clothes, stacks of pottery and ironmongery, every kind of produce. Here, precious music, the one treasure I still possessed, was reduced to a worthless, knockdown thing.

Was that why a panic set in? A bad one, the worst for months. Perhaps the faint odour of rotting meat from a nearby butcher's stall didn't help. And it was a warm day.

Mainly it was the eyes. Passing, staring, judging my pointlessness. I hammered out *Way Down East* on a discordant upright piano hauled onto the pavement. My absurd, tinkling voice lost in the heedless, crowded market.

Gladys Bannering and Ambrose Ackerley were busy handing out flyers. No help from them. The commissionaire must hate me for bungling his precious Valentine card; the usherette despised me even more. Sweat gathered on my forehead. My heart yammered with an urge to run. Right now. Anywhere.

Then I was slap bang back in Hell, Hull and Halifax. Up there! *There!* Five, six thousand feet above us, a huge, menacing shadow, a Zepp! Fitz pointing up the nose with every inch of throttle, anything for his blasted VC, any risk at all. We would stall and spin down, smash like a crate of sticks into the seething, clutching North Sea... 'No! We'll never reach it. It's too high, you fool!' The seaplane jolts. Lurches...

'Mr Young?' breathed a soft voice in my ear. Hands were twined round one of my arms. I sat, rigid as a pillar of salt, on the piano stool.

I met Gladys Bannering's anxious green eyes, inches from my own.

'You took a funny turn,' she said.

I needed air. She attempted a lop-sided smile. I breathed in. Out.

'I've sent Ambrose off,' she said. 'You know, to tell Mr Laverelli you've come over queer.'

I'd recovered sufficiently to notice people watching.

'Blow me! If it in't the chuffin' Phantom of the Opera!' called out a coarse voice. 'Look who's giving him a hug!'

Gladys hastily let go of my arm. I turned. A knot of young men in flat caps and red scarves crowded near the piano. Even light-headed, I could tell they had been drinking early. There was a local football derby that afternoon.

'Blow me if it in't Gladys Bannering an' all!' added the young man. 'How's that conchie brother of yours, Glad? Still yellow as Coleman's mustard?'

His mates appreciated such wit.

'He's braver than you'll ever be, Bob Markham,' retorted Gladys. 'At least he believes in something more than his wallet. At least he believes in peace for the world.'

'More fool him then,' replied the young man, to his friends' delight. 'We all know what *you* believe in, Gladys. Go on! Give us a kiss! You know you want to.'

He leaned forward and made a sucking noise.

I rose. Wobbled away from the piano stool.

'It's alright, Mr Young,' said Gladys, hands on hips. 'Never mind these *fatheads*.'

'Look here,' I said to the group of beery lads, 'you're upsetting the lady.'

Their leader laughed. 'Our Glad is no lady, mister!'

We assessed one another for a chilly moment.

'Any man who says so to an unprotected woman – and on the street – is no gentleman,' I replied, loftily.

An inspired line given how shaky I felt. A line acquired from the hero of some Edwardian penny dreadful devoured as a boy. It sobered them.

Her tormentor-in-chief was eyeing the girl hungrily (you could tell what he really wanted from her). But his pals pulled him away. In a moment, they were gone. I closed the piano lid.

Sod Laverelli. I, too, was done.

With that, I walked blindly into the crowd, leaving Gladys Bannering open-mouthed, a wedge of leaflets for *Way Down East* in her hand.

It took Gladys an hour to catch up with me in the public library. First, she had to get the piano pushed back into the Clock Inn then nip back to the Electric to explain. Then she looked for me in the Cricketers Arms, before taking a peek by the Ouse near the Museum Gardens, where I was fond of sitting by myself on a bench to watch the river drift by. Then she thought she'd pop into the library.

How did I know all this? Because Gladys told me in a rapid stage whisper that sent the librarian's eyebrows rocketing.

'Can I have a word,' she concluded. 'Private like?'

'All right.'

After a bad panic attack, the fluttering hollow in your gut can take a while to settle. Only to be replaced by a dull ache, heavy as thick chains across your chest. I was in the second phase.

Outside, I discovered a sunny afternoon.

'I like the library, you know,' she said, as we stood by the entrance.

I'd seen her in there once and hastily buried my head in a book. I assumed she was after romances with plenty of sauce and tickle; or returning her Mam's overdue loans.

'It can be full of surprises,' I said, darkly.

93

She didn't get the hint.

'Thank you for standing up for me. You know, with them lads. Sometimes I hate this town, it's so… ' She flapped her arms with a slight laugh. 'So *small*. It makes me feel like a linnet in a cage.'

'What did Laverelli want?' I asked to change the subject.

'Oh, it's not him! It's me as wanted to talk. You see, I thought you'd gone off sudden because of what Bob Markham said about me brother, Thomas, and… I wanted to explain.'

We drifted from the library in the direction of the river. Our feet took us through the gates of the Museum Gardens. Trees and flower beds were coming into full leaf, bees drifting lazily. Close to noon there were few shadows. One of the resident peacocks displayed its fan of bright tail feathers.

We passed York Observatory, a small square stone building with a conical turret on its flat roof. Within there was a telescope for scanning the constellations. Just then it was locked and silent.

'I wanted to explain, Mr Young,' she said, firmly. 'You overheard those lads – oh, that Bob Markham, he were a right bully at school! – talking about our Thomas. He's me big brother, by the way. And I were afraid, well, you'd think he was a conscientious objector for *bad* reasons. That he was yellow, like Bob said.'

She paused to draw breath.

'Mr Young, I know you must have suffered terribly in the war – and are still suffering – but I wanted you to know our Thomas was brave in a different way. Not that I'm comparing, but… ' She paused significantly. 'He had the courage of his convictions.'

I took out my fag packet.

'Mr Young, our Thomas, bless him, believes with his sincere heart the best way to defend ourselves from war is not to fight it. And that British workers shouldn't kill German ones, 'cos we're all the same.'

She shuddered. 'They beat him something rotten in the military gaol. It wasn't right. And now *he's* not right. His spirit is not right.'

She subsided with tears in her eyes. 'I just wanted you to know the truth. Before someone tells nasty tales. The way they always do in this town.' Her voice, usually so bright took on a bitter edge. 'Oh, I know very well what they say about them cowardly Bolshevik Bannerings. And… and about me.'

It was over. She dabbed ruined mascara with a finger. Expensive mascara she must have put on specially – and daringly – to match the glamour of *Way Down East*.

We had reached the ruins of the old abbey, deep in the Museum Gardens. What passions had been acted out when those monastic buildings were torn down to satisfy the greed of a tyrannical king? How many consciences had revolted at the outrage to all they believed holy? How many martyrs had suffered torture and imprisonment for their faith? Nothing changed. Then it was religion, now war, among the myriad causes people set against each other.

I had a vision of Gladys's brother in the glass house. The kind of men who guarded places like that could be the worst kind of bastard. Patriotic heroes hundreds of miles from danger. I imagined him shivering in a cold, dark cell, fed slops and forced to pick oakum until his fingers were numb. Daily humiliations to big up the bullies set over him. Forced marches in the snow and standing on parade until he collapsed. We'd all heard the stories what happened to conchies.

I offered my packet of cigarettes. She took one uncertainly. I lit a match. Held it out. She sucked hungrily.

The whole conversation was ridiculous. What on earth did she want from me? A belated certificate of exemption for her brother? But she had put herself in my power. My response to her words could either wound or heal.

'You know, of course,' I said, not meeting her eye, 'I'm meant to hate conchies like everyone else.'

I lit my own cigarette.

'I certainly used to,' I warned. 'These days I'm not so sure conchies are that different from those who enlisted. They just enlisted for something else. A different kind of war. One you fight with words and ideas, instead of bullets. They believed people can be better than they are. The problem is they always lose out to the men with guns.'

She was watching my face with her wide eyes. I kept my own averted. A charm of finches twitted round the abbey ruins.

Then I looked hard at her.

'There was something I wanted to ask you, Gladys. Why were you with Ernest Precious outside the Grand the other day? I was, well, I was surprised.'

'Oh, you saw!' she exclaimed.

'Yes, I saw.'

'Do you know why I went to see that great bag of dripping? It wasn't for me self.'

'Oh?'

'I went to beg him to give our Thomas a job. I heard they might need another projectionist. Only, he wanted something from me in return.'

She let the implication hang.

'And did Thomas get his job?'

'No. Whatever people round here say, I'm not... No, he didn't.'

I grunted. A migraine was coming on.

'Please tell Mr Laverelli,' I said, 'I might not make the six-thirty showing. Not today.'

She treated me to one of her bobby dazzler smiles. 'I will!'

Then Gladys Bannering leaned forward and popped a kiss on my cheek. It was chaste enough, lest you get the wrong idea. She was simply grateful I didn't hate her beloved conchie brother.

Her kiss was on the burned half of my face. It tingled like static.

My dreams and memories of the war weren't all nightmares. Seeing the B.E.2c circle over York reminded me of that. Though recollections of combat troubled me most, sometimes haunting the next day, not all brought out the sweats. Yet always I was the navigator; that was my fate. Three lives aside from my own hung upon my hurried calculations and judgements.

After my panic attack on Parliament Street, I anticipated a rough night. But the dreams started kindly enough...

A summer flight, early morning. A sky of intense blue, tinting sluggish waves. Up we climb and the world's a mirror of marvels. The distant fleet trails ribbons of smoke, brilliant white wakes like gossamer strands drawn across the ocean. A vast flock of gulls stream due south towards the coast of Holland. Fitz takes us right through them: they wheel around us like flying snow. There, a three-masted sailing schooner, tilting in the wind, canvas unfurled.

A moment later piercing through a summer cloud layer, dazzled by sunlight, longing to step from the cockpit and walk upon solid clouds...

Then the sky darkens. Rain lashes my face. I'm in charge of our route, our fate. The British Grand Fleet close now, directly below. But it's not ours! German warships form a long line driving north, shelled from over the horizon by the Royal Navy. Tall spouts of water rise white from the sea. We hear the shells whistle as they whoosh down.

What's that, high up and faint, like floating cigars? Zeppelins. Two monsters spotting for the German High Seas Fleet.

Fitz points and raises our nose, desperate to get a shot at them, desperate for glory...

And I awake, knowing how the dream ends, only too well.

Fourteen

I received an unexpected visitor. The lights had just gone up on the early evening show. As the audience filed out, a woman in a nurse's cloak and bonnet appeared. It was the Matron from Fitz's ward at the asylum.

I eyed her warily.

'Now that was real lovely,' she burbled in her pleasant Irish brogue. 'I thought me heart would burst when the poor dog got whipped. Little feller as he is!'

How often people are more moved by cruelty to animals than humans.

'Thank you.'

'Let me just say, Mr Young, I'm not here for the pictures only.'

'Oh?'

Her voice took on a placatory tone. 'I know you have every reason to be cross with the Lieutenant.'

More than you'll ever guess, I thought.

'The last time you visited us, he nearly broke your fingers with his queer fit. And you playing that old piano so beautiful an' all! He's such a lost soul, bless him. And way too proud to seek help where he needs it most.' She shot me a quick look. 'There's many a young feller like that as has come home.'

I glanced at the exit.

'Now the thing is, it would be grand if you gave him a second chance. Popped over to see him.'

I laughed. 'I'm not sure he'd be pleased to see me.'

'Well, that's where you're wrong.' She leaned forward conspiratorially. 'After your last visit, he came straight out to Dr Middleton. No prompting, at all. "I owe that chap an apology". Or something of the kind.'

I had no doubt he'd said nothing of the kind.

Louisa Mountjoy was ear-wigging as she packed away her music. Unexpectedly, I recalled meeting her and little Freddy among the flowers, trees, spring sunshine and caged monkeys in Homestead Park. She had said: *People see someone far worthier than you seem to imagine.*

The Matron watched me shrewdly.

I sighed. 'Very well. I shall pop along next Tuesday. Except I insist… ' It felt essential to escape that ward, its unhealable misery. 'I insist on being allowed to take him for a short walk in the hospital grounds. That is, if the weather is suitable. And if it will do no harm.'

'It'll do the poor chap a world of good. Dr Middleton *will* be pleased.'

I might have guessed he was behind her little arm-twisting mission.

That was how I found myself moving snail-like across the park at the rear of Bootham Park Asylum. A gnarled lump of a young man anchored my pace. His bulk was heavy upon my arm.

Sparrows, blue tits, chaffinches chirruped in bushes and trees. Fitz reeked of Dakin's Solution applied liberally to his burns as some ladies doused themselves with scent. A perfume that seemed to follow me around.

He contemplated something as we shuffled along. I didn't expect to learn what it was. But I was set for a surprise.

'Every day's the same here, Young,' he rasped, indicating the dark mass of the asylum with a twitch of his remaining eye. 'Except Tuesdays.'

The day of my visits. Was this a small nod of appreciation?

We reached a cricket pavilion. Daisies sprouted from the grass. I helped him onto a bench. We sat there like two old men looking out across the silent pitch.

'There'll be matches here soon,' I said. In case he thought I was volunteering to play chaperone, I added, 'Perhaps the nurses can help you watch one.'

Archie Fitzclarence had always loved sport of the hard, hearty, competitive kind. Rugger, cricket, hockey, soccer, he excelled at them all. And vied to lead the team.

'Yes,' he said.

I lit a cigarette.

'Damn bad habit,' he croaked. 'Kill you in the end.'

I laughed. 'Frankly, sir, I couldn't care less about the future.'

'You should.'

'Is that an order?'

'You should care, Young.' His throat worked for breath. He was thinking out reasons why.

I looked at him askance. 'Do you mind me asking something?'

His seared face wrinkled. A tiny bead of pus discharged on his forehead.

'Carry on.'

'There's something I don't understand.'

'What's that?'

'Dr Middleton says you are physically a lot better. I mean, when we walked here, you could have used a stick instead of leaning on my arm. Not that it bothers me. Why don't you go home? Hire a nurse to change your dressings.' I nodded at the asylum. 'Why stay on here?'

A longish speech for me. And exceptionally frank. He listened, his single eye goggling. I expected no answer. My question, impudent, by his standards, and perhaps designed to be, reflected my confusion about him. Along with distrust, I felt a clear sense of responsibility. We had shared much in the war. Too damn much. Perhaps I simply hoped to encourage him out of my hair by quitting York.

Fitz grunted. Again he surprised me. What happened next wasn't a lot, yet it changed our destination as surely as a slight shift of compass angle when flying over the North Sea.

'Funny thing, Young.'

He hesitated, peered at me again. Made up his mind. 'Pater and Mater don't know how to act around me anymore. Perfectly natural, of course. Don't blame 'em for a minute.'

I listened intently. Would he say more? Never had he shared such private feelings before. Indeed, almost any feelings. Then it occurred to me, neither had I. In that respect, we were as bad as each other.

'Look, Young, everything's gone to hell. I'm not myself anymore. Never can be. Not what they want.'

That I understood well enough. Those keenest to send us young men out there for England's glory were often the least welcoming when the mangled spare parts came home. My own dear Mother sometimes half pretended I wasn't in the room. When she did acknowledge me, a scared, wariness entered her eyes. A look no son should receive from his mother. All a child wanted was love, infinite love, and reassurance. A problem that worked both ways.

Fitz lapsed into brooding. I resisted the temptation to chain smoke.

'They expected me to manage the estate,' he said. 'First born, you see. Son and heir. Pater had ambitions for me in the political line. MP for Thirsk and Malton like himself. Crashing disappointment all round, I'm afraid.'

If only Dr Middleton could hear this! Fitz was delivering a soliloquy worthy of Hamlet. It suggested his silence up to now had been, in part, pre-meditated.

A more decent person would have tried to persuade him he was wrong. Mummy and Daddy *did* still love their little Archie. Even if he now resembled a shrunken prune. But it crossed my mind that instead of love they might only have pity, maybe irrational guilt. And pity is not love. I offered my hip flask of rum. He took it cautiously. Sniffed. Gulped.

Cough. Cough. Gasp.

'By blazes, I needed that!'

At last we had something in common.

For a good half hour we played pass the parcel with my rum, having run out of anything else to share. We even managed a laugh at the memory of a pet dog one of the other pilots took up with him on patrol. Then it was time to return to the ward.

Fifteen

Every Monday morning brought the Electric fresh gifts from Dreamland. Reels of celluloid in flat, round tins marked by handwritten, pasted labels. Soon after their arrival, Laverelli and I got busy in the auditorium, fitting the picture.

How many lost arts this spinning world has woven. Ghosts of human endeavour and ingenuity. Where now is the Egyptian pyramid builder or mummifier of corpses? Perhaps it means nothing, so much technological change. Yet back then, the art of fitting a picture was a craft I took great pride in. After all, I had little other reason for pride.

It worked like this: Laverelli set up a small hand-cranked projector complete with carbon arc lamp saved from his days as a travelling film exhibitor. I took a seat before the screen, notebook and pen poised.

That Monday morning, the auditorium was unusually busy. Not just Laverelli and me; also Louisa practising the piano. Her landlady, the Electric's charwoman, Bertha Kettlewell, was sweeping up Saturday's detritus. Little Freddy played in the rows of empty tip-up seats.

We soon got through the newsreel then Felix the Cat, and a weekly Western short starring Hoot Gibson – people preferred the same music on the whole for regular features. The main attraction, *Suds*, starred Mary Pickford. We anticipated a decent crowd, despite the Grand showing it at the same time.

I've often wondered how it would feel if you could fit the film of your own life. A brisk agitato when running for the bus. Tinkling, dreamy arpeggios as you sit at the window, cradling a coffee mug, wisps of steam evaporating with your thoughts. Not to mention your wedding day or the birth of a child. The possibilities are as limitless as life itself – and as time bound.

'Stop.'

Laverelli halts the cranking handle. The giant intertitle freezes on the screen.

> # N o hero here with passion pants –
> This is the tale of a humble shirt

I scribble in my notebook, check my stopwatch. Ah, for a comical trombone! Sometimes I dream of swollen orchestras and choirs, massed ranks of bongo players for jungle scenes.

'Carry on.'

The handle cranks. Street scenes busy with horse-drawn carriages, an occasional motor car, workaday people bustling. I want chirpy motion, comic anticipation.

'Stop.'

My fountain pen scratches. *The Merry Maker. Coates. 1:43*

'Carry on.'

Sometimes the handle cranks in reverse to replay a fragment. Scenes shift like dappled shadows cast by a wind-stirred tree. Always the music seeks to match the action, right down to sound effects on Maurice's rattles or whistles. Maybe a pratfall chord for comic effect from Louisa. Or a saucy glissando with my bow. Always our performance will be obsolete after the picture's run.

Freddy perches beside me in an adjoining tip-up seat, hypnotised by the gigantic, silent images above his head. I sense Louisa observing us together.

'Stop.'

Consult watch. Scribble.

'Carry on.'

Suds is the kind of story that will affect Louisa. Having witnessed her reaction at close hand to dozens of pictures, I can guess. A tale of a soap-sudded Cockney Cinders laundry girl. Poor, put upon Suds is forced to scrub and toil amidst mockery and disdain. Despite the slapstick, all the ingredients of tragedy lurk, as always, beneath jollity and farce. The pathos of failed dreams. A daughter rejected by her wealthy father for loving inappropriately, cast out into the cold night to fend alone...

But – for this is Hollywood – there is always the consolation of hope.

Imagination is God's greatest gift...
Even a hungry flea
on a toy dog may be happy
-- with imagination!

'Stop.'
Ave Maria by Gounod.
'Carry on.'
Of course, it was always about love, in the end, the eternal story.

It came to her swiftly,
poignantly - - - that he
would be ashamed of her!

Blast it, why not? A sop for the tearful hankie-brigade. Louisa will be happy for a change. *Hearts and Flowers. 1:15.*

$$\boxed{\text{W}\text{ho would love }\textit{me}?}$$

$$\boxed{\text{W}\text{ho could?}}$$

$$\boxed{\text{N}\text{obody never won't!}}$$

As I closed my notebook, and yawned, Ambrose Ackerley staggered down the aisle with a battered travelling chest secured by leather straps. At once, I was on my feet.

'Louisa,' I cried. 'I mean, Miss Mountjoy. The other instruments I told you about have arrived.'

A week earlier I had posted a note to Mother. The first proper letter, it must be said, except for terse postcards informing her I was 'alright', since my arrival in York. In the note, apart from a little bragging about my new role – one in the eye for Stepfather! – I had requested she send an old chest of mine. It contained clothes, oddments and something very precious to me, inherited from my father.

I fumbled with the leather straps. 'Now I can add a few unexpected touches, especially on the clarinet,' I told Louisa. 'My ukulele should be in here, too. I'll need to hire extra music when I go to New Century today.'

Glancing up, I noted approval in her smile.

'Here we go,' I said.

I looked forward to surprising them with the clarinet. They only knew me as a fiddle player and pianist. Laverelli might even give me a pay rise.

Opening the lid, I rooted around inside. Neatly-folded clothes, a few books, yes, all as requested, even my little ukulele. But the precious thing was missing: my clarinet.

Instead, there was a letter.

13 Mafeking Road
West Ealing
Middx
12th May 1920

Dear David,

We were very pleased to hear you have managed to find suitable employment at long last. Daddy (she still insisted on calling my stepfather 'Daddy', like Gertrude calling Claudius 'Dearest Papa') *sends his best wishes to you and says you must have done very well indeed, as there will be lots of better musicians in a town like York.*

We are very well here and busy with the front garden. Daddy's roses are splendid as usual and we expect he will win first prize at the church summer bazaar. Mrs Beecham from No.11 asked me to send you her regards, though she has lumbago.

I have packed all the things you asked for, apart from that old clarinet you have not played for years. Daddy says you will not need it if you are a conductor of an orchestra and only need a baton now. So he kindly sold it to Mr Topping at church (you will remember his poor son, Jacob, who got killed at the Somme). Daddy got a good price for it, 20 shillings, to cover the postage of this trunk. He told me to tell you, there is no need to write and thank him. There was even 5 shillings left over, which I am keeping for you as a postal order. Let me know in your next letter whether you would like me to put it in the Missionary Box for Poor African Mites.

Your Mama

p.s. I think you should send a short note thanking Daddy even though he said not to.

For long moments I held the letter, unable to grasp its significance. Then I hurriedly reread it to make sure.

'Are you… alright?' asked Louisa.

Had they really done this? Had *she*, my own mother? The clarinet, my father's clarinet, the instrument which earned him a decent living, even minor fame. The clarinet he sang through like a nightingale's bill before audiences and orchestras and bands all over London. No, all over England. Once, an extended tour of Germany and the Low Countries. How proud I had felt, watching from the best seats of the Albert Hall, as he performed Mozart's Clarinet Concerto at the Proms. I had applauded until my palms burned. How I had longed to follow in his footsteps, to stand where he stood.

Father's clarinet. The last thing I possessed that belonged to him, apart from some yellowing sheet music. Mother had sold anything valuable in her blind, tearful panic after he died. Watch, clothes, shoes, hats. But the clarinet had been saved. Father's deathbed request. And now it had been traded for less than a song to the bumptious Mr Topping at church.

I went dizzy. My mouth opened stupidly.

'David? Have you received bad news?'

I scarcely heard Louisa's voice. This was a brand new version of Hell, Hull and Halifax. Another world of shadows and memories, long suppressed…

In my mind – because I had just finished the intense fitting of a film – images and accompanying music whirled. Except those brief flashes of memory involved not just sight, or sound, but all the senses…

A gay, light intermezzo, the orchestra bouncing along with some comic pizzicato and knockabout woodwind. Ten years old, I stand beside Father in the living room where he likes to practise. His hair oil smells faintly of eucalyptus, his waistcoat of pipe tobacco. He is teaching me how to tongue a note on the clarinet, patient as he adjusts the mouthpiece. When I blow, the instrument squawks, shrills, quacks. Its long wooden body heavy, yet delicate in my hands, the metal keys fragile.

107

Try again, only don't blow so hard. Any instrument worth its salt is your friend, David. Make friends with it. You never have to try too hard with good pals.

He's right. Always right. As soon as I blow gently, music comes clean. Long, sweet, pure notes. I look up at him. He ruffles my hair...

Now the orchestra darkens. Sighing, minor chords of violin, cello, bass. Faintly discordant undertones from the brass section declare the tragedy. A lightning flash. Real or misremembered. All day storm clouds brood over the young suburb of West Ealing, its remaining fields and hedgerows ready to be portioned into building plots. Ready for the new, bold century ahead. The house in Mafeking Road silent as suppressed misery.

Darkness on the stairs as I ascend, shaking. Eleven years old. A big boy now. They tell me I must not cry. Because I am a big boy now. The shadows of dusk pool over the landing. I know Mother is resting on the sofa downstairs, worn out by tears. She is allowed to cry.

I push open the door to their bedroom. The door creaks. The curtains are closed. Yet enough light enters for me to see the body on the double bed. After the laying out by the local midwife, he is still as stone. 'Rendering the last offices' Mother called it. Father washed and dressed in a white shroud.

I enter a few steps, observe him in death through a lens of welling tears. Cotton wool stuffed into his nostrils. Pennies laid across his eyes. Chin bandaged so his mouth will be forever closed, unable to call my name. Ribbons round his body at the elbows, wrists, ankles, to hold his limbs straight. A prisoner bound, ready for the coffin. Outside, I hear the neighbour's children playing hoop in the street. Their mother calls them home to bed...

Angry stabs of chords. A serpentine oboe hints menace and villainy. Just a year later, Stepfather cold in his rages, shaking me so hard my teeth rattle. *You will do as you are told. You will do as you are told.* Mother hand-wringing to one side. *You really must do what Daddy says, dear. You're upsetting everyone.* But he is not Father! He is my enemy.

Only when I play the piano do I feel happy – that he dare not sell, for the sake of respectability – or when I play the violin Father left me explicitly in his will. Or take up his clarinet, feel the comforting weight, only then am I allowed peace. Even Mother, guided by the vicar who offers to pay for the lessons, insists I receive the tuition I need. Their cost is still begrudged to the last sixpence by Stepfather. When I make music, hours merge, aches of heartbreak and fear and loneliness are dispelled by magic...

Then those few strands of memory dissolved. The imaginary orchestra and images faded to nothing. The little boy was a young man once more, back in York and the shadowy belly of the Electric Cinema. Phrases from the intertitles of *Suds* echoed: *Who would love me? Who could? Nobody never won't.*

Without a word, I hurried to the exit, clanking down the pushbars of the double doors. In the alleyway I stood shaking.

At last, I grew conscious of company. Laverelli and Louisa were whispering by the open doors. She came over.

'I hope you don't mind awfully,' she said. 'But Mr Laverelli wondered if you would take me with you to Leeds this afternoon.'

Leeds? For a moment I blinked at her.

'He'd like me to learn how you do it,' she said. 'You know, at New Century.' Her false brightness faltered. 'If you wouldn't mind awfully.'

Actually, I did mind awfully.

Laverelli's motives weren't hard to fathom. He expected me to join Fitz over in Bootham Park Lunatic Asylum by teatime at the latest – thereby missing the 6.00 o'clock showing. The show must go on, with us or without us.

An hour later we were at York Station. I sat on a bench, staring rigidly into space. Not so Freddy Mountjoy: the little chap could scarcely believe his luck. Each time a sooty clanking iron and steel monster rolled past, smoke and steam billowing, he skipped for joy. His mama clutched his hand, warning him to stay clear of the platform edge.

I ignored them. Not from deliberate rudeness, though I most certainly was rude. Sick heaviness filtered through me like poisoned water. The loss of Father's clarinet magnified other losses, long nurtured, never accepted. Though Laverelli probably believed he had done me a kindness by sending Louisa as company, the opposite was true. I just longed to be alone.

'Do sit quietly, Freddy. The train will be here soon.'

She dragged him to my bench. I shuffled along to make room. This placed her on my left: I often grew edgy when people faced my left. The minute hand of the station clock ticked above our heads.

'If you would rather we didn't come, that's perfectly fine,' she said. 'It's just Mr Laverelli thought it would be useful. For me, if that's allowed. To make me a better musician in the orchestra. That's why he offered to pay my fare.'

'Did he offer to pay Freddy's fare as well?'

'Well, no,' admitted Louisa, 'I just thought… '

'You know the real reason he asked you to come along, don't you?'

I let my question hover. 'It's so you can replace me – and all the more smoothly – when I up sticks and toddle back to London.'

Louisa flushed at such frankness.

'Well, you can hardly blame him,' she said. 'Isn't that your plan? Upping sticks and toddling?'

'I suppose so.'

It crossed my mind a free trip to smoky old Leeds was an exotic treat for her. At least it got her away from Princess Street.

'I must warn you,' I said, 'I'll be very busy during the journey.'

I half-extracted the notebook containing my scribblings for *Suds*. Her face betrayed a flicker.

'Of course.'

'Good.'

'We could always sit in a separate carriage.'

'Well… '

'Or I could even take the next train.'

'I'm sure that won't be necessary.'

'I really would hate Freddy to inconvenience you in any way.'

The late morning was hot, breezeless. A nerve on my forehead began to throb. I returned to contemplating steam and smoke whenever a train clanked by. Father must have waited with his clarinet on summer platforms like this one. Waited for connections to concerts no one remembered now. How casually, like love, music dissolves into eternity.

Sixteen

We found seats in a second class carriage occupied by a couple in late middle age. Their clothes marked them out as respectable upper working class.

The woman's eyes brightened at the sight of Freddy. She whispered to her husband in a North Riding accent, 'Father, p'raps the bairn should sit by the window.'

This was soon accomplished with expressions of lofty gratitude from Louisa. Her Home Counties accent clearly impressed them.

I extracted my notebook to work on fitting *Suds.*

'You off to Leeds, love?' the lady asked Freddy.

The boy was watching the suburbs of York slip behind. He pointed at a factory spewing smoke. Everyone – except me – was laughing at his gleeful wonder.

A conversation began about the purpose of our visit to Leeds.

'We are going to a big library of cinema music,' Louisa explained. 'There, we will hire the music we shall perform to accompany next week's pictures.'

'You don't say, love,' replied the woman, suitably awed.

'It is rather complicated at times,' admitted Louisa, with false modesty.

If it didn't include *Hearts and Flowers* and *In a Monastery Garden*, it was more than just complicated for her. I concentrated on my notebook, aware 'Father', as his wife addressed him, was watching me through watery yellow eyes.

'Do you mind me asking,' he broke in, 'was it the infantry?'

He referred to my wounded face, of course.

'No.'

I fingered the notebook: *'Wooing' from Love Tales (Schertzinger) 2:35…
'Valse Melody' (Drigo) 1:58…*

'I wondered if you was ever out near Cambrai way,' asked the man. There was an edge to his voice.

'I'm sure the gentleman doesn't want to talk about that, Father,' urged his wife.

'No, I wasn't out near Cambrai way.'

'Oh.'

An uncomfortable silence settled in the small carriage. I became aware of a definite whiff of urine from the adjacent toilet. Then it had gone, lost among all the other aromas on a crowded steam train in summer. The sweet smell of dust. Cigarette smoke. Cheap perfume. Hair oil. And I wondered, are we just scents dispersing, too? After my memory of Father's laid out body beginning to decay, an uncomfortable thought.

'You see,' whispered the woman to Louisa, 'our only son, Eric, passed away over there. Near Cambrai, the telegram said.'

Louisa clucked sympathetically. She squeezed her eyes.

'So sorry,' she murmured.

That was enough to start the woman dabbing with a handkerchief. Even 'Father' looked fixedly out of the window. Yet I wanted to demand of them, no, shout at the whole stupid, cruel, heedless world. Why *did* you send Eric out there? Why did you send him and the rest of us out to face pitiless guns and machines? Did the question never occur to Louisa when she mourned her dead officer-fiancé? Even just for Freddy's sake, because his father could never be there for him.

'It's lovely to see your little family though,' said the woman.

She was trying to salvage the sunken mood.

'You must be proper proud of your Daddy, eh, son?' she said, turning to Freddy.

All eyes were on me now as the representative hero. I sensed Louisa dreading my response. It would have been simple to divert the conversation. Even tell a white lie. Or make some meaningless, conventional comment about the lads at Cambrai, their bravery for

King and Country. It would have been easy to evade the issue of Freddy's paternity for Louisa's sake.

But how could I pretend to be something I was not? There had been too much pretending since that bloody war ended. That victims were heroes. That civilization had somehow advanced through the carnage. That unscrupulous rich men had not grown even richer through the misery of millions. Did Louisa even expect me to pretend? What would Freddy's real father have said, if he'd made it through, only to be scrubbed out, replaced by the next convenient candidate?

'He's not my son,' I said.

'Oh.'

The woman glanced sharply at Louisa.

'Excuse me,' I muttered.

I stepped out into the connecting corridor. Behind me, I could hear Louisa finding fault with Freddy as a way of covering her confusion.

Near where our carriage connected with another, I lowered the window, lit a cigarette. We were chuffing past fields of crops and green hedgerows. Acrid smoke from the engine darkened the air. God knew what tale Louisa Mountjoy was cooking up about Freddy's daddy in the compartment. I felt relieved not to hear.

The walk from Leeds Station to New Century was conducted in sullen silence. Apart from when Louisa remarked on items of interest to little Freddy, like a tram or statue. Her tone pointedly excluded me from the family fun.

Leeds was a city of shadows in the summer of 1920. A century of soot had stained the buildings, from pub to brewery, commercial bank to joyless chapel. Although the worst years of industrial decline were still on the horizon and the mills were buoyed by the residual fat of war manufacturing, unemployed men hung around everywhere. All claimed to be veterans. Most were. Beggars with a leg blown off and a tin cup. Others chalking pictures on the pavement or singing for a few pennies.

Our walk across town brought us to Cookridge Street and the Coliseum Theatre, a concert hall converted into a cinema. Its frontage was modelled on a Gothic cathedral. Within, rich and poor alike could worship the Great God Dreamland for sixpence or a shilling.

The owners of the Coliseum, New Century Picture Company, had set up an extensive music library in its crypt-like basement. Every Monday, cinema orchestra leaders congregated to hire sheet music, having fitted their respective films for the week.

It paid to arrive early or the best pieces might be out on loan. Dragging Louisa and Freddy along had delayed me.

She stuck close as I stalked round the shelves and compartments, notebook in hand.

'Lorra books!' Freddy exclaimed.

'So this is how you choose the music?' asked Louisa.

Her expression was that of an obedient pupil anxious to learn.

'You have to know the pieces first,' I said, helpfully.

She crimsoned. The air of habitual discontent and distrust returned.

'I was hoping you would explain,' she said, haughtily. 'That is what Mr Laverelli intended.'

'I'm surprised any explanation is necessary,' I said.

A bowler-hatted man stepped round the corner of a tall bookshelf. He had evidently been listening in. I recognised him at once as Mr Cooper, the director of the Grand's orchestra. A *real* cinema orchestra, that is, not a humble trio masquerading as a proper band, but a full nine-piece with strings and woodwind and brass, including organist and drummer.

I almost read his thought: *blow me it's the Phantom of the Opera.* There couldn't be that many cinema musicians in the area with a mug like mine. He held out a hand.

'Mr Precious told me you turned down flat an offer to be first violin in my orchestra,' he said. 'No hard feelings, son.'

'Yes. Thanks.'

His eyes twinkled as he took in Louisa and Freddy.

'When you've had enough of playing nursery maid at the Electric, the offer's still open. You're good, Mr Young. I went specially to hear you play. And I was impressed.'

'Thank you.'

He winked. 'Us musicians need to look after each other. There's only so much steady work ever going round in a small place like York.'

He tapped his nose. 'A word to the wise. From what I hear, the Electric might not be what it was soon.'

He wandered to the desk to settle up his bundle of scores. I was left to smart at his description of me as a nursery maid.

The ache in my gut intensified. You see, I was not lacking in ambition. As Father's son, I owed his memory that much. At the Royal College of Music I had worked hard at composition and arranging, conscious I aspired to lead my own orchestra one day. Light music rather than strictly dance band appealed to me. That way, you got the best of both worlds. Back then, there was a huge – and profitable – demand for light orchestras.

'I'm done here,' I said.

With that, we paid and stepped out into Cookridge Street.

It was my habit to stop off for a pint or two at the Weavers Rest near the station before returning to York. Following my conversation with the Grand's musical director, I had no intention of breaking it.

'Look here,' I said to Louisa as we reached City Square, 'there are a couple of things I need to sort out. Perhaps you should go on alone. The station's just down that street over there.'

Freddy was pulling her arm, demanding something to eat.

'Oh yes,' she said with sudden passion, 'you jolly well go and pour more drink down your throat.'

I lifted my head in surprise.

'Seeing you were so beastly in there – and in the train – I can't think of anything Freddy and I would like more.'

'*Beastly*?' I sneered at the word. But her comment stung. As a young man I was horribly sensitive to people disliking me. Or considering me a fool.

'Actually, you are not the only one who… who lost things in the war,' she said. She added with proud dignity. 'Look at that poor couple on the train. Some of us lost our *loves*.'

What the hell did she know about my losses in the war? Not least, my dearest dreams. My laugh barked.

'Let's steer clear of your *loves*, Miss Mountjoy, shall we?'

A shabby, shabby swipe. She turned pale, gripping her bastard son's hand so he writhed.

'Some of us,' she said, 'have too many responsibilities to wallow... like a *hog* in self-pity. And drink!'

With that, she dragged Freddy off into the crowd, leaving me to recollect Gladys's tale of her fiancé dying before they could tie the knot. Only the most bumptious of prigs would condemn Louisa for that.

Yes, I had been beastly, and not just to her and poor Freddy. She was right, also to that couple on the train. Simply, I supposed, because Mother and Stepfather had been heartless to me. Was that how we were obliged to behave, hitting out blindly to appease our hurts?

Quite abruptly, I lost my appetite for a drink. She had read my intention in that regard easily enough. I saw how others must view my drinking. Not as something justified by the war, but as unmanly, weak, proof of defective character. Did that trouble me? No, I told myself, knowing damn well it did.

Self-pity is a mask without eyeholes for viewing the world. In a few words, she tore away a shield I sheltered behind. Yes, I had been hiding in my own personal catacomb like the Phantom of the Opera. Behind my own mask.

There, stood in noisy City Square, my thinking jolted. I had discarded my dignity. It came upon me with the force of a revelation. I did not need to live like this. I could change.

It may seem strange such obvious thoughts – ones I had chewed over many times before – affected me so deeply. But that's how it was. Every season of our selves prepares the next. I sensed a tipping point. Perhaps I had Louisa Mountjoy's honesty to thank for it.

Nevertheless, I took that drink in the Weavers Rest, arriving back in York just in time for the six o'clock showing.

Laverelli greeted me as I slouched down the aisle to the orchestra pit.

'I don't know what happened in Leeds, Mr Young,' he said, 'but I've had word from Miss Mountjoy saying she's far too poorly to perform.'

He let the implications dangle as I unloaded my small suitcase of musical parts.

'*Did* something happen, lad?'

'She didn't seem well,' I lied.

Without the luxury of sick pay, next week would be tight for her and Freddy.

'Don't worry, Mr Laverelli, I'll take the piano tonight.'

He hovered thoughtfully then returned to his station in the foyer.

'I hear Miss Mountjoy went with you to Leeds and came over poorly, sudden like,' whispered Gladys Bannering between films.

She gave me a look that might unsettle a guilty conscience. I fiddled with my music.

'Things aren't so easy for her, you know.'

'I'm aware of that.'

Gladys glanced round to confirm we were not overheard. 'Me and Miss Mountjoy might not always see eye to eye. But she's brave to sit up there every night, Mr Young. It's not easy for a woman in a world made for men.'

I thought unexpectedly of Mother and her hasty, frightened second marriage after Father died. I realised, too, why going to New Century that afternoon had been so important to Louisa. Here was a chance for education – not a thorough, formal one, admittedly – but a means to earn her place with dignity and respect as a musician. My self-absorption had merely confirmed she was trapped forever in the role of disposable underling. The male mysteries were as taboo as ever.

I decided there and then. When Louisa returned, I would teach her how to fit a picture well. Above all, I would apologise for my behaviour.

Seventeen

Louisa was absent from work for several evenings – an unheard of thing. She couldn't afford time off for any sickness milder than bubonic plague. In the end, I told Laverelli I would call on her.

'That's a good thought, lad,' he said. 'Buck her up a bit. We'd all be obliged.'

Dark outriders of cloud were advancing from the south-east. The air tense, charged for a summer storm. From Clarence Street I took a wrong turn into the Groves down a terrace so lowly and soot-blackened, it didn't warrant a street sign. It was dependent on a single rusty gaslight for illumination at night. The drains reeked in the heat. Urchins in ragged clothes and flapping shoes played marbles in the gutter. Their hair was close-cropped to expose nits. A scent of rotten meat from a tanning factory by the River Foss vied with the sharp, burnt aroma of chicory.

I soon lost my way. The route I chose down an alley choked with weeds, rubbish, cinders and dog shit led to yet another narrow terrace backed by dingy courtyards. Here, cramped houses surrounded a communal toilet block.

At last, more by luck than design, I reached the relative civilisation of Lowther Street. Seedy pubs stood alongside the essential social service of a pawnbroker's. A few grocers specialising in tinned food bought on tick put up a brave front. A pasty-faced young man leant against a lamppost, gasping for breath from an asthma attack. The hack and gurgle of his lungs told tales of gas out in Flanders or France.

There was little traffic apart from stray housewives with baskets. The men were either at work or indolent. Wednesday was washday in York, so most housewives tended coppers of boiling water and carbolic soap.

At the entrance to Princess Street, I read the darkening sky. In the war I had developed an acute weather sense as a navigator. It saved us several times, especially over Dogger and west of Heligoland Bight where winds congregate.

Should I knock on her door? Dare I? It was unlikely Louisa would be pleased to see me. I cringed inwardly at my snide reference in Leeds to Freddy's bastard status. An insult not easily discarded. Maybe that decided me, because I deserved a little punishment.

You could tell from mould on the damp, muddy cobbles how rarely the sun reached Princess Street. Yet for all the meanness of the squalid two-up two-down houses an endless, and ultimately futile, battle for respectability was being waged. The lace curtains fronting the pavement shone a bright carbolic white, no mean labour considering the quantity of smoke, dust and soot in those tiny homes. Doorsteps and spaces directly before the front doors shone from sheer elbow grease. All to show a brave face to the neighbours.

I knocked on Louisa's front door, hat in hand, and waited. A minute passed. Perhaps she was holed up in some dreary back bedroom, too ill to rise.

When the door opened, I leaned back in surprise. The young woman before me scarcely resembled proud Louisa Mountjoy behind her piano. Her long hair was down, the first time I had not seen it pinned up in a big neat bun. It was mousy and greasy. Her face was mushroom-pale.

Louisa took a slight step back, battling an instinct to slam the door in my face.

'Please!' I cried. 'Miss Mountjoy. May I have a word?'

She examined me. Shivered.

'If you must,' she said. 'Though I'm sure Mr Laverelli could have told me himself that I have been replaced. He didn't need to send a messenger.'

'It's not that,' I said. 'I am here for the very opposite of that.'

Reluctantly, she stepped aside to let me in.

There were two small rooms on the ground floor, both crammed. The front room was dominated by an old, sagging horsehair sofa and a rocking chair covered with a woollen crocheted throw. The empty grate had been recently black-leaded. Cheap pottery dogs and horses gambolled on the mantelpiece, upon a green tasselled cloth. Everything belonged to Louisa's landlady, Bertha Kettlewell. Of her own taste, nothing was on display.

Louisa appeared more nervous than I had ever known her.

'No one else is here,' she said, hurriedly. 'Bertha has taken Freddy out. She said I needed rest.'

She wrung her hands, reached up to touch her disordered hair.

'Please come back another time. Have you no message from Mr Laverelli? I'm not well, you see. I can't be seen playing in that horrid cinema anymore.'

Her agitation increased. 'All the neighbours will be whispering about you. They watch from behind their curtains. You really shouldn't come when I'm alone. People will talk.'

'Please,' I urged, 'take a seat. You are distressed. I did not mean to disturb your rest.'

She looked at me wildly for a moment then sank on the soggy sofa. Although a close, breathless heat smothered the streets, the house was cold. I sensed it was always cold. A small, handmade quilt lay on the sofa. I gently placed it over her. She gasped involuntarily.

'Please keep warm,' I said. 'May I sit?'

She indicated the old rocking chair. It creaked alarmingly beneath my weight.

Silent, miserable tears trickled down her face. She was frightened, very frightened. Drained of hope, too. The strength that kept her going as the Electric's pianist when she barely possessed the necessary skill had died. My low behaviour had been the proverbial straw on the camel's back.

'Miss Mountjoy,' I said, 'I have come to apologise for any offence my words or behaviour have caused. You see, just before we went to Leeds... Oh, it is hard to explain, but I will try.'

And I did, describing Father's death and what the loss of his old clarinet meant to me. That it was no excuse for my unkind words. That I hoped, in time, she might forgive me.

'Perhaps,' I concluded, 'when you spoke to me of self-pity, you taught me the real lesson I must take from losing Father's old clarinet. I must strive to win a new one of my own.'

When I finished, my own eyes were damp. Together we made what Maurice would have called derisively, 'a right pair'.

'I did not know,' she said. 'Thank you.'

We sat in silence. A terrible longing for a cigarette gripped me but I knew she hated the smell of tobacco.

'Nor do you know anything of me,' she said, meeting my eye. It was a challenge.

'That is not entirely true.'

I told her what Gladys had revealed of her lost fiancé, Freddy's tragic father.

'And I know,' I continued, 'you are a most intelligent, cultured, respectable young lady. One who is admirably devoted to her son. So you see, perhaps I do know what is truly important about you. Or some of it.' I bit my lip. 'Nor do I expect you to trust me with confidences I have not deserved.'

Louisa sighed. Her hands grew busy until the heavy bun of her hair was back in place.

'Thank you,' she breathed. 'But you do not know how I came to be in York, do you? You must tell from my accent this place is strange to me. As it is for you, David.' She hesitated. 'Although in my case, my home was in... Surrey, not London.'

I waited.

'You see.' She sighed again. 'Yes, I shall trust you. When – what happened with Freddy's father took place – my own father – he is a Dean of Cloisters, you see, in a famous cathedral, I'd rather not say which – my Papa declared that his religion and respectability – in fact, his position in the world – meant he could have nothing more to do with me. Papa said I would poison my sister's chance of a decent marriage, as well as hurt my brother's career in the church. He's a curate, you see, and Papa is very ambitious for him. He said I was a disgrace to the family. That he had no choice.'

She shivered, plucking at the quilt.

'It is cold in this house, is it not?' she said. 'Do you know, and here's a strange thing, there is not a single room that gets a ray of direct sunlight. Not one! The only spot is a corner of the backyard. I never imagined myself in a house without sunshine.'

'It will not be forever,' I assured her.

'Perhaps.' She frowned. 'But I was telling you how Papa would have nothing more to do with me. How he washed his hands of me. I was showing with Freddy by then. Luckily, I had a little money for the birth and afterwards. I also had a friend in York. Or thought I did. That's why I came here. Far away from all those happy to condemn me. To call me a lost, fallen woman.' Her face quivered and she spoke with sudden intensity. 'A *whore*.'

The word was doubly ugly rendered in her well-spoken way. She paused to breathe deeply, and wiped her eyes with a finger.

'But when I got here I discovered my friend had gone to Scotland. I had so little money left over after Freddy was born. I was lost, David, and I feared... the worst.' She whispered. 'I was afraid of the workhouse.'

'Well, you need never fear that again,' I reassured her. 'The worst is past.'

'Is it? Perhaps. It was still the war, you know, and nearly all the men were gone. Then I saw an advertisement for a pianist at the Electric. And I... I told Mr Laverelli all about Freddy. I guessed it was best to be honest with him. You see, he is a kind man. A tolerant man. He said it was not for him to stand in judgement on others. That there is too much judging in the world. All of us need a helping hand, some time or other. He found me these lodgings with Bertha and she is so good with Freddy, so patient. Such a treasure! She looks after him while I am at work. Then, a year after the war ended, you came along. I suppose it was inevitable in the end.'

We sat facing each other in the cold, damp little house. She had indeed trusted me. I saw how that trust had unburdened her a little – and knew I must prove worthy of it.

'Let me be your friend, please,' I said. 'You see, we had a small collection at work for medicines and such – that's how essential you are to our orchestra, Louisa – and doctors are expensive.'

I extracted a ten shilling note from my wallet and, rising, laid it on the mantelpiece beside a china cocker spaniel. She watched me strangely.

'That isn't necessary, David. I really don't need charity.'

'Well, the collection was for Freddy,' I said, 'we all wanted to give him a treat. Please set aside the money for him.'

'David... '

'Remember what Mr Laverelli told you,' I interrupted. 'All of us need help some time. Besides, it would offend your colleagues if you refused the money. Or, indeed, ever mentioned it again. Please say not a word more.'

Another sigh escaped from her. Was it one of relief? I believed it was.

'I shall make tea,' she said. 'Yes, let me make you tea.'

She went through to the narrow kitchen with its cast iron range for cooking, its scuttle full of coal. Excusing myself, I followed her and took the back door to the outside toilet. There wasn't room to swing a dead hamster in that tiny yard. A tin bath hung from a hook beside a small brick shed containing the copper for boiling water.

Surrendering to my desire for a cigarette, I searched for the tiny corner of sunlight Louisa had mentioned. A sturdy fern clung to the brickwork of a wall. That must be the single place the sun found. The plant, more a weed, seemed little enough, terribly little, yet it gave me hope for her.

What followed was a parody of the lavish high teas she must have known as a girl. Instead of bone china and cucumber sandwiches with the crusts cut off, instead of prim ladies in tea gowns pouring gracefully from silver pots, we repaired to the shabby, cramped front room of 5 Princess Street.

Louisa had done her best, even finding a couple of saucers that matched the chipped cups. Lacking cake, she rustled up slices of home-baked bread with a scrape of margarine and a plate of broken biscuits you got for tuppence a bag at the Saturday Market.

Having shared so much frankness, we had nothing much left to say. Some intimacies do not require words. Some understandings are always unspoken. As I left, I encouraged her to return to the Electric that very night, if she felt up to it, promising to take over should she feel faint. We were still maintaining the pretence her sickness was more of body than spirit.

'What a lovely tea,' I said, lingering in the doorway.

The colour was coming back to her cheeks.

'Wasn't it jolly?'

'I should say so.' I paused. 'In fact, I'd be delighted if you would take tea with me another time. Nowhere fancy, I'm afraid.'

'Oh, I do love a Lyons!' she cried, as though slumming it was her favourite pastime. It indicated the kind of establishment she thought I could afford. 'And please tell Mr Laverelli I shall be ready for the six o'clock showing tonight.'

Black clouds had gathered over York as I stepped into Lowther Street. Thunder rumbled at the edge of the horizon.

As I hurried to beat the downpour, people stood in doorways. Among them, Gladys Bannering and her conchie brother, Thomas. They'd poked their heads out to assess the laden sky. She watched me curiously but I pretended not to notice. My mind was full of Louisa and the confidences we had exchanged.

As I neared Gillygate, it came down, heralded by a boom of thunder that shook the town. A solid cloudburst, rain pelting in rods off pavement and street and gutter.

Without overcoat or umbrella, I was soaked in a few moments, water dripping from the brim of my hat. But the rain felt fine. It was washing me clean. At last, I was being washed clean.

I replayed the worst of my pack of dreams that night. Well, almost the worst. Nosing through clouds, the rounded snout of a Zeppelin…

A click of Morse (I am more than proficient at Morse, though on our bus Smittie mans the crackly valve-powered radio receiver in the narrow cabin behind Fitz). He scribbles a note and passes it to me: **ZEP STOP SIGNALS DETECTED STOP L42 STOP APPROX SOUTH OF TERSCHELLING STOP INTERCEPT.** Soon I'm calculating wind speed and drift, numbers in my head, like syncopated, overlapping harmonies…

In an instant, we are nearing the island of Terschelling, a dark line to the east. Tense as cats, especially Fitz. Here is his chance for a Distinguished Flying Cross, at the least. The grim set of his shoulders, head like a hunter galloping forward, frantic for the fox, tells me what's coming our way.

Then I see her, my young eyes so sharp. Twelve, fifteen miles off, a slender matchstick passing over the rhythmic flash of the Terschelling Light Ship. Stomach muscles tense. Should I tell Fitz? Indicate the wrong direction? In my dream I suffer treacherous thoughts.

In reality, I point dutifully, excitedly.

The Zepp is low, foolishly low, just five thousand feet, its one real protection being altitudes that wood and canvas planes cannot reach. We climb, dropping our bombs in the sea to lose weight. Two miles, one and a half…

The wonder of the thing close up! Long as two football pitches, sixty feet wide. Broadside to us now, heading due north. Then we're slipping behind it, a perfect position.

Has it seen us? No, or it would be ditching ballast, shooting up into the heavens to escape our Lewis guns. My gloved hands tremble as I check firing mechanisms, drums of special ammunition designed to ignite hydrogen. Closing, we're closing, Fitz throwing us into a swooping climb, up, up, approaching high-throttle, our wings vibrating before he levels off to rush the giant, the monster's huge dragon body and gondolas hung beneath, enormous propellers whirling…

Now the dream always slows, strange with horror, for we are just fifty feet below the rear gondola and they've seen us at last. Terror, terror among the figures scurrying within the long cabins, rushing to machine guns. I glimpse goggled faces, then everyone's firing, Gus, me, Smittie.

Fitz weaves to avoid the scything propellers of the beast. I let off a drum before my first Lewis jams. The second empties nicely. Then we're scrabbling for fresh drums, bullets tearing holes in our wings and fuselage. Fitz dives away. Just in time!

A slight glow has appeared in the long canopy of gas. Like wildfire it expands, flames mushrooming. I crouch in my cockpit, unable to look away. How swiftly the fire spreads! With a whoosh, half way along the beast, its belly caving in as the flames reach up. One gondola ablaze; and as we circle I see them, the nightmare seed we have sown.

One by one, specks of burning men emerge and leap into the air, twisting, turning, fallen angels cast down, down, from Heaven towards Hell. Slowly, ponderously, the dragon follows, spiralling in a cloud of fire. Gondolas with their bombs break free and hurtle into the sea beneath. Sprouts rise where they strike the waves. Still the monster descends. A pillar of smoke and ash reaches high above the burning metal skeleton as it is swallowed by the sea...

There the dream ends. No drunken celebrations, though they did take place. And I did receive my own piece of tin, a Distinguished Flying Cross. No newspapermen interview the Right Honourable Flight Lieutenant Archibald Fitzclarence, son and heir of Viscount Cleveland, as they did in real life. Eager to meet the strapping young aristocrat – England's finest – who (almost) single-handedly slew the foul Zeppelin. No dreams of the noble hero who duly received his Victoria Cross from the King's own hand. No, I never dream of the medals or the glory. Just men, imprinted on my soul, burning, leaping and falling, tormented by wings of fire.

Eighteen

'Morning, Mr Young!' said Dr Middleton as I entered the ward. The way he rubbed his hands together suggested I was anticipated. At once, I grew suspicious.

'A quick word?' He drew me aside. 'Concerning a splendid little idea of mine.'

A minute later I was incredulous. What had put such an infernal notion into his head?

'I'm really not sure it would do him good,' I countered. 'All those people around. Looking him over. To be frank, I fear the clientele at the Electric is rather too *common* for his taste. In fact, I jolly well know they are.'

A secret part of me – perhaps unkind – believed it would do the Right Honourable Archibald Fitzclarence a power of good to rub elbows with the lower orders.

'People are precisely what he needs,' replied Dr Middleton. 'Besides, you have led the way in that direction. Taking him out for walks and such. It would be extremely helpful from a medical perspective. Doctor's orders. Lay a few ghosts, don't you see?'

I didn't. Or didn't want to. He waited, his blue eyes beady. I licked my lips.

'It is Charlie Chaplin this week,' I conceded. 'He went out of his way to watch Chaplin when we were in the Service. There was a little cinema in Felixstowe he used to visit with other officers from the mess.'

Naturally, I hadn't been invited to the party. Too 'bottom drawer'.

128

'Splendid! I've already spoken to him about the need to venture beyond these walls. Let's put it to him, shall we?'

I stayed quiet as Dr Middleton explained his 'little idea'. Fitz listened gravely. At least, I assume that was his mood. Given the injuries to his facial muscles, it could be hard to read him. His face was often as immobile as an Easter Island statue, unless a nervous tic set in.

'Well, Archie,' concluded Dr Middleton, 'how does that sound? Do think hard about our little chat yesterday, there's a good fellow. It sounds like awfully good fun to me. One step at a time, eh?'

Fitz uttered a sound like a shuddering cough. Or a petrol engine phuttering. Heads turned all over the ward. The officer minus a nose stopped rocking silently. I realised Fitz was actually chuckling.

'Ah, the Little Tramp,' he said, at last. 'Damn amusing little feller.'

'Good lord, yes,' said Dr Middleton. 'Well done, well done. Leave all the arrangements to me.'

Fitz's remaining eye grew intent. An intensity I remembered all too well. It translated as a resolution to get his own way, whatever the consequences, inconvenience, or perils to anyone else. Especially me. Horribly wounded or not, he was never a coward. You could call him an insufferable snob and conceited prig, but never yellow.

'Dammit,' he said. 'Charlie Chaplin it is then. Carry on, Young!'

There is a Chinese proverb: no good deed will go unpunished.

The first leg of the sortie went smoothly enough. I joined Fitz on the pillared front porch of the lunatic asylum. Though it was a pleasant May afternoon, they'd wrapped him in an overcoat and trilby, complete with silver-knobbed stick.

A taxi-cab rattled up and we climbed aboard. Fitz's limp was pronounced but he could hop around, so long as you weren't in a hurry.

The short journey from Bootham Park to the Electric, less than a mile, was soon accomplished. He peered out hungrily, as though reminding himself the world existed: shops and terrace houses, a young couple walking arm-in-arm, a dog scratching its behind with a hind paw. How starved of variety he was in the officer's ward. Not all prisons are for criminals. Mostly we construct our own.

A moment later, the Electric was in sight. No turning back now. It occurred to me that warning Ambrose and Gladys in advance might have been wise. They could have guaranteed an aisle seat in the back stalls with a good view. I also realised there had been a grave misunderstanding: Dr Middleton assumed I would be able to play the role of nurse.

Sweat appeared on my forehead. What if Fitz needed the toilet. Or panicked and started moaning loudly. Or decided to slam down the piano lid on Louisa's fingers. What if he fainted. Or had a fit in the aisle. I'd be at the front, occupied with the music.

'Here we are, sir!' cried the driver, as the taxi-cab pulled up.

A queue stretched from the foyer. I jumped out, hurrying round the back of the cab to open Fitz's door. As he climbed out, his leg waved like a beetle's antennae, followed by the silver-knobbed stick. Fortunately, the cab driver helped me ease him to his feet.

Anyone inclined to complain about queue-jumping was silenced by Fitz's face. Compared to him, I was a positive Valentino. His hat obscured the burned off stump of an ear, but nothing concealed the bubbling skin like white maggots seared into a bed of raw purple flesh. As ever, the ammoniac stench of Dakin's Solution – a real nose-wrinkler – lingered in the air.

Eyes softened in sympathy, or the appearance of sympathy. People soon learned expressions for ignoring hideously maimed veterans after the war. Blends of distant pity and grave respect. Expressions conveying a resolve to not get involved.

'By 'eck!' I heard Ambrose mutter. He hurried over. 'Need a hand, Mr Young?'

'That would be good.'

Ambrose took Fitz's arm while I held the swing doors. I heard whispering behind us.

Fitz stared straight ahead, shoulders back, mouth firm.

'Carry on, Young,' he commanded. A fine, patrician drawl.

'Would you prefer a seat at the front or back, sir?'

He shot me a startled look. He was panicking inside. Maybe he regretted his bravado in coming here; if so, we were mid-air, far, far out over the ocean, no turning back to base now.

'May I suggest the front?' I said. 'We'll get special cushions put down.'

I didn't like to say it would allow me to keep an eye on him.

'Very good, Young.'

Tiny droplets of pus had formed like dew on his brow as he sweated. He was breathing hard.

In the foyer we encountered Gladys Bannering. My heart sank further. Her job as usherette was to conduct him to his seat, Ambrose's was to manage the queue. The silly girl might well recoil from the monster before her.

For a long moment she eyed him. Then me. Then Fitz again.

'You mind the queue, Ambrose,' she said, 'I'll take over from here.'

'This is Flight Lieutenant Fitzclarence,' I told her. 'He'd like to sit at the front. Near the band.'

'Leave it to me. I'll make sure he's right comfy. Then I'll fetch him a nice cup of tea. And I've got some very nice buns.'

Was that a grin stealing across Fitz's face? He was a young man, after all, despite his injuries.

'Would you care to use the gentleman's room first, sir?' asked Gladys, quietly. 'It's a long showing this afternoon. We've a special double feature, Charlie Chaplin, you know. It's very popular.'

'That little chap is why I'm here, my dear,' rasped out Fitz, as her slender arm replaced Ambrose's burly limb. 'About the, ahem, gentleman's room.' *Cough, cough.* 'A very considerate suggestion.'

He'd forgotten me altogether. I left them to it, taking my place with the orchestra. Gladys Bannering treated me to a bobby-dazzler. I replied with a grunt.

He had come to see Charlie Chaplin's *Sunnyside*, but more was on the programme.

An obligatory Felix the Cat then documentary one-reeler of time-lapse photography showing the growth, bloom and decay of a rose.

We serenaded it with the Intermezzo from *Cavalleria Rusticana* by Mascagni.

Next a fifty minute Western, *Riders of the Dawn*. The story concerned a handsome ne'er-do-well helping a poor orphan boy become a man and win back his lost inheritance. I wondered if Louisa was thinking of fatherless Freddy.

Lots of galloping and menace from the villains in black hats. A whole fusillade on Maurice's cap pistol during the final shoot out. I added to the bang-bangs on the timpani while Louisa maintained a tense series of arpeggios in a minor key. Finally, with an unresolved chord of C# diminished, the baddie took a fatal bullet. Silence apart from the piano echoing. Louisa held down the chord and worked the sustain pedal. Cue mad scramble by myself and Maurice to seize our instruments and play out a triumphant *Love March* by Meierstein as the worthy cowpoke embraced his girl and the orphan, happy ever after.

Maurice grumbled while Victor loaded a new reel into the projector. 'What's all this, Mr Young?' He waved the cue sheet for *Sunnyside*. 'There's more changes here than a bride's nightie.'

'*Really*, Mr Skelton,' chided Louisa.

'You'd know all about that,' he mumbled.

I privately resolved to have a word with Mr Skelton about his baiting of Louisa. It was becoming insufferable.

Back then, audiences literally howled with mirth at Charlie Chaplin. Aficionados of his 'comic business' (there is a know-it-all for every subject) waxed on the little touches he used to add emotion to the farce, indeed, to every gesture, from his rolling, duck-like waddle to the poignancy of dark-ringed eyes beneath an unruly mop of curls. All performed while the lower half of his face stayed inscrutable as the Sphinx.

Chaplin was hard to fit up well. Too many sudden shifts of mood and perspective. The guiding tension was between lightness of touch in the romping sections and abrupt, raw, outbursts of pathos.

Gladys had placed Fitz on a padded tip up aisle seat at the very front. She even personally delivered his cup of tea and iced bun on a tray, placing it across his knees so she bent forward to reveal plenty of bosom. Every so often she would nip down to check he was happy. I noticed people in the audience conferring *sotto voce* about him.

They say the essence of comedy is timing: that was doubly true for accompanying Chaplin. Luckily, Maurice caught the exact mood for once. Every time the little clown's appalling boss, the owner of a country hotel and store, kicked our Charlie up the backside he played a different sound effect with gusto: woodblock, duck call, even a resounding chime of tubular bells that nearly brought the house down.

Fitz loved it. Rather too much, in fact. I almost stopped playing in alarm when Charlie placed a live hen on a frying pan to lay his breakfast egg. Then milked a cow straight into a teacup. Was that coughing and gasping the fatal fit I dreaded? But Gladys appeared with a glass of water and he sipped gratefully.

A title flashed up:

It seemed rude not to introduce the band while the audience filed out.

'Hope you enjoyed the show, sir,' I said.

Mirth had unknotted the muscles on his face. Strange what comedy can do for a man damaged in his soul. That was the worst of his wounds. The physical would surely mend to a just about bearable degree in time. He was tough as an ox. Who knew about the scars inside?

'Very good, Young, very good. I had no idea you're so dashed talented. That bally fiddle of yours fairly sings.'

The highest praise he'd ever allowed me.

133

'May I introduce Miss Mountjoy, sir? A very talented musician in her own right, as you've just witnessed.'

'Delighted, madam,' he said, holding out his one functioning hand.

'How do you do?' she said, with a slight bob.

She loved his accent and title. Her eyes were bright as she watched us together.

'And this is Mr Skelton.'

Maurice was choking to discover my relationship with such a grand personage. It says much for Fitz's unerring ability to place a person on the social scale the cellist received a brief nod.

I helped Fitz rise and led him to the foyer. A few people hung around, notably Laverelli in his manager's dinner jacket and black tie.

'Captain,' he said. His fixed grin was uncharacteristically deferential. 'I trust you were made comfortable.'

I decided not to point out the correct rank was Flight Lieutenant.

'Very good, very good,' said Fitz.

I could tell he detected something 'oily' about Laverelli. Even before learning his foreign surname. Perhaps he caught a whiff of lavender water.

'A regular of ours recognised you as a hero, sir. A recipient of our country's highest award for valour. We're honoured to have you in the Electric.' Laverelli's eyebrows shot up. 'And he mentioned our own Mr Young, also winning a very special kind of medal. Flying out over the sea against them terrible Zeppelins. Which he's kept *very* quiet about, I must say.'

It may seem surprising, but I'd never revealed my exact role in the RNAS to anyone in York. Nor that I possessed medals of my own. Not through embarrassment exactly. I just didn't like to talk about it.

'I wasn't the pilot,' I said, hastily. 'Flight Lieutenant Fitzclarence was the pilot. I was just the navigator.' I cleared my throat. 'Really, I should be navigating him home. Your taxi's outside, sir. Shall we go?'

But Laverelli seemed reluctant to let so notable a patron escape his foyer. Perhaps he hoped for a mention in the Herald.

It is strange how chance anoints heroes. The vast majority of York folk had few direct encounters with the war – I mean real war that burns men alive and tears their guts out before your eyes. But it so happened that back in May 1916, a Zeppelin appeared one sultry night over York. The droning, reverberating hum of its great engines drew startled people out onto the street to gape. It came in low, just four or five thousand feet. For a few minutes it hovered above the race course, black smoke trailing from its idling engines. Then it advanced. Still low, for there were no anti-aircraft guns in York. The last time the place had been bombarded was the English Civil War. With engines throttled high, dense black smoke formed a train behind its monstrous body, obscuring the bright stars of the clear night sky. Towards the Ouse it floated, suddenly spewing out bombs. Eighteen fell in total, killing nine and maiming dozens more. Whole houses were flattened and countless windows broken. Within minutes, the behemoth had overflown the city and dwindled until only the fading rumour of its engines lingered – along with the screams of the terrified and wounded.

The memory of that night, however, did not fade. Little wonder a Zeppelin-slaying hero like the Right Honourable Archibald Fitzclarence, VC, DSC, DFC etc attracted a hushed circle of faces. And Laverelli knew the value of an eager audience. What could be better for business than the Phantom of the Opera's medal-toting pal gracing the centre stalls? Complete with eye-catching wounds for extra drama. Show business comes in many forms.

'A great honour to have you, sir,' he said.

'Very good,' repeated Fitz.

He was exhausted. The strain of chaperoning him had worn me out, too.

'Consider yourself welcome to a free seat anytime at the Electric, sir!' called out Laverelli, holding open the swing doors with great ceremony.

Gladys appeared beside me, her hand hovering an inch from my arm. 'If you like,' she murmured, 'I could see him to the hospital in the taxi. You've only got twenty minutes until the next show. You deserve a nice cup of tea.'

Her face was near my own. She smelt of cheap, musky perfume.

Then came a suspicion. It took instant root. How else could you explain her enthusiasm to climb into the back of a taxi with Fitz? Perhaps she hoped her face – and legs and shapely figure – would be her fortune. She wouldn't be the first. And he wouldn't be the first cripple to fall for a pretty nurse.

'No,' I said, more curtly than I intended. 'No, thank you.'

She looked a little put out.

'I just thought you'd have to run all the way back for the six o'clock,' she said.

As it turned out, she was right. I did have to pelt back to the Electric from Bootham Park Asylum, arriving breathless and five minutes late. Laverelli didn't seem to mind. He whispered as I straightened my musician's black dicky bow. 'Remember, lad, he's welcome any time. On the house.'

Nineteen

Laverelli shut the Electric, giving the staff an unexpected holiday. The annual inspection was nigh. He floated round the building with young Victor the projectionist, clipboard in hand. Back and forth they progressed, no job too small. Experiments with the two statutory sources of lighting, namely, the gas generator and mains, to prevent a blackout. The proper functioning of water closets and urinals. Testing the spring door of the fireproof box containing the projector and flammable celluloid reels. Sand and water buckets. The Pyrene extinguisher full of soda-acid. Exits and passageways all clear. Aisles unobstructed...

On my way out for a stroll, I encountered him. He was mopping his brow with a handkerchief.

'Going well?' I asked.

'There's no pleasing some folk,' he said. 'Do you know what, Mr Young, all I ever do is reveal the magic that lies in the everyday to souls as sorely needs it. Everything you need to make a sad world happy can be found at the Electric. Remember this, "Man cannot live by bread alone". And for the cost of a loaf, I serve it every night on a silver platter.'

I could not help thinking of John the Baptist's head served by Salome on a tray.

'I'm sure people appreciate it,' I said.

'It's to be hoped. Especially with this inspection coming up.'

'My friend certainly enjoyed the show. Mr Fitzclarence wants to come again.'

'Does he now?'

Laverelli seemed to take solace from the news.

Later, on a bench by the River Ouse near the Museum Gardens, I considered his words. What was this magic of the everyday? I suspected he meant entertainment, distraction, thrills. Above all, being taken out of yourself for an hour or two. But I was not so sure. What was the everyday magic that made life worthwhile but kindness? Small, inconsequential actions between people, nothing much in the vast scale of the universe, ripples of sunlight on the river. That's all we are, I thought, moments of shifting light reflected off a dark stream. The trick – and one I seemed not to possess – was revelling in that fleeting moment when you flash and glow.

Oddly, this elevated thought made my stomach rumble. I had discovered a remarkably fine pie emporium in the Shambles. Firm, slightly crisp, melting pastry. Cubes of steak and kidney with just the right amount of chew in glossy gravy. Let's face it, perfect gravy is something you can spend a lifetime seeking. If I couldn't attain happiness, I could compensate myself with a damn good pie.

I floated through an afternoon of soft, warm breezes where seeds drifted. Through the looming gatehouse of Bootham Bar, down a street of higgledy medieval houses to the Minster. In those days, York people spoke of their town as the three Ps: pretty, proud and poor. Its ancient centre had scarcely changed for centuries. Nor, as I was about to discover, had its baser amenities.

Ahead of me I spotted Maurice Skelton. The bandy-legged cellist walked with unusual vigour. My route coincided with his but I hoped to avoid him, so I hung back until he reached Grape Lane. At this junction two things happened. Maurice glanced round as though checking whether he was observed, whereupon I stepped into the doorway of a milliner's. When I emerged he was entering Grape Lane.

Grape Lane had formerly been known as Grope Lane – and for good reason. A dark, seedy little flag-stoned street, its concealed entrances – snickleways as Yorkies called them – led to small, dead-end courtyards and Tudor beam houses, some given over to the oldest profession.

I watched Maurice vanish down just such a snickleway. Curious now, I ambled slowly after.

The shadowy passage terminated in a tiny courtyard and a pair of tarts. They were smoking and gossiping by an open doorway, their trade advertised by plastered makeup, bulging décolletage and elevated hemlines. I'd seen enough.

Well, well, I thought, making my way to the Clock Inn after enjoying my pie. What a sly, mucky old hypocrite Maurice turned out. Always chuntering and grumbling about *oo-ers* when he couldn't keep his hands off them.

Half an hour later, who should walk into the Clock but the sinner himself.

By then, I had worked up a mild outrage against him. Not about the tarts, you understand. I was ex-Navy, and while my own tastes never ventured that way, any port in a storm. No, it was his constant, sly insinuations concerning Louisa's virtue. He revelled in making her uncomfortable, exploiting her past in a spirit of cruel mischief. High time to knock him down a peg or two.

After his exertions, a liverish tinge reddened his cheeks. His oiled hair hung in greasy disordered strands. Nodding in my direction, he bought a pint and a pickled egg on a saucer. Then he settled at a table on the far side of the pub. I carried my drink over.

'Mind if I join you, Mr Skelton? I saw you earlier in Grape Lane. Visiting a friend, were you?'

His pint paused midway to his mouth. He examined me over its froth, calculating how much I knew.

'Mebbe.'

'Actually, I did hope to have a private word with you.'

'Oh, aye?'

'I couldn't help noticing how often you make comments that, well, upset Miss Mountjoy.'

'What of it?'

'I'd like it to stop.'

'Would you now.'

It had been my intention to leave it there. Just warn him that, as leader of our happy little band, I would no longer tolerate him carrying on about *oo-ers* in front of a lady. But Maurice was the type who craves the last word. Especially with a pipsqueak like me. A bullish leer made his expression far from attractive.

'From what I hear,' he said, 'you'll be headin' back south soon any road.'

'Oh?'

'Aye.'

'Where did you hear that, Mr Skelton?'

'A good pal of mine. Chap who met you in Leeds.'

I recalled bumping into the director of the Grand's orchestra.

'Mr Cooper?'

'Aye, Herbert Cooper. Me an' him go back a long way. To when you was still playin' with a rattle.'

'So what exactly *did* you hear?' I asked, puzzled.

He tapped his nose.

'Rather not say.'

Maurice took a bite of pickled egg. Crumbs of yellow yolk clung to his upper lip.

'Very mysterious,' I said. 'I suspect it was nothing.'

We eyeballed each other.

'Nobody's fault but his own if Laverelli catches it this time round,' declared Maurice, brandishing the egg. He was enjoying himself now. Letting out pent up bile. 'Not that I care. Shame he likes employing folk with a queer reputation. P'raps because they come cheap.'

'Well, he employs you, Mr Skelton,' I said.

'I were thinking of the Bannering girl. Among others. Everyone round here knows she spread her legs where she shouldn't. Aye, a very public affair during the war. Flaunted it, she did. But I'll say no more, seeing you're so fond of the lass.'

A little of some people goes a very long way. By now I'd had a bellyful of Maurice.

'Good afternoon to you.' I drained my glass and rose. 'And remember what I said about Miss Mountjoy's feelings. I mean it.'

Maurice lay down the remains of his egg on the saucer. He tapped his nose. 'Thing about York, lad, it's not *what* you know but *who* you know.'

I bore that wisdom out into the summer afternoon, along with his warning about Laverelli. It crossed my mind to mention it the next time I saw my employer. Somehow it didn't seem worthwhile. The thoroughness of Laverelli's preparations for the annual inspection was proof he ran a tight ship.

More intriguing was Maurice's revelation about Gladys. Although perhaps it was no surprise. By an affair, he had clearly meant with a married man. I could not help comparing the injustice of Louisa losing her reputation when her fiancé died serving his country, to Gladys conducting some tawdry liaison. Probably with an older man who could slip her extra rations. Louisa had loved too well. The usherette had sought a profitable thrill. The revelation made me more determined than ever to make secure Louisa Mountjoy's position at the Electric. Also, to know her better.

🎬

Late one evening, I was making my way through the deserted auditorium, torch in hand, when a loud meow came from the darkness. A moment later, Clifton emerged from beneath a seat, his white bib and paws catching my torch beam. I went over to sit beside him.

'Any mice for supper?' I asked, scratching beneath his chin. 'How about a nice fat rat?'

He purred lustily, ears back.

Then the watery light of my torch caught a shape on the floor. It was half-concealed by monkey nut shells beneath the tip-up seat where Clifton had lurked. Stooping, I discovered a notebook, six inches by four with a stiff cardboard cover. The kind sold in Woolworth's for sixpence.

Idly flipping the pages surprised me with poetry. Someone had copied out verses in their best handwriting. A posy of classics amidst sentimental poems of the type you came across in the Sunday paper. Each was reverently labelled with the author's full name: *Lord Byron (George Gordon)* and *Percy Bysshe Shelley*, to name a couple of the better known. Also, bards long forgotten now, like *Jean Ingelow* and *Miss J.K. Effie*. Every poem tended towards the romantic. A few carried no author's name. I deduced they were the handiwork of the notebook's owner.

REMEMBRANCES

A sad Memory,
A Nothing!!
Except it burneth like coals,
Smouldering.

You walked past
So Proud!
Did not e'en see me
On thy Road.

Why Remembrance
This Pain?
Because every dawn
Bringeth it to me again.

I'm sure you get the idea.

The next afternoon I sat for an hour in Dean's Park beneath the looming shadow of the Minster and read the poems. Before the war I had been inclined to romance, fancying myself in love with one siren or another at the Royal College of Music. Shyness had stopped me pursuing my hot gushes – a damn good thing for the young ladies concerned.

Then the war put a stop to any kind of infatuation. Too many girls and women had showered white feathers upon me before I enlisted (including dear old Mother, though, in her defence, her feathers were reproachful sighs). I had developed an irrational distrust, even wariness, around females. Many a young man who made it home felt the same way.

Something softened and revived as I read. *She walks in beauty like the night... How shall I love thee? Let me count the ways...* Even the awful attempts at verse by the notebook's owner touched me a little. They possessed sincerity, however mawkish and vulgar.

Through the fog of my youthful egotism – and cynicism – I glimpsed something else. Somewhere out there in soot-stained York a soul hungered for beauty. The notebook's owner had sought out these poems and tried to preserve them, like dried, scented flowers pressed between its pages.

In fact, the book played a similar function to the notebook I used for fitting films. One garnered pieces of music in order to bring alive illusions on the screen; the other harvested illusions of the heart, passions borrowed like ill-fitting clothes. Both brought a little consolation to a predictable, monotonous life – a life of clipped dreams. Oh, our books were not so different.

The poems also made me wonder about my feelings for Louisa Mountjoy. True, I felt protective towards her. Was that proof of love? There was no denying attraction. Nor did I dare think of her as more than a friend, looking the way I did. Not to mention my clumsiness around her. Expecting anything more was stupid presumption.

I closed the notebook. Randy pigeons strutted and courted, puffing out their chests as they cooed and pursued.

Next evening, I asked Esther Jones if anyone had enquired about a notebook. She stored lost property in the little ticket office. Since the Valentine card incident, I'd avoided her whenever possible. So I was taken aback by motherly sympathy in her voice. Perhaps I had been forgiven.

'Don't think so, love,' she said in her woebegone way. 'Have you lost summat?'

The perfect time, of course, to hand over the notebook: certainly I had no right to keep it. I found myself saying, 'I've misplaced a little book I use for the films. Don't worry, Mrs Jones, I'll check my pockets again.'

'As you like, love.'

Plain, tired old Esther hesitated as though she wanted to say more. But I headed quickly back to the darkness of the auditorium.

Twenty

Fitz's courage at the Electric Cinema inspired me. If he could risk a few stares in order to re-join the crowd, what was holding me back? In my case, I only needed to win the approval of a single person.

But for all the buffetings he had suffered, Archibald Fitzclarence possessed a native confidence I lacked. The legacy of being born among the very highest in the land. My own inheritance after Father died had been suburban self-doubt.

Still, faint heart never fair lady won. All I wanted from her was afternoon tea. The rest would have to take care of itself.

Building up to it involved a haircut and the purchase of a new shirt. For several days, I evaded the question until we found ourselves alone in the auditorium. Oddly enough, it was Louisa who gave me the cue.

'David,' she said, awkwardly, 'it seems I have to thank you for something.'

I was sorting music into piles.

'Oh? I don't know what for.'

'The other day Mr Skelton made a rather beastly remark to me which I shall not repeat. Then he seemed to consider something. Indeed, he complained about you *sotto voce*. That you had expressed to him a particular concern.'

'Yes?'

'That his *gruff ways*, his words not mine, might be offending me.'

'Good. I did have a word with him.'

She smiled. 'He suggested I needed a thicker skin. But since then he has been almost courteous.'

I straightened the parts for the cello.

'I find that hard to believe. But good for him.'

She smoothed back a stray lock from her pile of pinned hair.

'Thank you,' she said, softly.

My heart quickened. I shot her a swift glance.

'I, well, I did wonder if you would care to take tea with me on Tuesday. Before the evening show.'

For long moments her blue eyes searched my face. For once I did not grow uncomfortable.

'Yes,' she declared. 'That would be jolly!'

'Then I shall look forward to it.'

She inclined her head gracefully. 'And so shall I, David. Thank you.'

It never crossed my mind she would bring Freddy. Perhaps she wished to signal they came as one parcel. Or she had cold feet at the prospect of an intimate *tête-à-tête* with me over buttered muffins.

All three of us were scrubbed and brushed in our Sunday best. Her face told me she felt as anxious as I did. Freddy, however, seemed more bothered about the tightness of his starched collar.

'How do you do?' she asked, shaking my hand lightly like a debutante at her coming-out ball.

Formalities over, I ushered them towards the Station Hotel. In 1919 it boasted one of York's grandest restaurants and tea rooms.

At the sight of the portico entrance, Louisa hung back.

'Are you sure, David?' she murmured, as though someone might overhear a dirty conversation. 'It's awfully expensive here. I thought we would go to a Lyons.'

'I'm quite sure,' I said.

Actually, given my rent-free attic, I could afford to treat them.

Her mouth opened as though to demur then closed. With a determined look, she stooped to speak to Freddy.

'Now, dear, we need to be very, very polite in here. Mr Young is being awfully generous.'

The boy kept on tugging at the stiff collar.

'Don't do that, dear,' she told him, sharply.

'I don't like it, Mamma! It *hurt*.'

The lad was developing a real Yorkie accent. Thick as a slab of lardy cake.

Louisa's forehead furrowed. Hers was a losing struggle on the battlefield of elocution. Bertha Kettlewell was the only source of free nannying for Freddy. The charwoman's accent would be replicated by a symphony of York voices all around him on Princess Street. We suck up talk's music at that age like milk.

'Shall we?' I said, indicating the grand entrance.

She took a deep breath and led the way in as I held open the door.

The Station Hotel's tea room was lined with oak panelling. Mirrors gleamed on the walls between heavily varnished oil paintings of Highland scenes. The linen was spotless and the cutlery shone. All the crockery bore the name of the hotel, embossed in gold. Waitresses in black and white hovered at the sides, overseen by a stately head waiter.

The room was busy with the kind of respectable types you would expect in a provincial city, along with better off travellers between trains. We were shown to a table by a waitress who smiled as if she knew us.

'I think you might have been recognised,' whispered Louisa.

'Really? Then it will be *we* who are recognised.'

A trio serenaded – piano, cello and violin – playing a metronome stiff waltz by Strauss. We fell silent to listen. I winked.

'Not as good as us,' I said.

She laughed uneasily, one eye on Freddy lest he misbehave.

The tone of our tea party was set. Louisa sat stiff and aloof. Manners and unimpeachably proper talk were her last rags of status. She proved an elegant hand at pouring the tea and wielding the tea strainer and sugar tongs. Throughout the meal, she observed me carefully. I hoped it might be to learn my good sides – whatever they might be – rather than any lapses in fine manners. I'm sure there must have been a few of those.

Meanwhile, Freddy's wriggling increased at the sight of so many cakes on a stand.

'Do sit still, dear,' Louisa whispered every few minutes.

'I think someone might be excited,' I said, winking at little Freddy. 'And so he should be. This is a significant moment in his journey through life.'

The kind of joke my father used to make. Delivered with easy charm and wit. It surprised me to sound a bit like him.

Freddy Mountjoy had every reason for excitement. He was about to taste ice cream for the first time.

'It's awfully good of you to treat us,' said Louisa again.

'Are you looking forward to your ice cream?' I asked Freddy.

Louisa and I had dried up when it came to conversation beyond polite noises. And I've never been one for small talk. That's why we homed in on Freddy as a safe topic.

'I scream's nice!' he piped.

'It's *ice cre-eam*,' she whispered, rattled. 'Remember what Mummy said about talking nicely.'

The poor chap seemed more confused than enlightened.

'I do think you'll like it,' I assured him. 'Ice cream is *very* nice.'

Louisa bit her lip. 'Of course, I would have bought him some before,' she said, 'but I was afraid of damaging his teeth.'

'You would have done well to find any, what with the rationing,' I said.

When the waitress brought over the fabled ice cream in a tall, cone-shaped glass bowl with a cherry and nuts on the top, we both made a fuss.

I leaned forward to Louisa and whispered, 'It better be damn good. We've talked up the bally stuff like the ambrosia of the gods.'

For a moment she blinked at my mild expletive. Freddy's spoon dipped, dug deep, rose to a cherub mouth. We froze. Then we were both laughing. Sheer joy lit the kid's face. He tucked in, smearing half of it across his chin.

'That's a relief,' I said.

'Do say thank you to nice Mr Young,' Louisa urged, wiping his jaws with a napkin.

I had been promoted to nice. Absurdly, I felt moved.

Following our trip to the Station Hotel, Louisa and I 'walked out' now and then. With evenings given over to work, we picked stray afternoons without matinee performances. A couple of Sundays we walked round the river or out into summer countryside, half an hour's stroll from the Groves's grimy streets. Once we gravitated to Homestead Park with its aviary and monkey house.

In the films we accompanied, men and women would meet and their faces light up with attraction. They would talk effortlessly, eagerly, full of animation. Perhaps silent cinema demanded exaggerated expressions and gestures. Our private cinema, if you can call it that, was a subdued affair.

We communicated mostly through brief, careful exchanges. Something inhibited intimacy between us: I blamed my own awkwardness. At the same time, I did really wish to know Louisa better. I hoped to share a little of who I was – or could be – and that she would share some of herself in return. Is that not a possible definition of love?

I found myself talking to fill the silence. Often I told stories from my past, while she stayed quiet about her own. Tales of Father's glory and Stepfather's petty tyranny. Anecdotes from the Royal College I hoped would make her smile. The war I steered away from, though she did probe about Fitz on occasion. Her questions revealed she knew a surprising amount about the Fitzclarences of Broughton Hall. I shared my dream of one day leading a light orchestra, gaining a residency in a top London hotel.

'Is that likely?' she asked.

There was no sarcasm in the question. She wanted to know my prospects.

'In terms of skill and talent, I believe that I am qualified,' I said. 'But I would need a wealthy backer to establish myself right now. But I'm young. And I'm not afraid of hard work.'

Louisa fell silent, seeming to ponder my words.

Almost always, she simply listened or offered a few mild interjections. Not because hers was a submissive nature. I reasoned it was because her family's heartless abandonment when she needed them most made her aloof and self-reliant.

Only once did she reveal a flash of temper. I had explained Mother's hasty second marriage after Father died when she broke in angrily, 'I can see you reproach your mother for her sacrifice. *You* the very person for whom she sacrificed herself.'

'You believe she sacrificed herself for me?'

148

'Of course. To provide you with a secure and prosperous home. To guarantee your education.'

I looked at her doubtfully. It had always seemed to me Mother sacrificed her freedom because she could not live without respectability.

'How easy it is for a man to be *pure* in his affections,' she said, not without scorn. 'To only consult the wishes of his heart.'

'Cannot a woman do the same?'

Her laugh tinkled. 'Oh, please do not be naïve, David. We are too old to act like children any longer. Only the very wealthiest woman can entirely disregard money or society. Even then, there is a cost to one's social position.'

Afterwards, I brooded about the justice of her remarks. It was not hard to see fear for the future lay behind them. I also wondered if she was warning me that I, a penniless musician with poor prospects, could not offer the security she longed for. Or status, for that matter. Louisa Mountjoy hated being forced into the working classes, every fibre of her being proclaimed it. Whereas, I saw good in most people, whatever their provenance. What are we but an accident of birth? And I believed that music had its own compensations unrelated to financial reward.

Louisa's comment about Mother did sting. Perhaps I had been unjust in my resentments? I resolved to try to understand her better. And for many years I did try. But it all ended the same way. The past had forced us apart when I was very young and the future turned out no different. I wept at my mother's funeral when it came. Not so much for her, but what might have been between us, and never was.

On one afternoon walk, I pointed in the distance. 'Do you see what I see?'

My question broke an extended silence.

None other than Ambrose Ackerley and Esther Jones were promenading beside the river amidst a dozen courting couples a third their age. The commissionaire wore his best suit. Even Esther's clothes were a splash of colour.

'How long has *that* been going on?' I asked, in wonder.

Louisa gave me a puzzled smile.

'Surely you must know.'

'I don't. Well, I knew about Ambrose wishing to woo Esther. I didn't know she returned his interest until now.'

'It all started after he put you up to write a message in that ridiculous Valentine's card.'

'You *knew* that I didn't write that? I thought... '

She covered her mouth with a gloved hand.

'Oh, David! Really, you are a silly sometimes. Straight after you hurried off to the Cricketers with a beaten dog look on your face, *our Gladys* badgered the mystery out of Mr Ambrose. Then she made sure everyone knew who was *really* behind the Valentine card. You know how she loves to gossip.'

'Ambrose could have told me,' I complained.

'I think he was too busy with *our Esther*,' said Louisa. She concealed a ladylike yawn behind her gloved hand. 'Actually, it's all rather sweet, I suppose.'

This revelation made me wonder how many other things I misunderstood.

I made a point of sounding out Ambrose. He explained that Esther's grown up children had as good as banned her from remarriage. Especially to a ne'er-do-well like the commissionaire. They seemed to expect her to live in respectable poverty and loneliness until she died or was forced by frailty to become a burden to one of them. All of which meant that outside working hours, he could only meet Esther in a clandestine way.

'She's afraid of breaking with her kids,' he said, adding darkly. 'Me? I'm afraid which bit of 'em I'd like to break in two. Aye, with me bare hands.'

Twenty-One

Another Sunday, I rose very late, as only the young feel they have time for. At that age, life stretched before me like a limitless horizon.

Yawning, I stepped into the auditorium, usually deserted on the Sabbath. Instead of silent gloom, scented by the previous evening's bodies and cigarettes, there was light.

Laverelli had set up his hand-cranked projector and arc lamp on a little table. The same apparatus we used for fitting the films each week. Indeed, the same machine he bought in his youth for two hour 'biographic performances' in town halls and theatres all over the North. Back at the turn of the century, it had been a wonder of its age. Twenty years on, it was antiquated, even curious. The technology of our youth ages alongside us.

He was staring up at the illuminated silver screen. A tumbler fed by a bottle of whisky lay close to hand. On the screen, a football match was in full swing. The players' haircuts and moustaches must have been fashionable a couple of decades earlier, likewise their style of kit. Every so often, the camera cut to the crowd – all male, heavily hatted and coated, most smoking – where, planted among them, a youthful version of Laverelli waved a trilby at the players to add a little drama. He stopped cranking. The clicking of the revolving mechanism ceased. The film froze on a close up of his face.

Silence settled. He took a pull at his whisky. Then he noticed me in the doorway.

'Sorry,' I said. 'I didn't realise you were busy.'

'Nay, nay, come in lad.'

His Halifax accent thickened under the influence of the whisky. I made my way over to his chair. Looked up at the frozen image on the screen.

'That were me at Bradford City versus Sheffield United,' he said. 'We commissioned that during the Boer War.' (He pronounced it *Boo-ah*). 'It played all over Yorkshire and Lancashire. A right popular match for a while.'

At his feet, there was a stack of reels in round cases. The dull tarnish on the metal suggested they dated to a time before the Electric Cinema.

'This little lot represents just a small part of the catalogue we advertised. Believe it or not, that were around the time a young chap like you was a nipper. They've stayed exactly the same while you've grown into a man. Yet both of you end up meeting here. Now isn't that peculiar?'

'I suppose you could say that about a lot of things,' I said. 'I'm a great believer in coincidence.'

'I prefer to call it luck, whether good or bad. These here films are the ones I care for best. We had packing cases of bloomin' reels at one time. Enough film to stretch from here to Morecambe and back. Sit yourself down, lad. Find a glass. I'll treat you to an old style show.'

Loading and cranking the handle, Laverelli played film after film. I drifted to the piano, glass and ashtray handy. There, I added chords and runs to create a mood, pausing for Laverelli's reminiscences.

A magic, unrepeatable hour; nothing in life comes twice. Not least because those nitrate films must have vanished long ago, like discarded clothes or furniture. And, at last, I learned the identity of the man in the framed photograph. The young man Laverelli kept hidden in his accounts closet.

Lancashire mill girls, cheap plaid shawls covering shoulders and heads. Men in flat caps and child workers, loosed en masse through factory gates. Tired faces lighting at the novelty of the camera. Some smile nervously or pretend not to see, suspicious of this strange, hand-cranked engine. Grime of soot and factory grease on clouts and clogs. Laverelli almost the gentleman in his showman's flashy suit. He herds the stream of workers towards the camera, forever heading home…

Fuelled by whisky, he chuckled as the past came alive. How quickly one world vanished into another!

'Laverelli and Brown Bioscope Company,' he announced, proudly. 'Me and Alfred Brown would hire a hall for as long as we could milk the town. Then we'd move onto the next. When I were your age, the travelling life was just the ticket for a chap like me. And Alfie, of course. There one minute gone the next! Aye, a grand enough life for a pair of rascals like us. We was young and free. At least, he was young. A fair bit younger than me, as you can see. But both of us tried our damnedest to be free.'

A horse-drawn omnibus passes before the camera, blurred by shutter speed. Men smoke and stare at the one-eyed lens. A close up of a poster reading, 'Oi Bill, that's me!' 'Did you see yourself on the screen at the Alhambra!'.

To be seen, to matter, be preserved. The children understood it best, urchins laughing and pointing, girls giggling and hiding their faces, delighted as they blush. You almost hear hobnails on cobbles, the rumble of iron-rimmed cartwheels, voices, ghosts like a candle's reflection marching back into a mirror.

Always among the reflections, Alfred Brown, partner in the business. Tall and handsome in overcoat and trilby, up for anything...

Laverelli grinned, his eyes wrinkling.

'You know, I used to ask Alf to pretend to have a scrap with folk in the shot. Just for a bit of action, you see. There was always a couple of lads game to show off. Natural actors, you see, there's never a shortage of those. And folk want a bit of action.'

Alfred again, this time at the seaside. Morecambe Promenade on a Wakes Week in July. Factory hands holidaying in Sunday best, a decorous procession of strollers and souls beside the palatial pier and horse-drawn trams...

'Me and Alf always liked to set up for a few weeks in Blackpool or Morecambe. Summer wouldn't have been the same without it. Look at them lasses! Dressed like the bloody Queen o' Sheba. Emptying their pockets for a bit of finery, those lasses. We'd advertise: "See yourself promenade at your very best! 6d or a shilling." And they paid. Oh yes, we'd leave Morecambe with a suitcase full of coins!'

Laverelli sloshed more whisky as he fingered a particular reel. I didn't like him playing with old, brittle nitrate film in his current state. It could ignite on a whim.

'This 'un is special,' he chuckled. 'You see, I'd left Halifax as a kid to join a travelling fair. Let's put it like this, under a cloud. I was an orphan, no one even noticed I'd gone. So when I got a chance to go back and film the annual Catholic Procession for May Day, I said to Alf: "Let's show them rotten buggers what we're made of!" And blow me, we did.'

The Catholics of Halifax proud behind a statue of Our Lady. Banners and choirboys and priests, the altar boys carrying the Virgin decked in white lace and flowers. A long procession filling the street with congregations, each led by their priest. The men in their best suits, mothers and daughters dressed as respectably as they can manage, representing their faith…

Abruptly the handle stopped turning. Laverelli was staring. On the screen a tall priest with a black, shiny top hat on his head.

'Monsignor O'Donnell,' said Laverelli. He laughed dryly. 'Oh, he were a right bugger with the altar boys, that one.'

Then the handle is cranking again, the people back in motion, pushing to get on the screen for a viewing that same evening at Victoria Hall. In the background, trams, bystanders, the world bearing witness. And there, yes, beaming at the camera, Laverelli and Brown, Horatio and Alf, on top of the world…

'I called the show "A Trip Around the World – via Halifax",' he said. His voice was heavy with pride. 'I'd come back home a hero with a modern marvel. Folk as wouldn't give me the time of day when I left there, tail between me legs, shook me by the hand like they never wanted to let go. I left without a bone button and came back with a diamond tiepin. Alf and me wore special new hats and suits sharp enough to carve a loaf. Alf even found me a gold-knobbed stick so I could walk like a toff.'

154

He sighed. Images flashed of hillsides and factories, chimneys smoking.

'It wasn't so long after as me and Alf realised the travelling biograph shows was on their way out. The novelty had faded, you see, of watching yourself on the screen. Folk wanted proper stories in their pictures, not just to see themselves. We'd made so much between us we had this place built special. All according to the regulations and bang on with the latest apparatus. We'd gone serious all of a sudden. Grown up. Alf wasn't sure York was big enough for him. But I wanted the Electric to be our own little cosy palace. Right down to the style of the plasterwork. But it were never the same as being on the road. Never so free.'

Laverelli stopped cranking. Placed his hands on his lap. By now, the whisky bottle stood empty between us.

'What happened to Alf?' I asked.

He made a small noise I couldn't quite read.

'Alf? You couldn't keep a man like Alfred Brown pinned down for long. It wasn't in his nature. Oh, he tried his best. And I tried. We both tried. But when the war came he had the perfect excuse. He signed up in September 1914. Among the first. He made it all the way through to the Somme.'

No need to enquire if he made it further. Then I understood why Laverelli had set up his show. This was the fourth anniversary of the Somme's first day, the newspapers were full of it. That blood bath unparalleled in history. Laverelli was putting on the show for Alf. So his ghost could watch their glory days again. Swap ribald remarks about familiar faces on the screen. Be revived by a breeze that had blown away. Most of all laugh and reminisce, sharing a drink.

Laverelli sighed. 'Well, we had what we had together. Saints get to heaven, though I doubt they have as much fun as me and Alf did. The rest of us get what love we can in the meantime.'

Finally I understood the double bed hidden in the privacy of an attic you could only approach by the creakiest of wooden staircases. A bed behind two doors, both lockable on the inside. Laverelli had remarked when he first showed me the place, 'A man as wanted a bit of privacy could be happy as a canary up here.' That went for two men.

I should have been shocked, disgusted, outraged. Maybe a small part of me was. The part clinging to suburban certainties, Mother's desperate faith in respectability. But the Electric had already shaken my prejudices. Louisa the so-called 'fallen' woman who I could not help admiring. Ambrose reformed from drink by love. Gladys Bannering, her tarty ways, Bolshevik family and conchie brother offset by a generous heart. Yes, even Fitz, though two good men's horrible deaths still lay between us. Two men with wives and kids who'd placed their faith in us.

'Let me help you put your old films away,' I said.

He rose unsteadily.

'Nay, lad, I'll ask Victor to keep 'em safe in the projection box. Lovely boy, that Victor, very helpful. They have to be kept somewhere fireproof. Can't be too careful with the inspection coming up.'

I left him haunted by lost faces, each unique and undiminished by the cruelties and generosity of time. Ordinary folk made special by the camera. Faces forever streaming through factory gates, or promenading by the seaside on a rare holiday, or watching a football match with pals and family, or dressed up for a parade, bound for eternity.

Twenty-Two

Then came a day that blew through the Electric like a flash summer storm.

The evening before had been one of shame for our little orchestra. My own fault, perhaps. In fitting the film, I had selected pieces at the borders of Maurice and Louisa's musical competency.

Predictably, when it fell apart, the audience started laughing, stamping and jeering. Mortified, I leapt to the piano, stilling the motion of Maurice's bow as he sawed on like a carpenter. Crouching beside Louisa at the piano stool, I commenced a thundering improvisation of runs, rills and arpeggios, one eye on the screen. The climax became *Land of Hope and Glory*. This went down well. I had saved the day but not our honour. The thought of Mr Cooper's amusement if they got wind of it at the Grand was mortifying.

Once the auditorium cleared, I apologised to Louisa for taking her place. But things had changed between us since the last time I stopped her playing. There was, for want of a better word, trust.

'I know you wouldn't have done it unless you had to,' she said. 'Actually, I never realised you could move so quickly.'

Maurice rejected my apology with an upraised finger. His eyes were bloodshot. Mouth tight.

'Let's understand one thing, sonny,' he said. 'You don't ever touch my bow again. Not ever.'

Now it was my turn to get angry.

'It is my responsibility to make sure the Electric's orchestra is a pleasure to hear. And not a laughing stock.'

He laughed. 'Oh, aye? Until you get your fingers burned.'

Inevitably, I wondered if he referred to my face. I was aware Louisa could hear every word.

'Very well, you leave me no alternative,' I said.

Maurice was quivering a moment later. I had proposed something virtually taboo in the provincial cinema world. In short, a rehearsal.

'Now you're going too bloody far, lad,' he said. 'I have never heard the like. Nor will I stand for it.'

'Mr Laverelli will be behind me on this,' I warned, though I hadn't consulted him.

Here was the moment of crisis between myself as leader and Maurice Skelton. And I was determined not to lower my standards or back down.

'Please be aware of this. *Anyone* not competent to perform tomorrow's pieces will see it reflected in their pay packet.'

Louisa blanched at the possibility of deducted shillings.

Oh, I was sick of music without the least adventure. Sick of not reaching for subtler, higher emotions. Sick of settling for coarse, obvious moods. Both of them *were* capable of the pieces I had chosen. They just required a little practice and determination.

'Trouble'll come of this,' predicted Maurice, packing away his cello. 'Trouble all round. Remember, he who laughs last, laughs longest.'

He gathered breath for an inevitable parting shot. 'An' you can tell Laverelli I said so.'

An hour before the first showing on Tuesday, the five-thirty, we gathered unhappily to rehearse. Maurice turned up in the end with an inscrutable leer plastered across his face.

Louisa seemed distracted, upset by something deeper than music. I had grown sensitive to her moods without really understanding them.

Maurice concealed not a huff of his discontent. 'I've complained to Laverelli about you, Mr Young. An experienced man like me never needs to rehearse. *Never*. It's a bloody insult. I'm taking it up with t'union.'

'Please do.'

I was determined not to be bullied.

'I really don't see what you have to complain about. I've made sure you get paid union rates to rehearse. Now let's get on.'

Before we could start, the swing doors of the auditorium banged open. Gladys Bannering ran down the aisle.

'Where's Mr Laverelli?' she cried. 'He needs to come quick. It's the police!'

▆

Now it may seem strange but I momentarily wondered if they had come for me. I could see Maurice looking shifty as well. It was how we were raised. Most ordinary folk were cowed by authority from the core of their bones.

'Mr Young,' pleaded Gladys, 'can you come?'

I followed her back up the aisle and into the foyer. There, three men waited.

The first was short, weedy and suited. Wire-rimmed spectacles had been jammed to the top of his nose; he carried a clipboard. I put him down as a species of clerk.

Beside him, were two burly, hard-faced customers. One wore the blue uniform and helmet of the York Constabulary. The other, an inspector or detective, sported grey, pin-striped civvies.

Clifton appeared from behind a cracked replica of a Ming Vase, generally reserved for cigarette butts. His agate eyes glittered at the policemen. His ears went back. Waving his tail, he stalked over to Laverelli's office door and scratched himself airily, without once slackening his vigilance.

My nerves vanished. Perhaps it was Clifton's sheer insouciance. Or the policeman's blue uniform, reminding me that I had been an officer and a gentleman in His Majesty's Navy.

'Good afternoon,' I said.

They examined me. The senior policeman raised an eyebrow. More than possibly he had sat in the darkness while the Phantom of the Opera serenaded some picture. There were only so many places to be entertained in York.

'We're here for the annual inspection,' he said. 'Laverelli around?'

I didn't care for his tone.

159

'*Mister* Laverelli,' I replied, 'is around. I am quite sure he will be offering every amenity.'

An ugly smirk appeared on the suited cop's face. 'Aye, he likes to do that.'

His colleague chuckled briefly.

Gladys was listening in, her pretty face flushed. It occurred to me her family must have suffered a fair share of attention from the police on account of her brother's conchie ways. Not to mention her railway strike-leading Dad.

The plainclothesman assessed me again. Lord knew what it took to raise a smile from that one.

'We'll be getting started then,' he said.

'Mr Laverelli just popped out for a Herald,' piped in Gladys, hands on hips. 'You really ought to wait for him, Inspector Green. That's just plain good manners.'

Her voice quivered with defiance.

So my guess was correct, the Bannerings knew Inspector Green. Her expression and puffed out chest told the story. But he also scared her. If her comment about the beatings Thomas Bannering had received were true, well he might.

All three fixed on her instead of me. She quailed a little. I stepped forward to stand between them.

'I'm sure Mr Laverelli is best qualified to offer assistance, gentlemen,' I said, my diction growing plummier by the word.

Gladys shot me a grateful look.

'And here he is!' I added, affably.

In bustled Laverelli with copies of the Yorkshire Herald and Evening Press. At the sight of the visitors, he pulled up short.

'Afternoon Bob,' he said to the uniformed copper. 'And why, Inspector Green! Can I help, gents?'

'Inspection,' said Green.

A complex silence followed. The clerk used it to push his spectacles up his nose.

'Carruthers,' he said, by way of introduction, 'from the Corporation.'

'Oh aye.' Laverelli turned to the uniformed constable. 'Normally it's just you, Bob.'

The latter shrugged uncomfortably. Perhaps a few free tickets had changed hands during previous inspections.

'According to the law,' said Laverelli, tapping his copy of the Yorkshire Herald as though it was the Magna Carta, 'it's not the Corporation as inspects, but the police.'

Carruthers fussed with his clipboard.

A sneery expression passed over Green's close-shaven face. 'There's some important folk in this town concerned about standards at t'Electric.'

'Folk who don't like competition for their new business?' suggested Laverelli. 'One that – so a little bird tells me – isn't bringing in as much as they first hoped?'

'Last time I saw you,' Green countered, 'you were hanging around the gents urinals in Parliament Street.'

Icy scorn crept over our employer.

'I believe a full bladder is not a crime yet,' replied Laverelli. 'Anyway, you'll find these premises clean as a nun's underwear. If you'll excuse the expression.'

The Inspector would excuse nothing. He and his colleagues marched into the auditorium. I was about to commence my delayed rehearsal when Laverelli grabbed my arm.

'Hang around, Mr Young, there's something fishy about this little lot. I'd like a witness.'

Licking Maurice and Louisa into shape seemed far more urgent. It never crossed my mind the Electric was in breach of any laws. I'd witnessed Laverelli poring over the place with Victor only a few days before. And his clipboard was quite as impressive as the clerk's.

'I'd be right grateful,' he added.

I sighed. Perhaps if we replaced the Rachmaninov and Debussy with *Hearts and Flowers* and *In a Monastery Garden* (bird whistles included) we'd get through tonight without being an object of mirth.

'Very well,' I said, 'do you think it will take long?'

They started from the bottom up. We trooped into the basement where the gas generator was situated.

'You've never checked here before,' said Laverelli.

The weedy clerk came back, quick as a ferret, '1901 Factory and Workshop Act, Section 20.'

'This isn't a factory,' pointed out Laverelli.

Carruthers sniffed in a manner reminiscent of my stepfather. '*That part of any premises in which electrical energy is generated or transformed for the purpose of supply by way of trade*,' he intoned.

'Oh, I see.'

The dynamo, motor, wiring and fan belt generated lots of scribbling on the clipboard.

'Happy?' asked Laverelli, as we trooped upstairs.

It was clear the clerk could not consider himself *unhappy* within the terms of Section 20. Calling him ecstatic would be to stretch a point. He was the type who strangles joy with a bird's nest of red tape.

Then things started to go wrong.

First stop, the auditorium. Here, Louisa and Maurice sat waiting. In the latter's case, glowering. Inspector Green asked to be shown all the light switches in the main hall.

'You'll find everything as it should be,' predicted Laverelli.

In order to prevent a blackout and deadly stampede in the dark, there was supposed to be two separate sources of lighting. Vigorous clicking revealed only one worked.

'That's impossible!' stuttered Laverelli. 'I only checked it last night. I check it before every blooming show!'

Scribble, scribble on the clipboard.

Next up, the fire exits. No one today will recall the tragedies where dozens of people burned alive in the early Kinemas and Biographs, or suffocated from smoke. That was why push bar doors opening outwards were introduced. Ours led to a service alley at the side of the building. Inspector Green duly tried to depress the push bars. Nothing. The latch had jammed.

'What the bugger!' cried Laverelli. 'I tested and oiled it me self.'

Now came the turn of *t'box*. This cast iron cube was designed to ensure that nitrate film bursting spontaneously into flame did not torch the whole premises. A wise precaution, particularly when the images were lit by oven-hot arc lights.

T'box was Victor's territory; Laverelli relaxed as we queued outside.

'Our projectionist's top class,' he said. 'Young but very promising. A clever lad with his hands. I'm sure you'll find everything in order. As I say, we went right over it last week.'

'Hummph,' opined the clerk, dodging into the enclosed space behind Laverelli. I waited outside with the two coppers. No one spoke. Suddenly a voice inside shouted, 'Sabotage! That's what this is!'

Moments later the clerk appeared in the corridor with Laverelli in pursuit. 'I'm telling you straight! I put those reels in the metal case me self. They're special stock from years back. Of Halifax, if you must know... '

'All I know,' said the clerk. 'Is the container was left open. Very dangerous to expose nitrate like that.'

He was gaining confidence in direct proportion to the quantity of notes on his clipboard.

'And the water buckets?' he demanded. 'All empty. As are the sand buckets. And even the fire extinguisher is empty. Very serious. *Very* serious indeed.'

Laverelli was sweating now. It was serious. And he knew it.

The coppers and clerk descended to the auditorium for an urgent whisper. Meanwhile, Laverelli and I waited in the foyer. I could see Ambrose Ackerley in his commissionaire's uniform marshalling a bigger crowd than usual for Tuesday teatime. Perhaps word had gone round about the orchestra's musical pratfalls the night before and people wanted a cheap laugh. Esther Jones watched Ambrose adoringly from the ticket booth. They probably blew kisses at each other when they thought no one was looking.

'Bloody 'ell!' muttered Laverelli. 'Can't you see what's happened? A traitor! That's what. I've been stitched up like a kipper.'

'You alright, Mr Laverelli?' asked Gladys.

At that moment, the inspectors emerged from the auditorium.

Laverelli must have known what was coming. He fought hard for dignity, a sad struggle. The Electric Cinema lent shape and purpose to his life. After what I had learned about his lost partner, Alfred

Brown, consumed by the mud of the Somme, perhaps it was all he had left.

'Right then, Laverelli,' said the Inspector. No chance of a *mister* now. 'Our report makes very bad reading. I've seen knocking shops better run than this place.'

The clerk nodded gravely as though he had inspected many a knocking shop.

'That's why we're closing you down,' concluded Green.

'But you can't! I've paid for advertisements in the Press and Herald all week.'

'Oh yes, we can,' said Green. 'These premises are to close forthwith as a place of entertainment pending the next petty sessions of the Magistrates Bench.'

'When will that be?'

'You'll be notified in due course,' chimed in the clerk. He paused for his coup de grace. 'In line with the Cinematograph Act 1909, Sections 6, 7(a) and 11(c).'

'What about all them folk queuing outside?' said Laverelli. 'They expect a show. We've been running a show every weekday for twelve years. They've come here for a *show!*'

'You'd best tell 'em it's not safe, hadn't you?' said Green.

With that, they departed.

Laverelli was too shaken to face his customers, many of whom he knew on first name terms. He hurried to his tiny office and closed the door.

Ambrose stepped outside to announce the show would not go on. A fair proportion of the queue drifted in the direction of the Grand.

We huddled before the silver screen like the survivors of a shipwreck. Ambrose stood protectively close to Esther, who had gone pale. Maurice glanced from side to side as though trapped. Louisa was evidently thinking about her lost wages, signs of panic rising through her usual reserve. Gladys Bannering tended towards outrage at the police. As for tight-sweatered Victor, he was whining to Laverelli how the fire equipment in *t'box* had been 'sound as a pound' when he left last night.

'I know, I know,' muttered Laverelli. If anyone risked going up in a puff of smoke, it was the projectionist.

We fell silent as our employer stepped forward. One among us had systematically sabotaged our safety apparatus. That much was plain as cabbages.

A bleak, noble expression worthy of a tragic hero settled on Laverelli's face. Even in extremity he couldn't avoid a touch of ham.

'Friends,' he began, 'this is a situation I am right sorry to see.'

Murmurs of assent.

'Right sorry,' he continued, in the same low, mournful voice. 'You see, I've always considered myself a fair man. A generous man, in my way. There is many here who might have struggled for honest work without the Electric Cinema.'

Half the staff grew positively awkward. Only Esther and Victor counted as purely respectable in the world's eyes. What with a propensity for excessive drink, fornication and children out of wedlock, dodgy relations and a history of violent brawling, the rest of us had quirks that might well put off employers.

'That's why,' said Laverelli, voice rising, 'I could wring the neck of the *traitor* who has taken fifty pieces of silver. Aye, like Judas Iscariot himself, to shut us down. Only, instead of the blinkin' Pharisees, he's taken his dirty money from Ernie-bloody-Precious at the Grand!'

'Steady on.' complained Maurice. 'You've no right... '

For some reason that did it. Never mind I couldn't stand the old hypocrite, this concerned justice. I wanted the whole world to know what I knew. Laverelli *had* been good to us. He'd certainly been good to me. Pansy or not – and the evidence pointed towards the former – I liked him. I turned on Maurice, my tone icy.

'I think we both know, Mr Skelton, what happened here today was no surprise to you.'

He bridled a little.

'Now hold on... '

'I think people deserve to hear this.'

As concisely as possible, I explained the warning I had received from the musical director of the Grand, Maurice's old comrade and pal, Mr Cooper. Also from Maurice himself over a pickled egg in the

Clock Inn. Namely, that I would need to seek new employment very soon.

'It's obvious to me what has happened here,' I concluded. 'It's a very shoddy business indeed.'

A courtroom stillness in the auditorium. One by one, people came to life.

'My!' exclaimed Esther.

'You bugger!' breathed Ambrose. I hoped for Maurice's sake he didn't plant a meaty fist in the cellist's face. Perhaps the influence of his beloved Esther restrained him – for now.

'How could you, Mr Skelton?' wailed Gladys.

'I want you out of here!' thundered Laverelli.

'I'll not 'ave this!' protested Maurice. 'I'll be speaking to t'union about this little lot. You owe me a week's notice, Laverelli. In me hand! I'm warning yer. I want that money. In me hand!'

'Get out, I say!'

Ambrose stepped forward. Maurice Skelton seized his instrument and fled.

Not long afterwards, we dispersed to chew over our respective financial worries. I suspect mine were less serious than most. Who did I have to look out for except myself? And my accommodation, rodents and all, came free. Emergency train fare back to London still lay secure in an old tobacco tin beneath the bed, along with extra savings.

'Louisa,' I called as she left, 'let me walk you home.'

We stepped out into the sunshine. Warmth lit our faces. Yet her cheeks were pale as swansdown.

'David, forgive me,' she said. 'I must go. There is no time to waste. Not now. I must write a letter, you see. One I have tried to avoid. It has come to it, and I must.'

She hesitated. 'You will hate me for what I am about to do. I know that. Yet I must do it. For Freddy's sake.'

With that she hurried in the direction of the Groves. The very set of her shoulders spoke of a resolve that excluded me. I felt a wrench in my gut not to deserve her trust.

Twenty-Three

I suppose Laverelli's disaster led me back to my own. That night it rushed through my dreams...

At first the dream is of the sea, infinities of sky. A pale dawn, a black-rimmed horizon of cloud. Booming out on a routine patrol after U-boats. Signals detected from a raider on the surface back to its base have confirmed a likely course. Out from its home port at Cuxhaven then through the North Sea before slipping round Scotland to the killing fields of the Atlantic.

Autumn, so cold out here. This alien desert of salt and spray and energy I'm beginning to loathe and fear. Yet the news from France suggests the Germans are beaten. Their last desperate offensive has turned to slaughter and retreat...

Even as we fly up from Felixstowe, the curving harbour littered with destroyers and light cruisers and minesweepers, I detect something strange. Hard to name. Is it how the twin-engines vibrate? A sound beyond hearing. Yet our bus responds fine as the Fitz takes her up to two thousand feet, optimum observation height. My job is to scan the sky hard, not fret.

An hour later. Fifty miles south east of Harwich. Over the North Hinder Light Ship, the centre of the spider web we patrol. By now the vibration – faint but discernible – is troubling our engineer, Smittie. He clambers up from the cockpit behind Fitz. He shares it with Gus, our wireless operator and gunner. Smith drags himself onto the wing between the two roaring Rolls Royce Eagle engines for a check. Fitz holds steady until he climbs down to report.

I join him in the pilot's tiny cabin to listen in. My presence irritates our CO. He wants me watching for Fritz, not questioning his orders. All of us stretched to breaking by days of patrols. This is our last before a week's shore leave.

'Odd rattle in the port engine, sir,' bellows Smittie. 'Can't place it. Fuel line was loose. Might be related. Suggest we turn back, sir.'

Fitz shakes his head. Waves us back to our posts. He wants a U-boat to trump his Zeppelin. Lord knows what bit of tin they'll give him for that.

When Smittie has gone back to join Gus, I shout in Fitz's ear. 'I think we should listen to Smith, sir. Remember what happened to Bates and Sanderson.'

Forced to ditch when their engine rattled and its fuel pipe came loose. A miracle to have been picked up by a destroyer. Two days and nights of hell: rolling, pitching, bailing water from their bus, pumping for dear life, every heavy object save their hearts thrown overboard to stay afloat. By the time they were picked up, one man had been lost to the waves. The rest clung to the wings for dear life.

Fitz grips the control wheel, works the heavy foot pedals, his fleshy cheeks quivering with the rhythm of the engines. He waves an imperious hand.

Back to your post, Young.

'But sir!'

'Get back, Baby! You'll miss the Boche!'

Some restraint breaks within me. Ignored, derided, sick of it. I can hear plainly the rattle in the engine. My musician's ear is sensitive to the slightest variation.

On we fly. I trace a route using the few guides we possess. Crossing and criss-crossing the North Hinder Light Ship, covering a patch of sea like a wedge of pie. When Fitz gets tired, I take over flying for half an hour. He slumps in the observer's seat, drinking coffee from the thermos, head bowed.

Yet it seems he is to be proved right. In these last days of killing, I spot one. The black lozenge of the conning tower rises vertically from the sea, cutting a distinct wake.

We swoop, lest it identifies us and vanishes underwater. This is my show as navigator, observer, bomb-aimer. I feel sudden disgust, shivering in my fur-lined clothes. Must we drown these men in salt water as we torched the Zeppelin crew with flaming hydrogen? The war will be over in weeks, they say

Fitz descends astern of the submarine to fly directly over. The U-boat is diving, white water churning as they blow out their oxygen tanks. For all my scruples, I aim to puncture their hull, allow the water to pour in, choke them until they float down to the seabed. I pull the toggles. Two of our four bombs fall away. Down they curve, the explosions spraying great gouts of foam like fountains.

Then we're banking round. Our quarry has vanished. No oil or bubbling air to suggest the hull has been breached. Missed, dammit, missed.

Behind me, I see Fitz cursing, banging his fists against the control wheel. And realise my mistake. I should have dropped all four of our eggs. With two left he has an excuse to punish failure. Hand signals indicate we will continue the patrol – for the U-boat must seek to preserve its fuel and stored electricity by surfacing, as soon as it believes we have gone.

Minutes stretch to an hour. We have been up for four now, the rattle in the port engine pronounced. Surely Fitz can hear it. Is he so mad for glory?

Twice I pass back notes scribbled on my pad, urging we return to base. To the north, a thick line of cloud, rain, maybe even fog darkening the horizon, rolling our way. Twice he screws the notes up. I'll catch sheer hell for insubordination when we get home.

Smittie's head bobs up from the rear cabin, listening hard to the engine. Then he's hauling himself up once more, gripping the joists between wings as he adjusts the petrol feed pipe. Once down, he waves to Fitz. Makes a throat slitting gesture: the whole engine might cut out any minute.

I point frantically at the cloud bank. Close now. Threatening to envelop us. At last, Fitz makes the signal for home.

Again, my show. Yet there is no sign of the North Hinder Light Ship, my only point of reference in this wasteland. As fog closes round us, rain spattering on our goggles, I cannot even use the air sextant. All I have is the compass, reliable as fool's gold.

My mind whirls with previous information. Jotted records from the instruments in my navigator's cabin. Flying time. Airspeed. Rev counter. Wind direction to estimate drift. Years of decoding symphonies and concerti with dozens of parts whirl to my aid. I remember the prevailing air currents, calculate the direction of the streaming fog and rain. Less than an hour's flying time left. No room for error. For a long moment I waver. Then the decisiveness of the performer leaps to my aid. I choose. Sick to my stomach, I choose. And scribble down a course for Fitz.

The great wings of our bus dip as he turns, rushing through a wall of swirling vapour. Minutes pass. Half an hour. The faint shuddering of the port engine becomes a stuttering as it starts to loosen internal parts. Fitz drops our remaining bombs to lighten the plane. For a third time Smith is up there, fiddling with the fuel line. Great belches of sparks and heat from the exhaust pipes as the engine strains. Then it happens. The nightmare we anticipated – everyone except the one who should. A whoosh of air-fuelled flame rises from the engine. Smittie screams as he is caught – I hear it in my dream – he stands gripping one strut, beating at flames on his flying jacket. Gus leans half out of the back cabin, spraying a fire extinguisher on the flames, hauling at him with his gloved hands, dragging him below. But the engine won't stop burning. Flames reach up to melt the varnished covering of our wings.

We're rushing in a dive, Fitz heading for a sea-landing, anywhere for a chance to fight the fire. Still we're in fog. Mist all around, but thinner. Even in my panic and terror as I fasten on the safety harness, I notice that. Then we're out of the fog, twenty feet above the waves. I screech, cover my head with futile, gloved hands.

Cliffs! I took us too far north of base. I'm thrown to one side as Fitz hauls us in a curve. Earth banks rush towards us. With a groan of straining wings we turn in time, arching downward towards a long line of shingle beach and surf.

Sparks and flames flow from the port engine like the tail of a firework. Every dream the same way. The petrol feed has ignited. We stall, too low to recover, the nose stabbing down. Too low, too low, flapping, shaking, blown sideways by the wind.

Down we go, down like a wounded, heavy albatross and bounce off the surf. Once. Twice. Bits of fuselage break off. Then the petrol tank goes up.

Wood and canvas tear, the planks of our wooden belly parting, splitting like a rotten barrel. We're grinding through grit and surf, through air and water, wind and fire. Instinctively, I release my safety harness, jump out as we jolt to a halt. A squirt of burning petrol hits my left cheek, neck.

I'm rolling in the sand and sea to extinguish it, screaming, howling. More from panic than pain. That will come later, as soon as adrenalin fades. When I stagger up, the bus is a crumpled mass of wing and fuselage, brewing up into a fireball. Black, acrid smoke billows. Out of it a man stumbles, his whole upper torso on fire, flapping, beating at the flames. I struggle to drag him onto the sand, cover him with wet clammy sand. My own clothes are smouldering, but it works. The flames die, splutter, smoke. They go out.

Even as I collapse beside him, I realise Gus and Smittie are trapped in the inferno of our bus. One of them screams and screams. It seems to take a lifetime for his agony to end. Machine gun rounds pop as flames ignite the drums. Waves crash, oblivious... There the dream always ends. It is over.

Twenty-Four

The next day I woke sick in my gut.

For a long while, I stood in the gable dormer window. Smoke rose in wispy ribbons from the chimneys of York; already a summer haze lay over the city – over my life.

Needs were working through me. Through every man and woman in that ancient town, every child. My own at that moment? I was still crawling away from the crash. Fitz's arrogant folly and my navigating error had branded me for life. I could not help resenting him as I stood there, gazing at the morning. I could not help pitying him. And, maybe, pitying myself.

Did he wake from uneasy dreams, as I did, aware he could have saved Smith and Gus? The family men who died because of our mistakes? We were their officers, pilot and navigator. Their safety was in our keeping. And the war was so nearly over. We had made widows of their wives, orphans of their children. Yet we were the ones who lived.

After a wash and shave, I set out for Princess Street. I craved reassurance. Louisa had warned me I would hate her for what she was about to do, that she must write a letter, no doubt begging assistance from her flint-hearted family. It was essential to discover her plans, to offer help. Perhaps I nurtured a vague hope help might come my own way. How badly I needed it that morning. Rarely had I felt so alone.

When I knocked on the door, I discovered Louisa in walking clothes. Bertha Kettlewell could be heard in the kitchen playing with

Freddy. Instead of inviting me in, Louisa stepped smartly onto the wobbly flagged pavement of the narrow, dirty street. She closed the door behind her.

'David, how strange! I was just thinking of you.'

'You are going out?'

'Yes, I have an important letter to post, you see.'

I could see it poking from the small drawstring bag she carried.

'I came to ask if you are well,' I said. 'I was worried about you.'

Louisa pulled on a pair of thin kidskin gloves – the sort worn by the best class of lady. She must have hoarded them in some hidden drawer or box from more prosperous days. There seemed significance in her digging them out today.

'Perhaps you have time to walk with me?' she asked.

'I have all the time in the world.'

'Let us get away from this horrible place.' She nodded at the smoky, cramped terrace streets and slum courtyards of the Groves. 'I know, let us walk on the walls.'

York's medieval city walls formed an elevated passageway round the centre of the town. They were easily joined from the Groves at Monk Bar, an imposing gatehouse. On previous occasions, when we followed its circumference, Louisa would grow silent and thoughtful. I realised how deeply she needed to think right now: it was why she suggested this route. Whatever terrible dilemma she wrestled with lay sealed in the envelope in her bag. That she should want my company at such a time flattered and comforted me. The ache in my gut softened a little. Somehow, there was hope for us both yet.

We climbed steep stone stairs beside Monk Bar then were on the walkway of the walls. Strange paradox! To feel wonderfully freed from the workaday town beneath us, its factories and gasworks belching smoke, its servile habits of money. At the same time to feel bound by the circle of walls you might trudge round forever like one of Dante's damned souls, trapped within a circle of Hell.

We walked in our usual quiet way. Whatever was on her mind stayed there.

After a mile or so, we approached Walmgate Bar. The lowing of cattle joined the constant thrum of factories and mills in this part of town. Here, just outside the walls, was the cattle market. We paused to watch a drove of Irish cows unloaded from train trucks then driven to pens adjoining the ramparts. Men with sticks thwacked the dumb, panicking beasts to keep them in order. Louisa pressed against my arm at the brutish sight. Did she fear being beaten and herded by the world?

'Let's go on,' I said. 'There are better views from the walls than this.'

We left the chaos of Walmgate behind. Still she did not speak of the troubles written on her face. Near Micklegate we looked out over a large area of tracks and sidings –York was a great railway town. Goods and passenger trains waited or shunted, laying down a barrage of steam and smoke. The tracks shone dully in the sunshine, destinations pointing everywhere. There is always a direction to travel, even if just to retrace one's steps.

At last, we reached the end of the circle, Monk Bar, where our little journey had begun. I could hold back no longer.

'Louisa, please hear me out. Something is on your mind. A weight pressing down on you. You must know by now that I am your friend. If you cannot confide in me, I would understand. I have not really earned your trust. But if you did trust me, perhaps I could help. And I would be glad to do so.'

I took her gloved fingers in my hands. She did not squeeze back. Her eyes were looking past me, beyond me. She was struggling inside, her breath quickening.

'Tell me if I can help,' I urged. 'I'm sure that I can.'

Slowly, she loosened her hands. Tears glittered on her long eyelashes.

'Thank you, David,' she said. 'You deserve someone far better than I… Someone simpler. I, I must think of Freddy.'

With that she hurried back towards the Groves. A tall red pillar box stood on the corner of Monkgate and Lord Mayor's Walk. For a long moment, she stood before it, wringing her gloved hands. She reached into her bag for the letter. Still she hesitated, glancing back to where I stood and watched on the pavement. Then, almost convulsively, she pushed it beyond retrieval into the slot.

What did it mean? I could not think. Dared not guess. Instead, for some irrational reason I knew the time had come to have it out with Fitz. My horrible dream of the crash had been a call to arms. It was time to test whether he was friend or enemy. If the latter, to be done with him forever.

An hour later I sat with him outside the chapel of Bootham Park Lunatic Asylum. We had found an old bench in its shadow. A dark, soot-stained building, the wall above us streaked with green mould where a gutter had dripped. How many poor, troubled souls had sweated in that house of faith – still did – unable to bat off the terrors of hellfire.

If he sensed my resentment, he gave no sign. Then came the familiar noise of an aeroplane engine. Moments later a B.E.2c flew low overhead, trailing a banner: **ROBINSON'S FLYING CIRCUS.** The same army surplus bus that had buzzed York with advertisements for the Grand. It swooped towards the Minster then banked back round to overfly the river.

Fitz stirred as we watched it circle the city.

'They're based near York,' I said. 'I once walked out to their little aerodrome. All ex-RFC men, a rum old lot. Rather too fond of the bottle, some might say.'

He grew oddly intent. His one eye swivelled round in search of nurses then he fished out a hip flask. After his nip he passed it over. Far better stuff than I could afford.

'Do you know, Young,' he drawled, leaning back to follow the plane, 'you once mentioned I should go home to Pater and Mater. Funny thing is, I have it all worked out. Send a telegram and tell them I'll be there in a couple of hours. That they should meet me in Mellors Meadow. It's near our old place, perfect for a landing. Then I fly in, land a bus, surprise the whole lot.'

Clumsily, he screwed the cap back on the hip flask.

'Toshy rot, of course,' he said. 'My flying days are over.'

I turned to him. 'Is that a bad thing?'

Still I did not approach the one topic on my mind. In a clipped, casual way I described what had happened to Laverelli, how the magistrate's hearing was a few days off.

'I don't imagine Mr Laverelli will have his licence renewed. He seems quite demoralised. He says that he can't afford a lawyer. So I'll be out of work.' I wanted to see how Fitz took this. 'I suppose I'll return to London. There's always work down there for someone like me.'

He appeared not to register I might fly south. Or he didn't care.

'Laverelli? The fellow looked like a pansy to me,' he said. 'You're well shot of him.'

I turned angrily to face him. He had offered just the excuse I wanted.

'I believe him to be a good man. Pansy or not, he has been kind to me. And generous to many others, including you.'

'He just wants money, Young, don't be naïve. They all just want money. Can sniff his sort a mile off.'

'At least he uses what little power he has to help those less fortunate.'

I let the implication dangle. For all his great wealth and connections, Fitz never lifted a finger for anyone but himself.

'Good lord!' he mocked. 'Steady on, Baby.'

That did it.

'My name is *Young*. David to my friends.' My tone made it clear he was not included in that number. I felt adrenalin pump. 'Do you know, *sir*, I have been thinking a lot about the war lately. How we both came to be here. Yes, about our last patrol.'

Now I had his attention.

'The more I think about it, the more of a bad show it seems,' I said. 'Either crass stupidity or sheer bloody-minded murder. Do you ever think of Smith and Gus? I'm genuinely curious. Do they ever cross your mind?'

He goggled at me.

'I thought not,' I said.

'Careful, Young,' he growled.

But I was in full flight.

'You were warned and warned about that damn port engine. If you had the slightest humility you would feel nothing but shame and guilt. Perhaps both of us should. We killed those men with arrogance then rotten decisions.'

'Smith was responsible for the damn engine,' he replied, wrathfully. 'Damn you, Young, it was his job to keep it working, not mine. His mistake is why I'm here.'

'What nonsense! We both know those engines were never reliable.'

'And what about you, Young? You were the navigator, not me. You led us nearly a hundred miles north of base. Straight into a ruddy line of cliffs! I would have landed safely without that, if you'd got us back to base.' He raised a shaking finger at me. 'And who paid the price, eh? Look at me! Who paid the price?'

'Smittie and Gus paid the price!' I cried. 'I paid the price.'

'Tommy rot and you know it. I trusted you, Young. One of the other chaps warned me. "Baby has a yellow streak," he said. And you lost your nerve in that fog. Let me down. Let the crew down.'

We tensed, glaring. For a moment I thought he might hit me with his walking stick. Then my anger subsided. In its place came sadness, a desire to cry. I had no intention of giving him that satisfaction.

We glanced up instinctively as the B.E.2c flew low overhead, on its way back to the aerodrome at Clifton Moor.

I rose, looked down at him.

'We both know why you won't go back to your parents,' I said. 'Back to luxury and pampering in that grand old house. It's you who has the yellow streak.' Then it came to me. It had run through him like a rotten vein amidst his triumphs and medals and recklessness in the war. 'You've always been afraid you're not good enough.'

I straightened my hat.

'Goodbye, sir. I do not believe we shall meet again. As I mentioned, Mr Laverelli's hearing is in a few days. He is sure to lose his licence. After that, I shall be gone.'

I turned, and walked towards the long, elm-lined avenue. It led to freedom from the lunatic asylum.

'Damn you, Young! Come back here. That's an order!'

I ignored him. He could navigate his own way back to the ward. And rot there.

Twenty-Five

We sat on a long bench in the corridor outside Magistrate Court No.2. Almost the entire staff of the Electric had rallied to Laverelli. Only Louisa and Victor stayed away.

Louisa's absence grieved me. She had more reason than most to be grateful to Laverelli. But I reasoned she was too sensitive, that the rules of conduct never apply universally. Hadn't the war taught us that?

Laverelli wore his soberest suit, which nevertheless trailed a miasma of cologne. He couldn't stop picking at the lining of his hat. Alongside him were Ambrose Ackerley, Esther and Gladys Bannering. The latter sported an uncharacteristically low hemline.

'I do hope Victor will come,' murmured Laverelli. 'He promised to act as witness. In fact, he's me only witness.'

'Does he live nearby?' I asked. 'You could send Ambrose to fetch him.'

Knowing the commissionaire, it would have been by the scruff of the neck.

'No, no,' said Laverelli, 'too late for that now.'

More people joined us in the corridor. Inspector Green and Carruthers from the Corporation, a cardboard folder clutched to his weedy chest. Then two people entered together. Who else but Maurice Skelton and Ernie Precious of the Grand?

Laverelli tensed. Precious had come to savour his downfall. Not for the first time, I wondered what exactly festered between the two men.

Although Maurice sat well away from Precious, no one was fooled. Ambrose went so far as to crack his meaty knuckles whilst eyeballing the cellist. There were many dark alleys and passageways in York. As Maurice Skelton might yet learn to his cost.

The previous hearing concluded. Out stepped a publican renewing his annual licence.

'T'bench are sharp as tacks today,' he warned. 'I'm lucky to still be in business.'

With that, he departed the halls of justice.

The usher summoned us into the court.

The back wall was dominated by a long bench. Behind it sat three Justices of the Peace, all aging men, respectable as a bank's facade, in wigs and scarlet fur-lined robes. The clerk of court perched in a den of law books. A moody devil he seemed, too.

What with plaintiffs and defendants and witnesses we half-filled the pews in the public gallery. My main interest was Maurice Skelton. What mischief could the sly hypocrite want here?

Then my attention was on the various submissions to the court. I shall spare you the legal ritual. It had one destination, inevitable as a lynch mob's verdict. But, of course, the evidence *was* damning, and it had all been gathered in strict accordance with the Cinematograph Act 1909. Section by subsection, Carruthers droned on. Then Inspector Green presented his case in a tone implying he'd nobbled a few bad 'uns in his time, and was delighted to add Laverelli to the list.

The Chairman of the Bench raised a fluffy, silver-haired eyebrow.

'Thank you, Inspector. Mr Laverelli, do you have a submission to make?'

After a brief swearing in, Laverelli took his place at the witness stand.

'Mr Laverelli,' began the worshipful alderman who chaired the Bench, 'we have heard damning testimony from Inspector Green.'

The gentleman in question acknowledged the compliment with a grave nod.

'As well as from Mr Carruthers of the Corporation. What have you to say in response?'

The courtroom hushed. Seconds of silence melded until the clerk of court looked up.

'His Worship has asked you a question. Please be so good as to address the Bench.'

Laverelli wrung his hands, sighed.

'What I have to say, no one here will believe. Even though I know it to be true.'

The worthies exchanged glances.

'But I'll try,' continued Laverelli.

'Please do,' ordered one of the magistrates, 'or we'll be here until teatime.'

'Well, it's like this, sirs. I've always taken me bounden duty for a safe, clean, honest establishment as seriously as any man alive.'

Was that a snort from the general area where Ernie Precious sat?

'That's why I undertook a thorough – and I may well say *painstaking* – examination of my premises preceding this 'ere inspection.'

Laverelli went so far as to produce his tick list and clipboard.

'So you see, Your Worships,' he concluded, 'the mischief lies not in the direction of the management. No, there has been a paid... ' His voice lowered. '*Agent provocateur.*'

He pronounced the last word *pro-va-cat-ooer*, but we got the idea.

The Chairman of the Bench leaned forward.

'Do you have a witness to support this assertion?'

'I did have, but he hasn't come today as he promised. I mean, young Victor, our projectionist. Victor Walker, that is, Your Worship.'

'Ah. So he declined to act as your witness.'

'He said he would then he didn't.'

'I see. And you claim this *agent provocateur. . .*' (Pronounced the French way). 'Went round your cinema sabotaging all the safety apparatus listed in Inspector Green's report?'

'What other explanation can there be?'

A faint smirk on the Chairman's face suggested alternative theories.

'On whose behalf, dare one ask, was this wicked spy in your midst working?'

'Him!' said Laverelli, pointing straight at Ernie Precious. His face reddened. I could have sworn the whites of his brown Italian eyes showed. 'I'm tellin' you it was *'im!*'

Uproar in the court. Precious on his feet. Fingers pointing, accusations flying. Ambrose boomed out like a kettle drum, 'It's a ruddy shame, that's what it is!' while Esther dragged at his arm to make him sit.

'Order!' called out the Magistrate. 'Order!'

When peace had resumed, he readjusted his wig. It had slipped a little.

'I will not tolerate this behaviour. Now, Mr Laverelli, I will give you one last opportunity to prove your case. Who is this *spy* you allege sabotaged your cinema's fire apparatus?'

Five pairs of eyes swivelled to where Maurice Skelton hunched at the end of a row, pale and surly. Before Laverelli could answer, Maurice shuffled to his feet. As he did so, I noticed for the first time that a clean-shaven man in a black suit had appeared out of nowhere to sit at the back. The stranger was observing the proceedings closely.

'I know who did them things,' announced Maurice. 'I know exactly who the *ar-gent sabotage-ooer* was.'

We stared in amazement. Was Maurice about to confess? His conscience must have got the better of him.

'Aye, I know,' he repeated with bitter satisfaction. 'I saw it with me own eyes.'

For the first time, Ernie Precious seemed a mite rattled.

'Do stand down, Mr Laverelli,' said the magistrate, 'it appears you have a corroborating witness for your fanciful claim.'

Maurice was duly sworn in and replaced Laverelli on the stand. He made a shabby spectacle, fidgeting and unable to meet a single eye.

Once his relationship with the Electric had been established, questioning began.

'So you *saw* an act of sabotage,' prompted one of the magistrates. 'That's a serious accusation, Mr Skelton. Endangering people's lives, I'd call it, to do such a thing.'

Maurice nodded. 'Aye, except I didn't exactly see it.'

'But you just said that you did.'

'I didn't need to see it,' he said. 'Except in me mind's eye.'

'Really?'

'Aye. You see, I heard all about it from a friend of mine. He didn't say much but he said enough.'

'And who is this friend.'

'I'd best not say.'

'But we insist on a name, Mr Skelton. What use is your testimony without a name?'

Maurice grumbled to himself. Whatever hope I had when he took the stand crashed to earth.

'I'd best not say,' repeated Maurice, doggedly. 'Only, he's in a position to know, if you see what I mean.'

Out of all the folk in that courtroom, I was probably the only one who *did* see. He meant Mr Cooper, the director of the orchestra at the Grand.

'Anyhow,' said Maurice, 'I can tell you the name of the lad who did the mischief. And a right rotten trick it were. Him putting the blame where it's not warranted.'

Maurice scowled accusingly our way. Injustice only interested him when it applied to himself.

'The lad's name is Victor Walker,' declared Maurice. 'And I think you'll find he were promised a job as projectionist at the Grand in return. Ask *'im* if you don't believe me.'

I need hardly say the *'im* in question was Ernie Precious.

In my early twenties, I was far, far too self-centred to be a reliable reader of minds. Even I could tell the bench was less than amused by Maurice's testimony. I also suspected they blamed Laverelli for it.

'I think we've heard enough,' said the chief magistrate, coldly. 'This hearing has taken too long already. We'll never get through the list at this rate.'

'Shall we, err, withdraw?' murmured one of his worshipful colleagues.

My pulse quickened. Every instinct argued against what I must do next. Not least a dozen people staring at my blistered face. No skulking in the dark, no hiding behind an instrument. It was why I had brought something to the hearing, hoping not to produce it. I reached inside my jacket, pulled out a row of medals which I pinned to my lapel. Prominent among them was my Distinguished Flying Cross, earned for *exemplary gallantry during active operations against the enemy in the air.* An ornate piece of tin with a bright, horizontal purple and white striped ribbon. My reward for turning a dozen Germans into human candles as they leapt from the fireball of their Zeppelin. There were other minor medals but that one crowned them.

I rose, calling out to the clerk: 'Sir! May I have permission to approach the Bench.'

Another phrase learned from penny dreadfuls like so much of my wisdom. The clerk frowned at my best suit, medals and Home Counties accent.

'Very well.'

After a short consultation I, too, was sworn in and took my place in the witness box.

'Your worships,' I began, 'my name is David Young. I hope you do not mind me displaying my Distinguished Flying Cross. I served as a Sub-Flight Lieutenant in the Royal Naval Air Service. I was awarded the decoration for my part in downing Zeppelin L42.'

Nods of approval. A clean take off.

'I would also like to explain, sirs, I am a graduate of the Royal College of Music and now have the pleasure of directing the orchestra at the Electric Cinema, employed by Mr Laverelli.'

Eyes hardened a little. A nicely spoken young hero was one thing: Laverelli quite another. I ploughed on.

'I'm afraid I cannot shed light on whom or what led to the safety apparatus being universally out of action on the day of the inspection. All I can say for sure, Your Worships, is that I have never witnessed a breach of duty in the entire six months of my employment at the Electric. On the contrary, I have always observed Mr Laverelli to be most meticulous in that regard. And I can confirm that he did conduct a very detailed safety check prior to the inspection. Indeed, he closed the cinema for a day so it could be done thoroughly. And that he was accompanied by Victor Walker in the role of his assistant.

'May I conclude, sirs, that I have always found him a kind and considerate person to deal with. I would urge you, if the law allows it, to give Mr Laverelli a second chance. In short, to renew his licence. I do not say that for my own advantage – it is my intention to return to my native London soon – but to give a decent fellow a break. That's all I have to say, Your Worships. Thank you for your attention.'

The best I could do. One look at the irritated, fixed expression of the head magistrate confirmed my fears. Back in the gallery, Laverelli shook my hand.

'That were good of you, lad,' he murmured.

Again the Bench prepared to withdraw. Only now, at the very stroke of midnight, a new personage entered the stage. The man in the smart suit sat at the back. He, too, approached the bench, though with far more assurance than I had. In his hand was a thick document. What it signified I had no idea.

🎬

'I trust Your Worships will accept a submission on behalf of my client,' he said. He had a deep, stately Edinburgh burr, every inch the Scottish gentleman. A level of dignity that didn't come cheap, either to hire or acquire.

'Who *is* your client?' demanded the magistrate, now plainly exasperated. He was almost certain to miss afternoon tea if proceedings dragged on.

The barrister, so he introduced himself, mentioned a well-known solicitor in Leeds. He raised his voice haughtily. 'I represent Sir William Fitzclarence MP, Viscount Cleveland.'

Profound silence in the court. Would it be an exaggeration to call it awe? Firstly, the employment of a distinguished barrister for such a petty case was like sending out a battleship against a fishing smack. Sir William Fitzclarence MP was none other than Fitz's father and he owned half of North Yorkshire. Your-Worship-Who-Wanted-His-Tea wasn't quite so thirsty anymore.

'We would be most pleased to hear a submission on Sir William's behalf,' said the Chair of the Bench.

'The submission takes two parts, Your Worships, the first being this written statement in my hand. It takes the form of an unimpeachable witness as to Mr Laverelli's character. I refer to Flight Lieutenant Archibald Fitzclarence, VC and DFC, Sir William's eldest son. Will ye look it over, when Your Worships withdraw?'

The agents of justice were all attention. Nothing was too much bother for Sir William and his noble progeny.

'And the second part of your submission?' enquired the chief magistrate.

'Ye'll also find that in the document Your Worships have kindly chosen to consider.'

The Scottish lawyer paused significantly.

'Your Worships,' he said, 'listening to this proceeding has minded me of the Judicial Oath, as I'm sure it has Your Worships.' He spoke clearly and crisply, '*To do right to all manner of people after the laws and usages of this realm*. Now it seems we've heard "all manner" of people here today. Quite a gathering, indeed. I was particularly touched by the brave young officer's testimony on behalf of Mr Laverelli's character and the facts he averred. All for no financial gain pertaining to his interests. His call for a "second chance" seemed to me, Your Worships, most appositely *to do right to all manner of people*. I shall commend the matter to Your Worships' wisdoms.'

With that the magistrates withdrew. The Scottish lawyer took a seat and consulted a folder of notes. Esther leant against Ambrose as though the trial had quite exhausted her. As for Gladys, she slid over to where I sat.

'Your friend has hired a fancy lawyer,' she whispered. 'Blimey, 'e's like a walking dictionary!'

That much was proven.

'Mr Fitzclarence must have *really* liked them films.' She shot me a shrewd side glance. 'Unless, of course, he did it for someone else.'

'It's as much a surprise to me as you,' I murmured back.

She patted my arm understandingly. I felt myself blush.

They weren't out long, those justices. Back they came, clutching Sir William's wad-like written submission.

My throat tightened. I hoped dearly for Laverelli's sake that whatever arguments the document contained were sufficient. After a pause, the Chair of the Bench cleared his throat.

'A most unusual case,' he said. 'In the light of the evidence and the late submission from Sir William, including his fixed determination to appeal any adverse judgement in this matter to the highest authority available, we considered three options. First, to close down permanently the Electric Cinema as a hazard to public health. Secondly, to give the premises a clean bill of health and renew its licence. Or thirdly, as suggested in Sir William's submission, to renew the Electric Cinema's licence for a temporary period of twenty-eight days – or as near a time as practicable – pending a fresh and thorough inspection of the premises, as set out in Section 6(ii)(c) of the Cinematograph Act 1909.'

The ticking of the clock on the wall sounded very loud. Then the Chief Magistrate spoke.

'The third option is the one we wish to pursue in this matter. Mr Waverley?' He addressed the Clerk of Court. 'Please record our verdict.'

Twenty-Six

We stepped out together into the sunshine. For a moment, I just gawked at Clifford Street. A horse-drawn brewer's dray rattled past, bearing a load of empty barrels. A two seat sports car followed with the hood down. A glamorous young couple in goggles sat behind the dusty windscreen and I was reminded of flying.

Then we were laughing, shaking hands. Laverelli, Gladys, Ambrose, Esther and myself.

'It feels like Christmas come early,' declared Esther.

'That's right, love,' agreed Ambrose Ackerley. He seemed to spend a lot of his time agreeing with her.

A shadow fell upon us. It belonged to Ernie Precious. His drinker's face redder than usual, spud nose prominent above the handlebar moustache.

He halted before Laverelli.

'You got away with it this time. You won't the next.'

We all fell silent. Though nothing had been proven, none of us doubted who had bribed Victor Walker to play so low a game. But then, being projectionist at the Grand was a prize worth gambling for, especially if you lacked scruples and had few other prospects. And now I thought of it, there had always been something sly and self-satisfied about Victor. Or perhaps hindsight detected those qualities. There was another possibility. That Precious had something on the lad. Once Laverelli had dropped a hint Victor was of a similar persuasion to himself. Blackmail was all too easy in those days for those whose very nature offended the law. The exact truth was something we would never know.

'You played a sharp hand, Precious,' conceded Laverelli. 'But the best man won. Like last time.'

'Still, I don't see no pretty boy Alfie Brown around watching out for you,' sneered Precious. 'Enjoy what you can, is my advice, while you can.'

He stalked off down Clifford Street.

'Nice feller, that one,' opined Ambrose.

Another person exited the Magistrates Court. Again we quietened.

Laverelli coughed awkwardly. 'Mr Skelton,' he said, 'it seems I owe you an apology. It was very good of you to stand up for me the way you did.'

'Aye, it was,' agreed the cellist.

'If you'd care to have your old position back, I'd be right pleased.'

'Mebbe.'

Maurice turned to me with cool defiance. Never had a man enjoyed his hour in court so thoroughly. In Maurice's mind, the only reason Laverelli wasn't in York Prison right now was his turn at the witness box. Nor was he the kind to relinquish such an advantage without wringing every last drop from it.

'Whether I come back depends on smarty pants over there.'

'Oh, nothing would delight me more,' I said.

'And no more fancy *rehearsals*?'

Maurice invested the word with infinite contempt.

'Not for you, Mr Skelton, clearly.'

'And it's been a while since I had a pay rise. A good long while.'

From the look on Laverelli's face, it would be a while longer yet. He wasn't *that* grateful.

'Then mebbe I'll be seeing you.' Maurice paused for effect. 'And mebbe I won't.'

Which, of course, meant he'd be back at the stand tomorrow. Worst luck.

As we headed in the direction of the Electric I heard the drone of an aeroplane engine and craned to locate it. There it was again! The B.E.2c from Robinson's Flying Circus out at Clifton Moor. It seemed to follow me around like a bird of omen. I recollected Fitz's longing to fly when we saw the same bus circling over Bootham Park Lunatic Asylum. It was then I glimpsed what I must do.

The very thought of it tightened a knot in my stomach. Had I not promised myself to never take that risk again? The person willing to risk life and limb for brief excitement had died on the shingle beach where our bus crashed. Yet I sensed such a sacrifice would not only liberate Fitz from that hellish ward. It might free me as well.

'You do realise the only reason you won the case?' I said to Laverelli, cautiously.

He seemed dazed by his good fortune and was uncharacteristically quiet.

'It was the barrister that Flight Lieutenant Fitzclarence's father hired,' I said. 'He put the willies up the Bench.'

'You're right there, lad. I'd say it entitles him to free tickets and monkey nuts for life.'

'I've a better idea,' I said, 'though it'll cost a few guineas. You know, to hire this and that.'

Don't say it, you fool, I warned myself. But it came out. After that, there seemed no way of going back without cowardice. He listened closely as I explained. With a grunt, he extended his hand.

'Done!' he said. 'And a bargain. You assure your friend the trip's on me.'

We were walking as a loose group down Parliament Street, market stalls of fruit and vegetables on either side. I sensed people's eyes upon us.

'How'd it go, Horatio?' called out a man behind a cheese stall. His hair was unusually bouffant.

'Justice prevailed,' replied Laverelli. 'I'll be seeing you, Winston.'

'I'm sure you will. Usual place.'

Laverelli grinned like the cat that got the fabled cream.

'I'm going to need a new projectionist,' he said. 'Someone not likely to turn Judas on me like Victor did.'

I had another idea. Perhaps it came from passing the Clock Inn where a drunk had taunted Gladys.

'I can think of someone,' I said.

'Oh, yes?'

'How about Gladys's brother, Thomas Bannering?'

Laverelli regarded me narrowly. 'You know he was a conchie, don't you?'

I shrugged. At the sound of her surname, Gladys had drifted close. By now, our party was passing York Minster. The stained glass windows of that noble building caught the sun. Gargoyles leered down at us as they clung to the wall.

'I suppose there's no harm in trying him out,' mused Laverelli. 'He couldn't put customers off if he was hidden away in the projection box.'

Gladys's head bobbed between us. 'Oh, Mister Laverelli!' she cried. 'Thomas is ever so reliable!'

Laverelli continued to ponder aloud as though he had not heard her. 'And I reckon he'd come pretty cheap. By that, I mean only expect a reasonable wage. While he learned the ropes, of course.'

'Oh, he would come pretty cheap, Mr Laverelli,' declared Gladys. 'You can be sure of that. He's ever so reasonable.'

'We'll be opening up again next Monday. Soon as I can get some films delivered and advertisements in the Herald. Tell him to pop by tomorrow morning for a powwow. Do you think you can do that, Gladys?'

'I do!'

He turned to Ambrose, and Gladys tugged at my sleeve to detain me. For once, she was out of words. She just looked up at me and smiled. There were tears in her eyes.

'I… ' she began.

'No, please don't say it,' I interrupted. 'After all, that sorry war is over for us all. Winners and losers. Time for a fresh beginning.'

'Yes,' she said. 'Yes.'

⬛

Laverelli treated us all to a celebration in the saloon bar of the Cricketers Arms. A slate was established by Alf and comestibles ordered. We were hungry and thirsty after the trial, and couldn't stop talking.

Alf's wife bustled up with a wedge of ripe Stilton cheese and thick slices of white bread and butter. Pickles and mustard were laid out in bowls to accompany a pork pie broad as a plate. It had a crisp crust, glazed with salty aspic. Scotch egg quarters came next, along with egg and ham tarts. There were slices of cold roast beef and a jar of horseradish sauce with a fine tingle. Needless to say, I paid each dish the tribute it deserved.

Amidst the jollity, I could not help wishing Louisa was there. Though I suspected such an ordinary pub with a mainly working class clientele would make her uncomfortable. Yet I longed to reassure her that her job was safe. That whatever fears had driven her to post her fateful letter no longer applied.

I drifted to my usual corner table. I was in no mood for drinking and hardly said a word, busy making calculations and a little list in the notebook I used for fitting pictures. In fact, my whole plan felt like fitting up a picture except in real life. Instead of melodies I considered necessities: equipment, maps, clothes, even provisions. Anxious energy drove me to make my list. I knew that I must put my plan into action without delay or lose my nerve.

Laverelli sat beside me heavily. He was onto his fourth double whisky and soda.

'I hope you're not working,' he said, recognising the notebook. 'Diligence can be taken too far, Mr Young. The only real job that matters, when the curtain starts to descend, is whether you was happy with the show.'

I dreaded to think what pearls of wisdom a fifth double whisky would provoke. But I had a question for him. One that needed an answer.

'Don't worry, I'm just planning that trip I told you about. There's a lot to organise. But, Mr Laverelli, there is one question I must ask. Why does Precious hate you so?'

The old showman's grin became slightly more fixed than usual.

'Oh, that's ancient history, lad.'

'Still, I would very much like to know.'

He sighed. 'You see, me and Ernie Precious were partners before I took up with Alfred Brown. We built up the original business together, as it were. Alf just worked for us. Precious took it right bad when we parted company. Claimed I swindled him out of a fortune. Though nothing came of it when he went to the police.'

'I see.'

Laverelli winked at me. 'I wouldn't call it a fortune though. Just a tidy sum. Enough for me and Alf to set up on our own behalf.'

'You mean?'

'Just what I say.'

It was as near an admission of sharp practice – if not downright fraud – I was to get out of the man. I can only assume a sense of triumph lowered his guard, along with the double whiskies. But I never thought exactly the same way about Laverelli after his revelation.

Not that I was allowed time for thought. Gladys Bannering appeared at my other elbow. Her own connected with my arm, so that I was forced to stop writing. She had a blissful smile on her face not unrelated to the quantity of port and lemon vanishing down her throat. The slate behind the bar was turning into a veritable scroll.

'Writing a poem, Mr Young?' she asked, mischievously.

'No. Well, not exactly.'

When I explained my notes she inched closer along the bench. I glanced nervously at the door. Somehow I expected Louisa to burst in and catch me in close proximity with Gladys. The worst of it was that her warmth – and I think I have mentioned her natural fragrance – inclined me to let her press as close as she liked.

'Do you know,' she said, 'I would love to fly. Sometimes I watch the pigeons circling round the Minster and I wonder how the world looks to them from up there. We must seem like little puppets with invisible strings. Strings a bird flying free can't understand.' She giggled and finished off her port. 'And do you know what? I don't understand it either.'

'Maybe there's not much to understand.'

She smiled a little blearily. I could tell she wasn't used to drinking.

'Oh, I understand one thing.'

'What's that, Gladys?'

'One way or another I'm going to fly free of this town. Just you see! The world is as big as you make it, my Dad always says. Not that he's gone far. But I don't want to live his life. I've got me own.'

For her sake, I hoped she was right.

Then Ambrose, who had been whispering with Esther, stood up. She flapped her hands as if to say, no, no. But he was having none of it. Unlike the rest of us, you couldn't blame his enthusiasm on alcohol. He was drinking lemonade. But there are many ways to be drunk in this world and many intoxicants.

He tinkled a fork against his glass for silence. Esther seemed torn between embarrassment and pride as she gazed up at him.

'Now then,' he began, 'me and Esther have a little announcement. Seeing this is such a special day all round.'

He cleared his throat. Took a pull at the lemonade for courage.

'There's some days you hope to see but never really expect to. I think of them days as dreams come true. And we all know how rare that is. But I'm happy to announce that for me, my dream *has* come true. All because of the loveliest lady in the world.'

I felt Gladys stiffen with excitement beside me. She knew what was coming next.

'Oh, Ambrose!' complained Esther. 'You are a one! Sit yourself down.'

But we could tell she was loving it. From what I had heard of her dead husband, the Primitive Methodist fond of using the back of his hand, who could blame her?

'I will shortly,' he declared. 'But first I would like to announce that me and Esther are officially engaged to be married.'

Laverelli led the applause. Other drinkers who had arrived for the late afternoon slot joined in. Gladys went over to Esther and gave her a hug of congratulation. Ambrose, beaming as though his mouth might burst, sidled over.

'Mr Young,' he said, softly. 'I have a favour to ask.'

Recollections of the Christmas present and Valentine card incidents made me cautious.

'Yes?'

'You see, there's something about Esther only I know.'

'Yes?'

'Before she married *him*, she used to sing solos at the Methodist Chapel. You know the one, where Clarence Street becomes Haxby Road. Since *he* died she's been singing there again. It's right... ' He struggled for the *mot juste*. 'Right uplifting.'

'Yes?'

'Well, I've asked her to sing something today, just for me, and she agreed. Like a kind of engagement gift to me. Though I suppose I don't warrant it. Do you think you could accompany her on the piano over there?'

I followed his glance across the pub to where thin, faded Esther Jones sat listening while Gladys chattered away. The woebegone expression I had noticed in her when I first arrived at the Electric was gone. She had gained something intangible yet real. Love had given her confidence. It had revived the embers of her squandered youth.

'You told me her grown up children had threatened to reject her if she remarried,' I said. 'Is that sorted now?'

A sudden hardness entered Ambrose's face.

'There have been words between us,' he said. 'Harsh words have been spoken. But they'll come round in time.'

I decided that I'd better not ask more.

So I found myself at the piano with some sheet music Ambrose had brought along. There were, of course, many protestations before Esther could be persuaded to step up beside me. But she'd had a couple of port and lemons herself (Gladys was a bad influence).

'Not too fast, please,' she whispered to me.

I expected her singing voice to resemble the way she spoke. As I have mentioned, Esther had a subdued, mournful way of speaking that made me think of dried old newspaper being crumpled into a ball.

'I'll be led by you,' I said, as any good accompanist should be.

I ran my eye over the score. It was a very spare arrangement of an American spiritual. Simple enough. Just a few chords then she was in.

'Ready?' I asked.

At her cue, I started. She drew breath and sang out. And I nearly fell off my piano stool. A full, rich mezzo-soprano voice poured from the little woman, as powerful and deep as the river she sang about.

Shall we gather at the river,
Where bright angel feet have trod,
With its crystal tide forever
Flowing by the throne of God?

My head span. Was I hearing correctly? I must confess that Esther Jones was someone I had written off as grey and inconsequential. Yet here she was, exploding with musical sparks and colour. Then I glimpsed something else. Even if she had been the plain person I first considered her, and could not sing a note in tune, Esther would still have been emitting fountains of light. Inner ones, true, but still sparking fiercely.

Ere we reach the shining river,
Lay we every burden down;
Grace our spirits will deliver,
And provide a robe and crown.

Her diction was perfect. Her vibrato – wonderfully controlled – trembled with such sincerity. I followed her dynamic choices and was glad to. The wooden floorboards and bare walls of the pub resounded then softened then resounded again for a triumphant climax. I glanced round to see if anyone else shared my astonishment.

Gladys sat clutching her hands to her chest, as though beatified. Ambrose gazed adoringly. Laverelli seemed torn between amusement and awe.

Soon we'll reach the shining river,
Soon our pilgrimage shall cease;
Soon our happy hearts will quiver
With the melody of peace.

And for all my cynicism – indeed, professionalism, for it is a poor professional who gets carried away when accompanying – I felt tears well up into my own eyes. Yes. It was time for peace. High time for the melody of peace.

When I looked up, the pub was full of applause and Esther was leaning on the arm of her aged fiancé. Both seemed the happiest lovers in the world. I wiped the tear from my eye; laughed at myself for it.

I became aware Gladys Bannering was watching me closely. Her eyes, too, were bright with tears. You see, not all tears are unwelcome. Some are harbingers of lighter moods. Even of joy.

And somehow Esther's song made me determined to carry out my plan. Discard my fears and go on a pilgrimage I never wanted.

An hour later found me walking through countryside, serenaded by hedge birds and the rustle of ancient oaks, amidst the scent of wayside weeds and flowers. In my pocket were a few fivers provided by Laverelli. I followed a dusty lane towards the aerodrome at Clifton Moor.

Twenty-Seven

The morning mists had cleared when I arrived at the aerodrome two days later. A brick barn with widened doors formed the hangar, beside a long wooden hut where the boys from the flying circus bunked and messed. All were young, ex-Royal Flying Corps, washed out and making a virtue of recklessness and drink.

As flying circuses went, it wasn't much of an outfit. There was a Morane-Saulnier monoplane, the ubiquitous B.E.2c, and a Sopwith 1½ Strutter. Near the end of the field hunched the remains of a peculiar kite with a push propeller behind the pilot's seat. Its wings lay broken, nose buried in a ditch.

'Pre-war experimental model,' explained the young fellow who had appointed himself my guide. The eponymous owner of Robinson's Flying Circus was sleeping off a hangover in the bunkhouse. 'Robinson bought her for two bottles of whisky and a tin of cigarettes.' He grinned cheerily. 'Lucky to walk away from that prang.'

We crossed the long, dewy grass to the B.E.2c. *BEATRICE* had been painted on the side. They were wits in Robinson's Flying Circus.

'She's a good old girl,' he explained, patting the varnished fabric of the fuselage. 'Not much of a stunter, of course, you know how those 2c's handled out in France. Sitting ducks. Still, she's good for a loop-the-loop, so long as you leave plenty of room. Not that I'd recommend trying it until you get used to the way she purrs.'

I didn't like the sound of that. 'Engine not steady?'

'Steady away, old chap. Just don't flood the tank and you'll be fine. She's touchy down there. Look, I'll rustle up the other chaps. Why not give her a final once over?'

While he 'rustled', I conducted a close inspection, much like a nervous soloist scanning the score. My heart quickened to be so near an aeroplane again. The last time I flew a B.E.2c had been pilot's training, three years earlier. After that, my flying had been almost entirely in our Felixstowe flying boat with its dual controls.

My negotiations with Robinson the previous day had included ten minutes in the cockpit to remind myself of the dials and pedals. Compass, altimeter, spirit level to check you were on an even keel, airspeed and rev indicators, plus the oil pressure gauge. Far fewer instruments than our two-engine flying boat. Ironically, the B. E. 2c was heavier to handle, lacking the nip needed for tight turns. Its virtue was stability. Even so, I recalled a few bumpy landings to fill my flying log with the necessary hours. And unless you were mindful of side winds, she could swing and wobble on take off.

I sat on the lower wing. Why was I doing this absurd thing? It might end up killing us both.

Just then a taxicab came bumping along the dusty track.

Fitz wore a thick leather coat and scarf. He'd donned a pair of riding boots and carried leather gloves. He, at least, looked the part. My own flying gear had long ago been hocked or sold so I made do with long johns, woollen trousers, two pairs of socks, woolly jumper over my shirt, topped by my jacket and old overcoat.

'Morning, Young,' he said.

I smoked while the ground crew assembled. The swallows flitting low over the grass seemed a good omen. Did my hand shake as I lifted the cigarette to my lips? By God, it did.

He, too, looked nervous.

'Have you sent the telegram?' I asked.

We had it all worked out, timed and plotted like a bombing raid.

'I did.' He guffawed. 'I wrote: *Have picnic lunch waiting in Mellors Field. Including pie. Leave plenty of room for landing.* That'll jigger 'em up.'

He peered at me with his one eye. We had decided to pretend our quarrel never took place. The day after Laverelli's hearing I'd set out my plan to him on a visit to the ward. When Dr Middleton got wind of it, he almost pressganged Fitz to agree. It had been months since his patient really benefitted from being there. Every fledgling must take flight or is abandoned to starve in the nest.

My own motives in offering to help him leave York remained complex. Fitz had explained – but only after a great deal of stubborn questioning and prompting – how he telephoned his father to hire the lawyer for Laverelli's case, promising to come home in return for the favour. I certainly owed him one there. But I also wished to see him settled, and off my conscience. In short, I wanted the best for him.

'Think they'll be waiting for me, Young? You know, when we land?'

'I suppose that depends whether your family are all at home. They might be away somewhere.'

'Dr Middleton telephoned yesterday, as you suggested. He confirmed with Rankin, our butler. Everyone's home.'

'We'll see then.'

His blistered young face wrinkled. A tiny droplet of pus caught the morning sun like the dew on the grass blades at our feet.

'Don't know if Pater and Mater will consider me coming home this way to be good form,' he muttered. 'Not exactly the done thing, is it?'

I took his point. Instead of allowing them to control the process by sending their limousine, this flight was a bold gesture of independence. Fitz was sending a strong message by returning his own way, and not just to his family, but the whole neighbourhood. There would be chuckles in the pubs when word got round how Archie Fitzclarence made light of his terrible wounds. You can't keep a good man down, and all that.

'They won't have much of a choice,' I said. 'Besides, it's still not too late to change your mind.'

A large part of me hoped he would.

'I suppose not.' Some of his old spirit returned. 'If they're not waiting in Mellor's Field, I'm going to bally well fly back here myself.'

We both knew that physically he couldn't. Nor did he have anywhere to go. He had officially discharged himself from the asylum.

'It will be fine,' I said, looking north. Was that a smudge of dark clouds?

'Sure you're up to this?' he growled. 'You seem damn shaky, Young.'

The fact I had lit a second cigarette from the embers of the first might suggest nerves.

'Yes, I am,' I snapped. 'What about you? Fixed at your end?'

He tapped the map case. 'Never could see why you navigator chaps made such a fuss. A child could find their way there.'

I had become pilot, he navigator. Why did my guts gripe at the prospect?

'We have three hours and fifteen minutes of juice,' I pointed out. 'Let's hope you're right.'

🎬

Manoeuvring Fitz into the observer's seat proved no joke. A quirk of the B.E.2c was the navigator sat in front of the pilot, involving a clamber onto the bottom wing of the biplane to take your seat. After several failed attempts at hauling himself onto the lower wing, I formed a human stepladder by kneeling on the grass and Fitz managed to scrabble up. From there, it was easier to feed his gammy leg into the cockpit, followed by the rest of him.

The young pilot appointed as my assistant watched with undisguised amusement. Of Robinson there was still no sign.

'That's the spirit!' he declared, once Fitz was settled.

A mechanic span the stiff propeller to spark the plug. *Phut. Phut.* Reluctant ignitions weren't unusual but by the fourth attempt the gripe in my stomach tightened.

'More choke,' advised the young airman. 'Beatrice is a thirsty old girl. Only don't flood the tank.'

So much was obvious.

Phut. Phut.

I was about to climb out of the cockpit when a muffled growl came from the old engine. Fuel fired, grunted. At once the four-blade prop was swirling. I felt the aeroplane tug gently at the chocks keeping it in place. Two bored chaps from the crew grabbed hold of the wings and tail, just in case I over-revved.

I tapped Fitz's shoulder and he turned with great effort. His stiffness didn't bode well. A good observer needed to crane this way and that for landmarks. Wind from the propeller flowed over us: we adjusted our goggles.

I had no intention of launching yet, not after the engine's sluggish start. I revved gently to warm it up, listening for stutters. It was singing alright.

Fitz turned and pointed at the runway impatiently.

Leaning out, I indicated a final ailerons test to the young chap assisting us. He slouched round the plane, checking each flap as I worked the controls. Lighting his cigarette near a can of petrol, he gave a thumbs up.

So that was it. Engine revved, rasping, chugging. Nowhere left to go but up. Unless I lost my nerve and clambered out to drown my funk in the Cricketers Arms. Just eighteen months since I last flew: it felt like eighteen centuries.

My turn to deliver a thumbs up and point at the chocks. Fitz ducked in the forward cockpit. Then the chocks were away. I gunned Beatrice, building her up until she rolled down the smooth grass runway, every instant gathering speed and momentum. My heart beat as furiously as the pistons. I could feel the imminent lightness of lift off. The tail rose with a surge of throttle. I held the stick well back. We were charging a line of low alders near the wrecked push propeller model in its ditch. Then we were airborne, climbing up, up, the prop chattering nicely. A slight cross-wind caught us. The bus swayed and I kept my eye on the spirit level that served as a gyroscope. Every few seconds I worked the rudder foot pedal, what we called 'pressing the ball'. We soon evened out as we gained speed. No more need for corrections. Up I nosed her, up towards the heavens.

Again, I tapped Fitz's shoulder. Five hundred feet on the altimeter already, and still climbing. I pointed vertically. It was a question. He raised his thumb in agreement. Settling in my seat, I kept the stick pulled back, our angle of ascent gradual. The last thing we needed was a stall.

Beatrice had a maximum ceiling of ten thousand feet but I didn't care to push her half so far. A steady fifty-five mph ascent to five thousand feet took us nearly twenty minutes. I scanned the rev meter continually and kept adjusting the throttle, a simple push pull knob, every time the dial flickered downwards. Beatrice's engine was not young, and she needed plenty of coaxing.

By now we were rushing along at sixty miles an hour. The nose rose naturally, increasing drag. Every so often, an air-pocket shook our wire-tensed wings. We passed a long, ragged stream of seagulls heading inland which struck me as strange: perhaps a storm was brewing out to sea. Then we were flying up through wispy clouds, moisture clinging to our goggles, faces, clothes.

For some reason the cloud layer brought on a panic. I wiped condensation off the oil gauge and my breath quickened. The pressure seemed to be dropping. By now the air was thinner and the revs almost on red. I eased back slightly on the throttle and used the mixture control, another push pull rod, to feed some juice. Still the oil pressure flickered. Would the engine fail? What if it died? Down, down we'd spin and corkscrew, gathering speed with each moment that passed. Unless I somehow pulled her into a helpless glide, found a soft place to crash. But the oil pressure slowly rose and the motor clattered steadily enough. The revs were constant. The altimeter showed we had reached a ceiling that felt comfortable for the old bird.

Then my nerves dissolved. Exhilaration and pride flooded through me. I realised how many of my deepest, most hidden fears had been conquered to bring me here, joystick in hand, feet working the rudder pedal, no longer in the observer's seat. Yes, I *was* the pilot at last.

Ahead of me, I could see the back of Fitz's head in the flying helmet he had borrowed from Robinson's circus. A few feet in front of him the propeller whirled, framed by the wing struts and a wonderful panorama of blue sky merging upward to white infinity.

By God, Beatrice was handling well. I barely needed to touch the controls. She wanted to float like a kite of her own accord – so long as I didn't try any sudden manoeuvres.

A few hundred feet below us white clouds shone with sunlight, forming and reforming as I watched. The compass pointed north and I kept that bearing, aware from the air speed reading we would soon overshoot our destination and have to come round. It didn't seem to matter. The clouds were left behind and ribbons of silver lay beneath us, fields and woods and the dark smudges of villages. The altimeter read six thousand feet.

Meditative minutes passed. I tapped Fitz on the shoulder. My gloved forefinger painted an 'M' in the air – our old, ironic signal for *map* when we flew over waves where maps meant nothing at all. The gesture also signified: *Where the devil are we?*

He spent a long time fiddling with the map in its case. Meanwhile I worried how far we had overshot our target. Then he pointed east.

The coast lay east, a fairish way from our destination. Of the three hours juice we started with, nearly an hour had been drunk.

To turn east was to bank and retrace our steps a little – or no longer fly north. I began a gentle curve, simultaneously losing height. It didn't take long to find the blue horizon of the North Sea over a line of hills. We both knew the Yorkshire coast passingly well from training in the flying boat. I guessed Fitz was still floundering over the map and decided to seek a landmark. Soon enough I recognised Flamborough Head, and yes, that town to the south must be Filey.

Fishing out my own map, I made a quick calculation then turned Beatrice due west. Fitz was belatedly indicating the same direction.

It took twenty or so minutes to find the small market town I guessed to be Malton. Lowering the nose, I came at it from five hundred feet so my navigator could take a long hard look. His thumb rose stiffly and I used the compass to nudge us south west. He was craning this way and that, seeking the landmarks of his youth. In the distance, purple and brown moorlands formed a line on the horizon. A train puffed below us, dragging a great ribbon of steam across the land.

Fitz pointed excitedly and I banked. There it was, Broughton Hall, an extravagant stately pile with two wings and plenty of outbuildings. A gravel garden walk surrounded fountains worthy of Versailles glittering in the sun. There was a sizable lake and follies and Grecian temples scattered round the parkland. Oddly enough, the main building's central portion reminded me of Bootham Park Lunatic Asylum. Walled gardens and hothouses were attached to the house.

Half a mile off, stood a home farm with barns and a scattered herd of white cattle.

I spotted a flat water meadow divided by a meandering river. Fitz turned and pointed at it. This must be Mellors Field.

Was this the 'perfect' landing place he had promised? For a start water meadows could be unexpectedly boggy. It looked flat enough. But the river called for a tight landing unless we fancied a swim.

For some time the petrol gauge had troubled me but now I could relax. On that score, at least. I circled to find the land's lie then chose an angle of approach.

There are two potentially messy moments in most flights: take off and landing. The first had gone well but I was less sanguine about the second. The tussocky field might be as rough as a convict's hairy backside.

For a second time I circled. Fitz wriggled in the forward cockpit to point down. I could guess what he was thinking: I'd gone yellow on him. And he was damn right.

Now I lowered the throttle and flaps. The grass rushed at us. But the B.E.2c was as stable as ever. With a lurch we bounced – the classic moment to tilt forward and prang your nose in the turf – then I cut the propeller and we were bumping along. The tail touched earth, jolted, decided not to rise again. Only then did I realise we were heading for a bend in the river. With a buzzing clatter we slowed. Slowed and stopped. I flipped a switch and the engine juddered to a halt. We had made it. Just a dozen yards lay between us and the riverbank.

After so much engine racket, the silence that followed felt profound. I unbuckled and rose in my seat, legs wobbly. Fitz was still struggling with his belt.

'You're home,' I said, master of the obvious as ever.

The tension in his face made me wonder if he quite agreed.

Twenty-Eight

For a start, his magnificent home turned out to be deserted. Fitz may have sent a telegram requesting a picnic in Mellors Field – with pie – and Dr Middleton may have given due warning of his patient's unorthodox return, but no bunting greeted us. No expectant crowd of relatives and forelock-tugging dependents gathered. Perhaps they thought the telegram was a prank. It did come from a lunatic asylum, after all.

Our sole reception committee: a dozen heifers. The beasts bucked and fled, alarmed by our engine noise. Crows cawed in fields surrounding the meadow. A few stalked round cow pats.

'Your message must not have got through,' I said.

He struggled to look around, still trapped in his observer's tight cockpit.

Then a young man came running towards us from beneath an oak where he had been waiting. He wore the long, black tailcoat and stiff, starched white shirt of a footman. Halting at the side of the aeroplane, he gawped at it – until his eyes found Fitz.

An entirely different expression fell across him. I had grown so used to Fitz's hideous appearance, I barely noticed it. This lad was seeing the new version of the Young Master for the first time. His reaction was disbelief, horror.

'S-sir?' he stuttered. 'Master Archibald? Is that you?'

'Yes, it's me, Ackroyd,' growled Fitz from his elevated position. 'Where is Sir William?'

'H-he sent me to await you, sir.'

'I deduced that, dammit. And Lady Fitzclarence?'

'They told me to tell them when you arrive, sir.'

'Did they not get my message?'

'I believe they did, sir.'

The poor lad still could not help staring.

'Well, go back and tell them I'm here, Ackroyd. Run along.'

'Yes, sir,' cried the footman, relieved to be dismissed. 'Right away.'

We watched him hurry down a track in the direction of the mansion. Its high roofs and turrets rose above a line of poplars.

Fitz struggled to pull himself out, useless arm and leg trapping him in the cockpit as effectively as a coffin. He swore in frustration. It crossed my mind a ladder would be useful. Also, that he must not be discovered by his parents in this helpless state. The main point of his daring manner of coming home would be undone.

Getting him into the cockpit had been assisted by gravity. Getting him out required all my strength. Still, he had lost weight in the asylum. His once proud sportsman's muscles wasted away by inaction. With some strain to my back, I dragged him over the rim of the cockpit and onto the wing. After that, it was merely a question of swinging his legs round and easing him onto the grass.

'There you go,' I said, breathless. 'I'm sure they'll be along soon.'

He fixed me with his single eye.

'You don't know them like I do.'

'Oh, come, sir!'

'Stiff necks. Family failing, Young.'

'Well, it looks like pie is off the menu,' I tried to joke. 'Good job I packed some sandwiches.'

'Yes. Pie certainly *does* seem to be off the menu.'

I retrieved his stick from the plane and we waited in silence.

He limped over to the grassy bank of the river, staring moodily into the waters. A swift running stream for such a dry summer, with lots of swirling eddies.

'I used to swim here as a boy,' he said. 'You had to be damn careful. The current over there can pull you down. When I was a boy, one of the stable lads drowned there.'

From nowhere, I had a presentiment of tragedy. My eye was drawn to the dark centre of the river. Was Fitz thinking of himself drowning?

Of being dragged down by forces he had grown too weak to master, his useless arm and leg struggling in vain? There was no river more dangerous than time and where it delivers us.

I felt a need to talk. Ever since my walk round the city walls with Louisa when she posted her mysterious letter, I had thought of little else. It came back to me now.

'You once mentioned a fiancée,' I said, awkwardly. 'One night in the mess.'

'Ah, yes.'

He glanced back at the house.

'Know what, Young, it wouldn't surprise me if she was still prepared to have me.' He laughed bitterly, pointing his stick to indicate mansion and grounds. 'I'm still the heir to all this, you see. Even though my younger brothers are salivating to get hold of the estate. My family own half of Malton and Thirsk. Little wonder Pater gets elected as MP every time. I told you once before, Young, for most people it's all about money. Women in particular.' He looked at me queerly. 'D'you know, you're the only chap I've ever met quite above that.'

My turn to laugh. 'Well, I do need to work.'

'But you don't care about money, Young. Not at heart. When you turned up at the asylum, I thought, here we go. Baby down on his luck. Wants to touch me for a few pounds. I misjudged you badly. Always did. Always did.'

Tears touched my eyes.

'Thank you, sir.'

'Nothing to thank me for.' His brooding gaze returned to the house. 'All the other way around.'

Somehow I found myself talking hurriedly about Louisa. How we were walking out together. That I was considering a proposal to her.

'You see,' I concluded, 'it is rather complicated. She has a son already.'

I paused, embarrassed. Only a cad impugned the honour of a lady. Especially his potential wife.

'The piano girl at the cinema?' asked Fitz. 'Damn young to be a widow. War, was it?'

'Well, the son came about in a not quite regular way,' I said. 'Her fiancé – infantry officer, as it happens – got sent out before the knot could be tied. Never came back.'

He listened with full attention.

'Do you like her, Young?'

'I believe so. Very much. But somehow I wonder if I know her. Well enough, I mean.'

'From good stock, is she?'

'A cathedral dean's daughter, no less.'

'Are you asking my advice, Young? Chap to chap?'

I took out a cigarette. Was I? The idea was absurd. What would he know about it anyway? But yes, I was seeking his approval, if only to disagree with him.

'I suppose so.'

'Well, the business with the boy wouldn't stop me. Not if I liked her well enough.'

'Wouldn't it?'

I didn't believe him. Archibald Fitzclarence was more conventional than the Archbishop of Canterbury.

He chuckled in his gravelly way. 'Would have done once, I'll admit that. I've learned the error of my ways.'

I would have liked to hear more. At that moment, a Rolls Royce appeared on the track from the house, heading our way.

I was expecting Sir William and Lady Fitzclarence. In fact, the car's occupants were a chauffeur and a woman in late middle age wearing a nanny's uniform.

'Good lord,' he muttered, as the car pulled up by the aeroplane.

'I think your parents are not at home, after all,' I said, quickly.

He grunted.

When the woman got out of the car, she cried out at the sight of her former charge. Bonny, handsome little Master Archie had been replaced by an impostor. She began to sniff, brushing tears she could not keep in – and hated herself for.

'Oh, what have they done to you?' she sobbed, wiping her eyes with a corner of stiff white apron.

'Where are my parents, Nanny?' asked Fitz, ignoring her tears. 'Why did they not come?'

She pulled herself together, came over to where he stood.

'There, I'm quite done now, Master Archibald,' she said, in a kindly North Riding voice. 'It was just the shock. Let me help you back to the house. I've been told to help you with your dressings. Sir William wanted to remind you luncheon is at one o'clock. He would like you to join him in the drawing room half an hour before the gong.'

'Would he now?'

Hard to read as his face had become, I sensed understanding flow through Fitz like a dark stream. He knew now, or could guess, what he had returned to. The incomprehension and confusion, even horror his wounds would always provoke. Above all lingering, unspoken grief for a young man destroyed yet inconveniently alive.

By God, Fitz had been right to say his parents had no idea how to behave around him anymore. They were communicating through the servants and strict, unalterable household routines. Without conscious cruelty, they had deflated his dramatic return in a new-fangled aeroplane, symbol of the new age, his brave gesture of independence. He was not to be allowed even that. Not even that. Little wonder there was panic in his eyes: perhaps even despair.

The resemblance of Broughton Hall to Bootham Park Asylum took on a sinister shadow. Once through those doors, he wouldn't be coming out again. Odd trips, perhaps, for medical treatment, otherwise it was a life sentence. Once more I thought of the murky river.

Then I knew what I must offer. I could not leave him here. Burden as he was, in every sense – for I still did not find him pleasant company, however much we had shared – I could not abandon him to such a fate.

I touched his arm.

'A word in private, sir?'

He blinked at me like a wounded Cyclops. I led him to the other side of the aeroplane.

'Have you got your hip flask?' I asked.

He produced it, casting a wary eye at Nanny. She was spying on his every move. We took long nips and I lit a cigarette.

'Come back with me to York,' I said. 'You have lots of money for a decent hotel. This isn't your only option. I can help arrange it all. And find a nurse for hire to change your dressings. If we can't find anywhere with a vacancy tonight, you can stop in my digs at the Electric until you've booked a suitable place. There's plenty of room. Oh, and I won't take a shilling in return, in case you're wondering. Just say the word, sir.'

Fitz goggled at me.

'Are you serious, Young?'

'Yes.'

For long moments he considered my offer.

'You've never really liked me much, have you, Young?'

I did not know how to respond.

'We're very different,' I conceded.

'Thought so.'

He took another pull at the flask.

'Which is why I won't forget you making that kind offer,' he said. 'Thank you.'

With a harrumph, he turned to face the Rolls Royce. One thing was for sure about Fitz, neither Pater nor Mater – not to mention Nanny – would be getting things all their own way. A terrible anger burned beneath his apparent helplessness.

'Good luck, old chap,' he said, holding out his hand to shake. 'Stay in touch, I insist. In fact, I've got a little idea of my own for you. Seeing what you told me about that girl of yours.'

He laughed hoarsely. 'Remember when we joked with Gus and Smittie about Hell, Hull and Halifax, eh? You know, before each patrol. At least we made it this far, eh? Even if Heaven didn't care to preserve us.'

I squinted up at the sky. Dark clouds were gathering in the north. I sensed a change in the air. Time to get back to York. I was also troubled by the fuel gauge. Half gone from the tank – assuming the petrol gauge was reliable. Even the simplest instruments on those old machines could prove fickle.

'Well then, Young,' he said, 'ready for the off?'

I nodded, patting the leather flying helmet and goggles in my pocket.

'Don't like the colour of those clouds,' I said. 'I'd like to get ahead of them.'

He grunted approval.

'You always did get us there and back again.' He hesitated before adding, 'It was I who crashed our bus, not you.'

I met his eye. 'It was just a machine that stopped doing what it was told.'

'Perhaps. Still, I was the skipper, wasn't I? And the skipper is meant to get his crew safely back to port.'

His good hand shook a little as he clasped my own.

'I'd better see to Nanny,' he said. 'She's looking quite alarmed. And it wouldn't do to be late for luncheon. Pater is ever so punctual. D'you know, I've built up quite an appetite. Quite an appetite. Fly safe, Young, for us both.'

🎬

Take off turned out hairier than landing. Beatrice coughed as though deciding whether to stall. But I got airborne and swept low over Fitz. He was still waving his stick when Broughton Hall vanished behind me.

Then I was flying solo, no one to help me. Reliant on the same adrenalin and nerves you get playing a cadenza, a big audience before you, the orchestra sensitive to your slightest error. Here my audience was cloud vapour and air; my instrument a box of fabric, engine, wood, wire. Below, should I crash like Icarus, waited earth and fire.

Given the arrow of the petrol gauge, there could be no false turns. Nor did I waste fuel by climbing high. *You're good at this*, I assured myself, ticking off landmarks from a mental list.

Louisa returned again and again to my thoughts. It was days since I had seen her. In the meantime, I had called at 5 Princess Street twice. On the first visit, no one was home. On the second, Bertha Kettlewell answered the door. She had eyed me suspiciously, Freddy by her legs, staring up. The little chap was subdued.

'She's not 'ere,' announced Bertha, brawny arms folded.

'Do you know when she will be back?'

'She's away.'

'You mean from York?'

The charlady in her pinny and housecoat sniffed. 'I'm not sure it's any of your business, young man. Any road, she asked me not to tell a soul.'

The door had closed in my face.

Summer glinted from every shiny surface as I flew. Lakes and rivers, glass houses in gardens, railway lines. Because I flew low the tops of trees seemed like meadows waving and catching the sun. Children jumped up and down on a bridge as I passed overhead, arms windmilling. Fields of green crops gave way to valleys dusted with yellow flowers. It felt as though I was flying over summer itself.

Yet I felt a strong urge to be back in York; that city was where my destiny would be settled. I brooded upon an image of Louisa, imprisoned by the sooty brick walls of Princess Street and came to a resolution. One with the potential to redirect our lives forever.

The Minster's lofty towers appeared on the horizon and I traced the curves of the River Ouse to Clifton Moor. A bumpier landing than at Broughton Hall followed. Pulling myself out of the cockpit, I felt like a bird emerging from its egg. Or an egg emerging from a bird, take your pick. Something told me I would never play pilot again. I must fly in other ways.

Twenty-Nine

The black clouds I had glimpsed north of Broughton Hall pursued me to York. All night rain tapped the roof slates of my attic room, gargling through gutters. I sat by the card table with a pot of tea and cigarettes, imagining the future. Anticipation and excitement mingled to keep me awake. The oil lamp cast its soft glow and a candle drowsily burned out its nodding nimbus of yellow light. Around midnight, a scratch at the door announced a visitor.

I opened it to allow Clifton to come in. He sat on my knee purring, digging his claws into my legs as I absent-mindedly stroked his head. The rain must have lulled me to sleep; when I awoke in the armchair at dawn, the clouds had cleared. I took the weather-change for a sign. Clifton regarded me curiously as I stretched and yawned. It was as though he had watched over me all night.

I waited until mid-morning before returning to Princess Street. Louisa answered the door.

Dark rings rimmed her blue eyes. Voices from inside the little house revealed the faithful Bertha Kettlewell entertaining little Freddy with a nursery rhyme. He squealed his delight.

'Bertha told me you called while I was away,' she said, glancing at the neighbours' windows.

I hovered on the doorstep. Would she invite me in?

'I was worried about you,' I said.

She focused on me then, as though reading behind my face. Perhaps she noticed I wore my best suit and had polished my shoes. Whatever she saw resulted in a long sigh.

'I'm grateful,' she said. 'You have been a good friend to Freddy and I.'

Her dull, resigned voice fell queerly. Her mood was distracted, edged by fever, I couldn't tell which.

'Can you leave Freddy for an hour with Bertha? Come for a walk with me. I have something important to say. Let's walk on the city walls. It's your favourite place to think and make decisions, isn't it?'

'Perhaps it is too late for new decisions,' she said. 'I really do not want to walk on the walls again. But I'll go with you. You deserve to hear what I must say. You deserve that.'

'Let's walk by the river instead,' I suggested. 'It might ease your mind.'

Mine, as well. The river was *my* favourite spot for reflection: a flow of messages and life without words. Like music, I suppose.

We walked through that ancient city in our customary silence, past timber-framed houses on streets laid down by Romans and Vikings. We might have been ghosts passing through, leaving no trace of our footfalls. No echo.

We reached King's Staith, a cobbled wharf by the river where barges unloaded. Still I waited for her to speak.

Leaving the wharf behind, we joined a long riverside path through ornamental gardens called New Walk, once a popular promenade for Regency ladies and their beaux. The high walls of the castle and prison overshadowed us. Louisa took my arm, her pace quickening. I could tell her thoughts had reverted to the workhouse.

When we left it behind she slowed again, releasing another long sigh.

'David, there's so much I have to tell you – to tell someone – and you are the only person I know who might understand. But I'm afraid you will hate me.'

I shook my head. And squeezed her hand resting on my arm. 'I very much doubt that.'

'You are wondering where I have been these last few days, and I will tell you. First I owe you a confession.'

214

Again, I waited.

'David, sometimes a mother must, well, *dissemble* for her child's sake. In my case, for Freddy's sake. Do you see that?'

Given the rough start that lad had been allotted, I understood too well.

'That is why – oh, you *will* hate me for this, whatever you say – I lied about Freddy's father. To you and everyone. He was never my fiancé. Nor was he an officer who died in France before we could marry. Freddy's father did not die in the war. He did not even fight in the war. He is very much alive.'

Now I halted. 'I don't understand… '

She stood with head bowed. Speculations came feverishly. 'Louisa, you are married and he was a brute to you. Is that it? You fled here to escape, to keep Freddy safe.'

'No,' she said, 'we never married. He was never a brute.' She bit her lip. 'He was already married.'

'I don't understand.'

She helped me understand soon enough. I sensed Louisa wanted me to know her fully, without illusions. Perhaps telling her story was a test, a trial by honesty. So I believed. A test of my love for her. Maybe her own for me.

Hers was an old story, I suppose, ancient as Abelard and Heloise.

It began when she won a place at St Hilda's College in Oxford. Her father, the saintly Dean of Cloisters, had agreed reluctantly to bankroll her studies. The discipline she chose was Philosophy, with lashings of Latin thrown in for good measure. Her chief Latin professor turned out to be three decades her senior, but still young-looking and energetic.

'I admired him.' Her voice combined defiance and pride. 'He was so clever and encouraging. His conversation so lively. You see, he paid me special attention. One afternoon I called unexpectedly to his room – I wanted to return a book he had lent me – and found him distressed. I believed he had been crying. When I asked if he was unwell, he told me… He told me about his wife, who was an invalid, almost a cripple. He joked of her abominable temper, hinting that

215

even in her healthy days, they had not been suited. They were childless because of his wife's choice. Oh, I understood all *that* implied, I mean about their relations. Perhaps I was meant to. He... he swore me to secrecy, and said that he knew he could rely on my discretion. I promised that he could.'

The rest took its course. Maybe Louisa found a father-figure, her own being something of an unapproachable prig, far more interested in his clergyman son than his two daughters. Mutual attraction became a stolen embrace. A kiss. Until the inevitable happened. She never told me where. I imagine the deed occurred in his rooms at the college, overseen by beetle-browed philosophers in leather bindings. How many times? She gave no clue. Once would have been enough.

'You must not think of me as a victim,' she said. 'I loved him passionately. Or believed I did. I was so young, inexperienced.'

Then she fell pregnant. I could imagine the tearful scene – how he feared for his position and reputation in the world. Desperate, she sought her family's support, refusing to reveal the father's name, and was spurned. Then Louisa was ejected from the college. Lost and alone, feelings I remembered too well after my discharge from hospital. We were alike in that. In many things.

'He offered me one hundred pounds, David,' she said. 'At first I refused. You see, I was beginning to hate him a little, though I understood the awfulness of his position. But I took the money in the end. What choice did I have?

'Then, carrying the baby, I mean, Freddy, I came here. After that, everything I once told you is true. I came to York to seek the help of a friend from school in whom I had confided. But she had married and gone to join her new husband in Scotland.

'The rest is as you know it. The war seemed as though it would go on forever. I was employed by Mr Laverelli and came to live with kindly, dear Bertha.'

'Did Freddy's father know you were in York?'

'No, to him I had vanished. I did not want him to know anything about Freddy. I even kept his name from the birth certificate. You cannot imagine how beastly the clerk was at the registrar's office.' Her voice descended to a whisper. 'He treated me like, like a *whore*.'

She shook her head, as though to clear the memory.

216

'I was afraid someone would take Freddy from me,' she said, 'or place him in a private orphanage.'

'But his father might have helped you. Given money.'

'I did not want to live beholden to him.'

We had reached halfway along the gravel path of New Walk. Here, not far from the river bank, stood a moss-covered stone well house. Behind it, overlooking the river, a row of plush Victorian villas.

'People once believed this well could cure sicknesses,' I said, as we paused outside the dark, damp entrance of the well house. It contained nothing now but wet mud, moss and stones. 'Let's sit over there.'

The bench in question was on the embankment. For long minutes we watched the wide, slow river flow towards the ocean, world without end, over and over.

We could not think of our lives from such grand perspectives. Our time was too fragile, too short.

📽

'Is that where you went,' I asked, finally, 'these last few days? To visit Freddy's father?'

A dull ache had settled in my gut.

'Yes, I went back to Oxford. I had learned something from an old college friend. Something that changed everything. And perhaps nothing. She mentioned it quite casually in a letter, not knowing its significance.'

'What did she write?'

'That… It was very sad, she was an invalid, as I have mentioned, a cripple really – I mean Freddy's father's wife.' She paused. 'I learned his wife had died. A few months ago.'

My heart quickened. 'That means he is free.'

'Yes.'

'So you went to see him?'

A new strength entered her voice. Behind it lurked confusion, anger at the neglect she had suffered; and shades of fear.

'Yes, I did go. I went for Freddy's sake. Who would have thought Mr Laverelli might win his ridiculous court case. That my horrid job at the Electric would still be open to me.'

'So you asked for his help?'

I did not mention money. Perhaps Fitz's cynicism was right, after all. It always came down to money in the end.

'No,' she said, with a shade of triumph. 'He was very contrite, David. He claimed to have no idea of all I had suffered – though he made little enough effort to find me and his child while *she* was alive. He said he wanted more than anything to see his son. His "son and heir", yes, that was the phrase. But I... I said no. I may have sought him out now but I would not be taken advantage of again. I was no longer a silly girl of eighteen.'

Her voice quavered. 'I set him a test. Yes, to see if he was *really* worthy of my trust.'

'Did he pass your test?'

'I don't know,' she said, softly. 'We shall see.'

The facts were horribly clear: freed from an uncongenial wife, 'Daddy' could claim an attractive, fresh, fragrant replacement thirty years his junior. Complete with a ready-made family. Louisa had said his ex-wife refused to have children, implying he wanted them. *Voila!* Along comes Freddy, the perfect bargaining chip from Louisa's point of view. Logical enough and perhaps inevitable, yet sordid to my young, unworldly mind.

'What was your test?'

Did my own voice crack slightly at the question? I fear it did.

'I said he must come here to York, in person. That he must take us away from... this ignoble, common life I have been forced to lead.'

'He agreed?'

'Yes. He has promised to come tomorrow.' The note of wary triumph was back.

'And will he marry you?'

'Yes. He will. He has promised. In writing. Which, I believe, has legal force.'

My shoulders slumped. No need to ask if she had accepted his offer. The very fact of his coming to York was answer enough. One thing niggled beneath my surprise and distress. A clear, unbidden memory of the day my stepfather took possession of Father's old house, not least a grieving, frightened little boy.

'Then he must have decided to acknowledge Freddy as his son?'

Now Louisa grew confused.

'He cannot do that, David, the scandal would make his position impossible. I do not ask that sacrifice of him.'

'Not part of the test?' I countered, a little cruelly.

'No,' she said. 'He has promised to bring up Freddy as his stepson in the world's eyes. But Richard has assured me – you'd have no doubts if you had heard how earnestly he spoke, David, and took my hand! – he will treasure Freddy all the more for the deception.'

It seemed shabby to me. Shabby as hell. Oh, I knew the difference between a real father and a stepfather, how it would change Freddy's life, haunt him forever. To always be a bastard, inferior to others in just about everyone's eyes, grieving the supposed lack of natural ties with the man he was forced to call Daddy.

And if other children followed? Louisa had proved herself fertile. She would most likely desire more children to secure her position as wife. I was convinced her youthful fecundity must be a major part of her charms to him. Except then, Freddy would be doubly inferior to the 'legitimate' new-borns replacing him as the centre of attention.

'I suppose that means the poor officer-Daddy who never made it back from the front is back,' I said, bitterly. 'Is that what you will tell Freddy?'

She looked away from me in distress. Neither did she deny my guess. 'I knew you would hate me,' she whispered.

'This man,' I said, 'this philosopher, with his Latin and Greek and whatnot, should acknowledge his own son. Bugger the consequences. Anything else is cruel to Freddy.'

'I did so hope you would understand. I need someone to understand. Please help me, David.'

I was in full flow now. Twenty-three bars – and years – into the cadenza of a hopeless romantic.

'Do you love him?'

'How can I? After everything that has happened. But for Freddy...'

'So you are sacrificing yourself for your son?'

'Yes... I mean, no! David, I cannot live any longer in Princess Street. With its insects and smells and damp and hopelessness. It is not where I belong.'

'You do not love him, Louisa! You have just said so.'

She began to cry; silent, bitter tears. I saw how impossible she found every possibility.

'Other men will love you honourably,' I said, taking her hand. 'For the woman you are.'

Louisa stared at the river. For a moment her hand closed on my own. Then the bells of the Minster tolled the noon hour, long, reverberating booms over the city. She started. Released her hand from my own.

'I must go back. I must go back to Freddy. There is so much I must do.'

We retraced our steps along New Walk, back past the castle walls and prison. My head and heart were too full to make sense of all she had revealed. We parted near the towering bulk of the Minster. I watched her hurry away from me.

There is a perverse comfort in massive buildings like York Minster when you feel small. I found myself drawn through the South Porch beneath the famous Rose Window, stepping into the cool, gloomy interior of that ancient cathedral. Masonry shot up in pillars and cliff walls to arch across the painted roof. A sooty, grimy old place in those days, before the proper advent of electric light, illuminated mainly by candles and daylight filtering through the stained glass windows.

I took a seat on a pew facing the organ and ornate carved rood screen that hid the choir stalls. Few folk were around. York was not much of a tourist town straight after the war.

She had told me everything, I felt sure of that. I believed her honesty was a test to confirm my loyalty and love, just as she had presented a test to Freddy's father. One he had passed, if his word held good and he arrived to pick her up from Princess Street on the morrow.

Perched on my pew, I was confronted with a choice. Did I even wish to pass her test? Hers was not a praiseworthy story. Especially when judged by the harsh standards for women at that time.

Yet I could not condemn Louisa. *Her* mistakes had not cost innocent women and children their lives when a bomb flew astray.

Deciding to seek out Freddy's errant father and marry him without love was logical in the world's eyes. Indeed, it was prudent, wise.

So why did my heart revolt at her marrying for money and security? Too many ridiculous romances flashing on a screen, you might say, too many sloppy poems and novels with happy-ever-after endings. All to satisfy the lingering iris shot of love.

I rose and walked down the long cathedral, reading names and dates on tombs. No possibility of love left for them. Their dance with the seasons was over. All that remained were carvings on marble or granite, not even a living relative to recall their faces, moods, unique scents.

I paid sixpence to climb the Minster's central tower: a huffing, coughing climb for one who smoked and drank too much. Up there, I gazed at the ancient city below, its roofs and thoroughfares. Beyond that spread a haze of horizon brought closer by the overcast day.

There I made my resolution. It was not too late for me. My rival had not carried her away just yet. I would call on Louisa, first thing the next morning, before he arrived.

Thirty

I rose early to wash and shave. Once more my best suit was brushed down. The sun was braver than the day before: it gave me heart.

On the way out, I paused before the long mirror in the dressing room at the back of the stage. A slight patina of dust furred its surface. Since the crash I had avoided my own reflection but now I wiped the glass clean. A tall, rangy young chap was revealed, hair boyishly ruffled (I never went in for the hair oil fashionable back then), brown eyes sharp yet indefinably rueful. Mostly, I saw the purple, mottled stain running down the left side of my face and onto my neck.

'You're a fool,' I assured the Phantom of the Opera setting out to win a pretty girl's heart.

I walked quickly through the dark auditorium, its familiar smells of must and old cigarettes. In the foyer, Laverelli was directing a team of painters and decorators in anticipation of his spectacular reopening. One battle with Ernie Precious and the Grand may have been won, evidently not the war.

'I was hoping for a quiet word, Mr Young.'

He drew me to one side.

'I've plans to expand the orchestra when we reopen,' he said. 'Naturally, you'll be the one who auditions new players. And I mean to introduce variety acts between pictures, a comedian, performing dog, plate juggler, that kind of thing. What *The Biograph* is calling *cinevariety*. It's all the rage down… '

His voice trailed as he read my face and best clothes.

'Off anywhere special?'

There was no time for delay. My own rival might already be approaching Princess Street.

'I must go, Mr Laverelli.'

His face adopted a speculative air.

'Heading down the Groves, by any chance?' he asked. The shrewd devil! 'Well, give her my regards. Good luck to you.'

How much exactly did he guess? It was almost as though he offered his blessing. With my emotions screwed tight as a drum skin, I felt touched and emboldened.

I left him supervising the tradesmen.

'No, not there, Sid!' he cried. 'If I wanted a queue to block the ladies' lavs I'd hand out loo paper at the door.'

Down Gillygate then Clarence Street I hurried. How would she respond? Surely she knew my feelings by now. That was why she had shared her story. I must convince her of many things. How deeply I respected her honesty. How her intention to sacrifice herself for Freddy was needless. A loveless marriage with money would be far greater poverty than a little hardship with one who truly cared for her. The more I considered it, the more I convinced myself.

⬛

I had arrived in time. No car waited like Cinderella's carriage outside the narrow terrace of Princess Street. I knocked on the tatty door of No.5. It opened almost instantly, as though she had been hovering on the doormat.

Louisa wore a stylish, brand new travelling dress and coat, every inch the respectable young lady – proof significant cash from Freddy's errant Daddy had already flowed her way. A small pile of new bags lay in a pile in Bertha Kettlewell's tiny front room, obscuring the soggy horsehair sofa. I heard footsteps in the room above, Freddy's excited voice through the floorboards, followed by Bertha's broad York tones. He had been hidden up there like a new bride, to emerge when the groom – Daddy, in this case – arrived to claim him.

Louisa was pale, her face tense and drawn. A sleepless night showed round her eyes. She had removed her thick spectacles.

'I must speak with you,' I said, casting a wary glance over my shoulder. No sound or sight of a car yet, just a rag and bone man crying out his wares from a horse-drawn cart.

A-ny old ir-on! Clip clop. Clip clop. *A-ny old ir-on!*

'I cannot, David! You know who I am expecting. He may come early. You shouldn't be here.'

'I must speak with you. I insist. It is very important.'

A hopeless look came over her.

'Come with me then.'

She led me through the kitchen. How they had made that place shine! Demonstrating that although Cinderella may have been forced to dwell among ashes, they were jolly respectable ashes, poor but honest ashes. We stepped out into the backyard.

I sought out the sturdy fern growing from the wall. It still clung to the one window of sunshine penetrating that little house and yard. Still growing tough, fibrous leaves like a hand reaching for glimmers of sun.

Otherwise, the yard was just the same. Outside toilet and brick shed with a copper vat in which clothes were boiled. A small pile of coal in one corner. It would always be the same. Year after pinching year, until Louisa's youth and looks and hope faded. Or until I set her free.

She stood near the back door, listening for a knock on the front. So small was the house, she didn't need to listen hard. My throat tightened.

'Louisa, do you know why I have come?'

'I am afraid, David!'

'In your heart, you must know why I have come.'

I had her attention. She knew alright.

'Right now,' I said, 'the man before you might not seem much. And my face.' I waved a hand at it. ''Is not pretty.'

She listened, watching me.

'Louisa, I know my current station in life is not grand like that of some. Certainly compared to a professor. And at Oxford University, no less. But I am young, not without talent. I will rise in my profession. With a good woman beside me, I could rise very high. I have so many plans and schemes. The war... the war distracted me. But standing here before you, I am myself again. The man I could be.

224

Winning a good life for us both and Freddy would spur me on. It would cure my bad habits... '

'No, David... '

'Please, please, hear me out. You know Freddy likes me. And I would soon learn to love him dearly. I would cherish such a fine boy, give him nothing but encouragement. Think what I have told you of my stepfather's bad example. I would be the very opposite. I would be as loving as my own father was to me.'

'David, you must help me... '

'Louisa, I must speak now before it is too late. Before he comes. You see, I do love you. I wish to marry you. And build a life together. Sometimes I feel we are afraid of revealing ourselves to each other. The heart of ourselves to each other. And yes, we are different. But I believe we complement each other. I know how much your misfortunes make you dread poverty. But Louisa, I believe love to be the best sort of wealth. I learned that from its lack as a boy. Please accept what I have to give you.'

It was done. There was nothing more I could offer. Just the best of my self. Tears started to her eyes, glistening on her cheeks.

'Oh, David,' she whispered, 'why could you not make this easier for me? You are my friend. You have made it so hard now.'

I grasped her hand.

'It is easy. Marry me.'

'I cannot!'

'You can. It is easy. Marry me.'

'I... I dare not.'

She slowly pulled her hand from mine. Both of us were breathing in ragged gasps.

'It is too late,' she said, gathering her strength. 'I cannot. You must go, David. He will be here any minute. Please. You must go right now.'

I nodded. She was shaking, rubbing her eyes.

'Louisa,' I said, 'of course I'll go. But bear this in mind. All morning I shall sit at your old piano in the auditorium of the Electric and wait for you. All the time, I'll play *Hearts and Flowers* and *In a Monastery Garden*, even though I hate them like stink.'

She laughed despite herself, tears starting again.

225

'Please!' she begged. 'I must compose myself. You are making this so hard.'

I walked blindly through the little house and out into Princess Street.

On Lowther Street, my own eyes blurred. A long black limousine drove past, a chauffeur in the front and silver-haired man in the back. Distinguished as a statesman or bishop, he looked straight ahead, distaste for the neighbourhood written across his clean-shaven face. His car purred through the Groves. Slum kids in ragged clothes, some lacking proper shoes, chased after the limousine. Cars were rare enough in that part of town. This specimen was fit to carry King George. The long car turned slowly into Princess Street then was gone.

Images flashed in my mind like pictures on a screen. A crowd gathering outside the terrace houses as Cinderella was whisked away by her belated Prince Charming. Murmurs, whispers, even a scatter of applause when Freddy and Louisa emerged from No.5. There was something of the fairy tale about it.

'Now then, Mr Young!' called out a voice from a doorway. 'Seems I need to thank you for getting me a job.'

Thomas Bannering. The conchie. He had extended his hand for me to shake.

'You alright, Mr Young?' he called after me as I hurried past.

Wiping tears from my eyes – how ashamed I felt to weep in public – I kept on walking like Felix the Cat, weaving round a tank-like perambulator full of twins, an old lady with elephantine hips, a grocer's boy riding on the pavement with a basket of parcels at the front of his bike. I kept on walking, to get far from Princess Street, to escape the constriction threatening to choke me. I kept on walking, afraid no one would ever love me. That somehow, without quite knowing why, I didn't deserve it.

The auditorium of the Electric was dark as a tomb, save for the faint glow of an electric strip light attached to the piano's music stand.

There I sat. Hadn't I promised to wait? A dull emptiness in my spirit knew she would never come. Each minute carried her further away.

I could imagine them in the back of the limousine, specially hired by Daddy to truly pass Louisa's test. Little Freddy clutching his Mama while everything he'd ever known fled behind him. His first ride in a motor car! Such excitement. The poor kid had marvelled at a humble branch train to Leeds as though it was a rocket to the moon.

What about the severe, iron-haired man on the opposite seat? I heard him address his son in that patronising, benign way men unused to children generally do. I didn't doubt he was working out the swiftest method to part Freddy from his Northern accent. Sending him away to a boarding school would be just the thing.

And Freddy? The boy would sense Mama's anxiety about the stranger without understanding it. He had so little experience of men. His world dominated by two women and occasional visits from Davy McPurple Face, who bought him I Scream.

I brooded. Not just about Freddy. Louisa staring determinedly ahead into the affluent, respectable future she craved. The handsome professor's youthful wife, admired and maybe envied by the better class of girls admitted to St Hilda's College for an education before wedlock. You could guess the official line about their marriage taking shape. *So good of the Professor to take on the poor girl and her boy after his dear wife passed away... The little chap's father was killed in the war, you know, so sad... Yes, she was a former student of his. Must have made a big impression on him. Well, she's awfully nice, her father's a Dean of Cloisters, you know...* Polite, insincere murmurings while everyone knew the truth.

Clifton padded out of the darkness, his tail swishing. For once the cat did not seek a warm lap. He perched on the stage, lifted a leg and began to lick his backside. All the while he seemed to be watching me closely.

Voices reached me from the foyer: Laverelli remonstrating with the painters and plasterers. Even in the midst of desperate emotions, someone is always busy with their own affairs.

That thought made me try to see Louisa's choice through her own eyes. She had allied herself with someone of proven success and wealth. Little wonder she had turned her back on the Electric when all it offered was insecurity. To her, I was merely part of this dark auditorium trading in fantasy and dreams. For Freddy's sake she craved the reality of a solid suburban home and position in society. A housemaid. A cook. A car. Tennis parties on the lawn. Afternoon tea with the other ladies in an elegant tea gown. Dressing for dinner each night even when there were no guests. The vicar calling round to solicit her charitable contributions. Yes, that was it. She had chosen reality over the improbable.

Then suddenly it seemed alright. Or, if not exactly alright, bearable. Louisa had made the right choice for herself. Good lord, yes. Who was I, after all? The kind of chap who offered a small flat or house and called it romantic. Evenings spent alone with Freddy while I sawed away in some cinema or dance hall, returning and rising late.

When I was a boy there was a sweetshop where lemon drops or humbugs were weighed out on old-fashioned scales. The same kind of scales used to depict justice. Little ounce weights determined how many sweets filled the paper bag. I understood my weight on those scales. My place in the world. It was quite alright. I must convince myself her choice was alright. Because no one else would magically appear to shake me and say, *Bugger the scales!* Say to me, *Be happy with your own weight, heavy or light.* Say, *Be yourself. Unto thine own self be true.*

I sighed, weary of the dark auditorium. I'd let this place grow too familiar. Like Louisa, I wanted more than the Electric. I sensed my time there coming to an end. Perhaps I should join her on the long road south. Perhaps my proposal to her was my leaving speech to York. Wasn't your whole life a leaving speech, from the moment of birth?

Reaching out, I played a few idle chords. Then I noticed the briefcase of emergency music I kept by my stand. I'm sure my intention was to find something to pass the time – I had promised to wait until noon and, absurd though it might be, I clung to my word.

The first thing I discovered in the briefcase was the Woolworth's notebook full of hand-copied poems. The irony of it! Guileless *l'amour* oozed from those verses – the last thing I inspired in women. Leafing through the pages by the feeble illumination of the strip light I came upon one clearly authored by the notebook's owner.

YOU

Your Eyes.
Mysterious pools
Of gorgeous
Light.
Yet, alas!
They looketh at poor me
With less
Than delight.
Your Eyes.

Your Hands,
Fingers strong
And nimble
Like a deer.
Oh, harshest dream!
Your hands
Will not
Holdeth me, Dear!
Your Hands.

Your Kiss,
A daydream drear
Because afar, afar
As Bright Stars!
Oh, 'alas, Your Kiss,
YOU ne'er dream of
Burneth like fire
My dear!
Your Kiss.

I guffawed. The poem reminded me of intertitles flashed up on the screen each night between handwringing scenes – only set to rhyme. Its author must lurk in the sixpenny stalls between visitations from the Muse, sucking up Hollywood romance like one of those new-fangled vacuum cleaners.

In disgust, I tossed the notebook onto Maurice's chair near the piano, raising my hands to hammer down a diminished chord. It echoed round the hall.

Then came a creak. A fateful creak.

Behind me, the auditorium doors were pushed tentatively open. I sensed eyes upon me. I went still, staring straight ahead. My fingers hovered above the keyboard. I knew it must be her. Louisa had come! A long laugh formed in my soul. Of course she had come. Months of watching faithful hearts win through every night had taught us both the necessary ending. I had been a fool to doubt it.

Yet I did not dare turn. Not just yet. I felt shy.

I began to play, my heart beating harder with each phrase. What did I choose? You can guess, *In a Monastery Garden*, the piece she had played when I first watched her perform with Maurice Skelton after my journey from Hell and Hull. I embellished it with rills and runs and ornaments. It was my call to her, the nightingale singing in the garden. I offered myself to her through the music, and awaited her response...

Thirty-One

This morning I woke early and switched on the television. Such astonishment! A space rocket climbed through a roar of flame and smoke. Mankind reaching to the heavens, the sheer wonder of it! I grew moist-eyed, wishing my wife sat beside me to witness this miracle. She always thrilled at signs of progress. Part of the optimism that kept her young, right until the end.

Apollo 11! Astronauts in a tiny capsule, hurling themselves up into the atmosphere, just as Fitz and I and poor Gus and Smittie once risked flight. Except, those astronauts flew not for war, not to bomb women or children, or turn men into human torches. They flew for knowledge, science. They gambled their lives for all mankind. For truth.

I grew tearful all over again to see the Earth's continents and oceans unroll like a map beneath the camera, the moon rising from the curve of our planet as the spacecraft approached. Craters and arid seas reflected the sun. And then, there he was, a man, a mere man, walking on the moon.

When Neil Armstrong hammered the American flag into the moon dust I did wish it had been a different one. Not because I hate Americans, as some do since their war in Vietnam. I have worked with many wonderful American musicians over the course of my career and found them fine people. No, I longed for a flag that has never yet flown. One representing our whole race rather than a single nation. In that belief, I must confess myself influenced by my wife's deeply held convictions – it is heartening yet fragile how people endure through others when they are gone.

■

After a nap, and so much emotion, I walked along Chelsea Embankment to a favourite bench beside the river. Since retirement there has been time at last to really look around me. Of course, I know the area well. We bought the flat here a few years after the last war, our bank account bulging from the sale of several film scores. By then, the kids had left home to start lives of their own and we wanted a fresh adventure in the heart of the city. My wife always loved London, especially the West End.

In fact, my lucky break as a musician came in London not long after we married. The twenties were really beginning to warm up; anyone capable of happiness was busy putting that terrible war behind them. A happy time in my own life. I had secured a good job that paid well: first violin for the Savoy Hotel Orchestra, playing light music for diners and dancers.

One evening, I noticed a small party at a table near the front. Two young men and two women, all wearing the elegant evening clothes you expected at the Savoy. But the finest Saville Row tailors could not disguise Fitz's blistered face.

Between performances, I risked the wrath of the conductor by going over to pay my respects. Fitz was with his fiancée, who had come to London to order her trousseau from select couturiers. It was a brief enough conversation, but one that changed my life.

'Still sounding top hole as ever, Young.' Fitz's voice slurred. He was drunk, quite possibly to cope with the constant pain from his wounds. 'Good man.'

'Thank you, sir.'

'Glad I've tracked you down,' he growled. 'Only found out you were here through that wop chap you worked for in York.'

I had sent a postcard to Laverelli with our news not long before.

'Expect something in the post,' he said, swaying a little.

His fiancée took his arm sternly. 'You do look squiffy, darling. Perhaps you should go up to your room.'

He glared at her with his remaining eye and I feared a scene.

232

'Poppycock,' he muttered. 'Expect to hear from me, Young.'

At which point I resumed my place with the band. It was the last time I ever saw Fitz.

When his letter came a week later it contained a cheque. Enough capital to set up an orchestra of my own. Soon after, I secured a residency at the Mayfair Hotel in Berkeley Street and my career took off. Radio broadcasts, tours all over the country and on the continent, and later, with the advent of talking pictures, a profitable line as a composer and performer of film scores. My time 'fitting' films at the Electric had trained me well.

I can no longer put off how it ended with Fitz. We had lost contact a few years after his generosity changed my life. His fault not mine. I did write once a year at Christmas to update him on my growing family, but he never replied. He, too, was married by then and living with his wife and parents in Broughton Hall. He had learned to manage his injuries to some extent and even had a son of his own.

What happened was reported in the newspapers as a boating accident. I never believed that. For one thing, it transpired he had changed his will to leave me a strange bequest the week before. Namely, I should be given all his medals upon his decease. This I refused, saying they should go to his son.

I have often imagined what happened to him, piecing it together from the reported facts. Sometimes I dream of that fatal day in November.

It begins with scarcely bearable pain, as all his days begin. He no longer shares a bedroom with his wife; partly because he hardly ever sleeps, partly because he only married her out of duty. A duty fulfilled by producing a son and heir.

It is a grand bedroom with tasteful furniture and soft furnishings. But he loathes it like a prison cell. Standing at the window, he watches light mist creep across the parkland of Broughton Hall. The trees are bare. No birds sing save for the cawing of rooks.

This, he decides, is the morning to put into action a plan long contemplated. A plan that offers a respite from pain and frustration; from the polite revulsion and disappointment he inspires, most of all from those who love him.

Filling his overcoat pockets with coins, he takes his stick and limps painfully down the servants' staircase so no one encounters him, exiting the old house at the rear. Then he makes his slow way over the gravel walk, past fountains choked with ice and the remnants of windblown autumn leaves, to a path leading down to Mellor's Field.

Frost paints the grass white and stiff. His breath labours and steams from the exertion of walking. The friction of his shirt on his burned torso enflames the pain; his face itches as always. Determined, he walks as quickly as he is able, afraid he will be spotted and pursued.

At the river, he reaches the wooden jetty where boats are tied up. Tarpaulin covers them until spring and it is hard to untie the knots with one hand. He resorts to his penknife, sawing through the cord. By the time he has finished, he is exhausted, drenched with sweat.

One last task remains. He struggles into the boat, collapsing on the bench so that it rocks alarmingly. Gasping, breath coming in grunts and gouts, he manages to lift an oar, shove the little boat out into the lazily flowing stream.

It floats slowly, revolving in the current, carrying him through Mellor's Field until he nears the place where he once climbed out of a B.E.2c. His final flight.

The boat is over the deepest part of the river now, where grasping currents swirl. The place a stable lad drowned. Where once, even at the height of his youthful vigour, he felt himself pulled underwater and needed all his strength to make it ashore.

What does he think? What does he feel? How little it seems to matter in the end. He is not a man for deep thought; his nature made for action. Now there flashes across his mind images from another man's life, for he was not always this wounded, scorched shell. A boy running rugby ball in hand, shouldering aside all who block him to touch down between the posts. A handsome, uniformed young officer bowing to the King as he receives the Victoria Cross, his proud parents looking on.

Does he feel grief to know that young man is already dead, that nothing he can do now can kill him? Perhaps he registers the trees in their winter bareness and remembers how they rustled and smelt in the full leaf of summer. Perhaps he wishes that somehow, through some miracle, he could go back to being that young man. Even if only for an hour. Just as an old man might crave to reclaim beauty and youth. Reclaim the chance to live life again, without mistakes and compromises and misfortune's accidents, all the time aware it cannot be granted. Our lives are only ever an iris shot that shrinks from full screen, slowly, slowly, into a tiny dot of light in the blackness – until even that pinpoint of light, like a star in the infinite darkness of the universe, goes out.

Perhaps he wonders about love itself. How elusive it proved. Does he blame himself for being too selfish or distant or cold? No matter. It is too late to win love now.

Awkwardly, because even this final act cannot be done with grace, he rocks the boat back and forth, back and forth, the momentum gradually building, until it tips over. His heavy body, weighed down with layers of woollen clothes and coins splashes as it enters the icy stream. He does not struggle. His one good eye is closed. He is determined not to struggle, to fight the water. Even though his instincts command him, shriek at him to fight for breath. He will have this last victory. He gulps a lungful of water and sinks. Lungs burning, brain like a coal dimming, dimming, until its glow is ash.

That is how I imagine poor Fitz on his last day. Often when I think of him, I remember Esther Jones singing in the Cricketers Arms, her voice transformed by the power of music:

Soon we'll reach the shining river,
Soon our pilgrimage shall cease;
Soon our happy hearts will quiver
With the melody of peace.

It is late now. Very late. As I stand on the balcony of our flat, a ribbon of moonlight lies across the Thames. The day's warmth lingers over the city. Bright lights are fuzzy in the haze. Cars and buses pass and stray couples walk home together after an evening out.

Clifton appears and rubs against my legs. Stiffly, I bend to scratch his ginger fur in the place he likes best, behind his ears.

235

My story is not quite finished. Not yet. I'll fish out that whisky bottle and the old fountain pen I used for decades to write up scores. Even the Woolworth notebook with its faded, yellow pages has been preserved to give me inspiration.

Where did I leave off? The swing doors of the Electric Cinema's auditorium creaked open. A long, cautious creak. I knew, just knew who had come to find me. I played *In a Monastery Garden* – it could as easily have been *Hearts and Flowers* – with all the hope and yearning I possessed aged twenty-three. Believe me, a great deal. I faced the blank screen above my head while cautious footsteps drew near. I sensed her presence behind me. My breath quickened, grew shallow in anticipation. Then she spoke.

Thirty-Two

'You alright, Mr Young? It's just our Thomas said you'd come over poorly.'

Not for me Louisa's cultured, mellifluous tones. It was Gladys.

In a Monastery Garden ceased. I swivelled on my chair. She hovered nearby. Though her features were shadowy in the dim light, I detected concern, along with worry that she was intruding. You got what you saw with Gladys Bannering. She wasn't a one for keeping up a front to impress the neighbours. It's doubtful she cared what the neighbours thought at all.

She looked different without the usherette's uniform and hat. Older, somehow more dignified. Her cheap woollen midnight blue skirt and white blouse contrasted with the splendid new travelling outfit Louisa had displayed in Princess Street, waiting to be scooped from the life she hated. Gladys Bannering would never be scooped from the Groves. No matter how far life took her from that close-packed community. The Groves had seeded and brought her to fruition.

She stood with a kind of defiant pride, favouring one leg. As I have mentioned, Gladys Bannering had a certain way of assessing you.

I became aware Clifton was also watching from his perch on the stage. His cold, agate eyes glittered where the strip light caught a reflection. The damn cat seemed to be enjoying my discomfort.

She laughed her nervous laugh. 'I wouldn't have bothered you like, but I saw what happened. You know, in Princess Street. The whole of the Groves saw. Blimey! That car were bigger than the Lord

Mayor's. Bigger than a Zeppelin! Then Thomas told me you'd been round there to call on Miss Mountjoy, and that you... you seemed right – I hope you don't mind me mentioning it – upset. So I thought, perhaps, I should look in and just check – seeing I was passing.'

She went quiet. I regarded her with the animation of a basset hound. Wordlessly, I extracted a pack of cigarettes from my jacket pocket, and offered her one.

As she stepped forward to my match I caught a scent of her hair. She pulled back. We puffed away.

'I'm fine.'

'Oh, good. I thought I'd just check. Then be on my way.'

'That was good of you.'

She blew out smoke, her head bent up towards the screen, a hand rested on her hip. It was a pose I recognised from numerous pictures.

'Why not sit down?' I said.

'Are you sure?'

I gestured at the front aisle. Instead, she went over to Maurice's chair beside the piano.

'Well, if you don't mind.'

Glancing down, she cried out. '*There* it is! I looked for it everywhere.'

I followed her pointing finger to the Woolworth notebook of poems. I had tossed it onto the chair in scorn: unless it was despair. My basset hound expression deepened.

'Are you saying that book's yours?'

She laughed her little laugh. 'Who else's should it be? The milkman's?'

I watched her pick it up and flick through. 'Where did you find it? I looked everywhere. Actually, I worried some strange man would read it. You know, a nosy parker.'

I wasn't quite sure how to take that.

'Clifton found it,' I said. 'At least, he mewed and I went over to where it lay hidden under one of the back row seats.'

'Well, it were very good of him, I'm sure!' she declared.

A sudden thought made her blush. She took a hasty drag. 'You haven't read it though, have you?'

I could have lied. Very easily. The thing about Gladys was that she wasn't the kind of person you did lie to – without risking her being 'right disappointed' in you. Somehow, that was to be avoided.

'Yes, I have read it.'

'All the way through?'

'Pretty much. I like poetry.'

She wriggled on the edge of Maurice's chair then laughed.

'Oh well.'

'I never realised you were a poet. A bard.'

She shot me a quick look with her green eyes.

'There's a lot you don't realise about me.'

She was right. I had to admit that. Blinded by the snobberies of my suburban upbringing, I had hardly seen beyond her broad York accent and manners. Her faulty grammar. But was it so faulty when you considered? It was correct enough to communicate exactly what she felt. Correct enough to formulate her own opinions. Correct enough to find out about other people and learn from them. There she sat, a girl with the scantiest of educations, who had discovered poetry in a public lending library and copied out Byron, Shakespeare, Keats.

A thoughtful silence followed. We watched each other smoke in our individual ways. She took a pull without swallowing then blew out a quick puff. It was oddly appealing.

'Actually, I find poetry beautiful,' she said, defiantly. 'You didn't think I could like poetry, did you. Or think anything beautiful.'

Not a question, a statement. Never mind Louisa's little tests, here was one from Gladys Bannering. Whether I took her seriously.

'I seem to recollect,' I said, evading the question, 'old Johnny Keats saying "a thing of beauty is a joy forever". Or something like that. And a nightingale coming into it. Or a steadfast bright star. They usually do.'

For the first time that day, I smiled. She smiled too.

'Unless it's that one about a Grecian *urn*,' she said, flapping a hand at me.

The Yorkshire way she elongated the 'r' in *urn* sounded very musical. I was surprised I hadn't noticed it before.

Then Gladys apologised again for interrupting 'my practice'. She launched into a breathless account of all that happened in Princess Street. It transpired she had popped round to see Bertha Kettlewell and learned the whole story.

'It seems the rich uncle of her dead fiancé – you know, the poor infantry officer – heard about Freddy. It had been kept from him before. He drove all the way from London to pick them both up so that Freddy can have a proper life. It's like something out of a fairy tale.'

It was that alright. More than she could know. And I wouldn't be the one to enlighten her. It seemed even Bertha had been excluded. For some reason, I was the only person in York with whom Louisa had shared the true story. This puzzled me. Perhaps she had wanted to test me out, half-anticipating that 'Daddy' would fail his own test and not whisk her to Oxford like a mature version of Prince Charming. Perhaps I would have been the consolation prize. More likely, I was just being unfair and bitter.

To my surprise, Gladys was dabbing her eyes.

'Are you alright?' I asked.

'Oh, I'm just being silly.' She sniffed. 'You see, I always felt badly for Miss Mountjoy. I lost someone I loved of me own in the trenches. We was engaged to be married, as well, though we were both too young really. I was seventeen and he a year older. I didn't want Harry to volunteer, though I never told him. He was so proud of that uniform. He didn't last a month out there.' Her voice descended to a hoarse whisper. 'That rotten war.'

I listened, my neglected cigarette burning in my hand. Suddenly I recollected her crying when we watched *Comradeship* together at the Grand. At the time, I had assumed her feelings to be shallow, even false. Now I grasped her sincerity. Perhaps she even had a miscarriage like the girl in the film: hence her ruined reputation in small-minded, provincial York. And why the sentimental drama on the screen meant so much to her. The irony glared at me like a searchlight. While Louisa's lost love consumed by the mud of the Western Front was a convenient fiction designed to maintain face, Gladys's was stark truth. With all the lingering sorrow it entailed.

'I'm very sorry,' I said.

She attempted a small laugh. 'Oh, it were common enough back then. Four years ago now. It's hard to believe how the time's passed. We was both too young.'

I could see how that kind of tragedy made you grow up fast.

Then I recollected that I, too, was meant to be heartbroken. Gladys must have sensed my thought, for her expression grew solemn.

'Anyway,' she said, 'I'm glad to see you're alright, Mr Young. I was just passing.'

'It was kind of you to stop by and ask.'

She rose; I also stood out of politeness. Gladys looked up at the dark screen.

'Do you know, I always think there's something sad about it when it's blank. Like a mirror reflecting nothing back.'

'Just the darkness, I suppose.'

She smiled. 'Depends if you put the lights on.'

I became aware how small a pool of illumination the strip light on the piano cast.

'Funny, isn't it,' she said. 'The screen's just a piece of board covered with silver. But it lets people and places come alive. Stories that can never be. Stories you wouldn't imagine possible.'

I nodded. 'Not just people,' I said. 'What about cartoon cats. Think of Felix and how he keeps on walking.'

We both instinctively watched Clifton. He was licking his white paws.

'It's daft really,' she said, 'but so many nights I've stood at the back with my tray and imagined myself inside the screen. Far, far away.'

'In a place where there is always a happy ending?' I offered.

'Of course! What's the point if there's no happy ending? Or a chance of one?'

Such logic is hard to dispute.

'Though sometimes,' she said, 'when the picture ends it just makes you feel worse. When you wake up from your daydream. Do you ever find that?'

We stubbed out our cigarettes, stood awkwardly.

'It's very dark in here,' she said. '*Gloomy*, I'd call it.'

'I suppose it is.'

'Do you like sitting by yourself in the dark?'

I shrugged. Now there was a question. One, I realised, that should have come up far sooner.

'Not really. Who does?'

'I see.' One of her eyebrows rose. 'Why do you do it then?'

'Because… ' I grew confused. Because of the war. Yes, that was it. And because of Father dying when I was just a boy. And the oppressive years in West Ealing. And now, because of Louisa. She, too, would become another reason to sit by myself in the dark.

'I've got into the habit, I suppose.'

'Oh.' A tiny line on her forehead cleared. 'You could always switch on the lights, you know.'

'Mr Laverelli doesn't like to waste electricity.'

She laughed, not nervously this time. 'With all the money he's saving on our wages, the old skinflint can afford that much. He's sharper than a packet of pins, that one.'

I offered her another cigarette.

'You know there's a window, don't you?' she said.

'Where?'

'Here. In the cinema. Did you never notice it?'

It seemed there were lots of things I hadn't noticed.

'I'll show you.'

Gladys rose and walked over to the curtain that framed the screen. Pushing it aside revealed a rope and pulley with a little handle.

'Look!' she cried. 'I'll show you how it works. It's right clever. Look up!'

She cranked the handle so the ratchet clacked and clicked. A flat sliding door on coasters began to open. A line of light appeared above my head. It was like an iris shot. Not one where the picture shrinks to a dot then is black, blank, lifeless. The other kind. The happier kind. A shot of life that starts in darkness and opens out slowly to show the whole world in all its baffling glory. With each ratchet of the handle, more summer sunlight spilled into the shadowy auditorium. Textures on the tip up seats and carpets were revealed, the varnish on the piano gained a patina of light, even the silver screen glowed. As did our young faces.

She walked back to join me. Gladys Bannering had a certain way of walking. You might even call it grace. She stood in the pool of brightness beside me, smiling up at the skylight.

'See!'

I did. I saw. But I was looking at her. She was a thing of beauty alright. I don't mean her face. Or figure. Or her arch vivacity. True, they were appealing enough. I mean the soul that shone from her eyes as she gazed up, a natural well of hope. Some indefinable quality that just might be a joy forever.

'Gladys,' I said, 'you know in your notebook there's a poem called *You.*'

She stiffened a little. 'Is there?'

'Yes, there is.'

I waited for her to reveal what I wanted to know. Then I realised she was waiting for me to lead. All I had to do was ask. Even then I almost failed, afraid how fickle it made me appear when a few hours earlier I'd been asking Louisa Mountjoy to marry me. But I felt myself drawn onward. The auditorium was very quiet and still. Even Clifton had stopped grooming himself and was watching us. I asked.

'Who did you write it for?'

For a moment I thought she wouldn't answer.

'It's in the title,' she said.

I breathed out very slowly. Looked up again at the skylight. It promised to be a fine afternoon. One I was determined not to spend alone in the dark. I lowered the piano lid. Met her eye uncertainly. What harm could there be in asking her to join me for some fresh air, strictly as a friend?

By rights, someone heartbroken like me should make polite noises until she got the hint and left. Then mope around with a bottle for company. Besides, my past behaviour towards her could hardly encourage her to join me. I had been patronising and rude. Still, there's no accounting for taste. That much was in my favour. She did seem to enjoy my company enough to seek it out. And we did have something important in common. I was mourning for Louisa and Gladys was mourning for her lost fiancé. The *You* in the poem's title could never be me.

243

Ah, what tricks we play on ourselves. And that's not always a bad thing.

'Would you care to take a walk with me by the river?' I asked, abruptly.

Her eyebrows lifted.

'Are you sure?'

'If you are.'

'Oh, I'd love to!'

And we did. We did take a walk by the River Ouse as sunlight caught ripples and swans floated lazily. We did get to know each other better, little by little, laugh by laugh, month by month, talking about this and that – there was always something to talk about between us.

What of Louisa Mountjoy? I never heard from her again, though it would be a lie to say I never thought of her or little Freddy. As my career and prosperity blossomed, an unworthy part of me wondered if she knew. And whether she regretted turning me down when I was poor and unsuccessful. My name featured on broadcasts from the newly-formed BBC, as well as in newspapers and film magazines for a while. She might have read *Music by David Young BA Mus ARCM* at the cinema as the credits played. I thought of Freddy when air raid sirens wailed in September 1939 to announce another season of killing. He was just the right age to get conscripted. I hope he made it through. But the decades faded her memory until very recently when it came back to surprise me. I trust she was happy in the life she chose.

And Horatio Laverelli, what became of him? The Electric Cinema carried on trading in cheap dreams until he retired to Morecambe after the war. Ambrose and Esther Ackerley were with him until they, too, qualified for a pension. Laverelli was an old man by the time he sold the place, his life's work. Its new owner immediately changed the name to the Plaza. With my wife's connections to York, we made a point of fitting in a show at the Electric whenever we visited her family. Laverelli aged gracefully enough – and never quite succumbed to competition from the Grand.

But I was talking about my walk with Gladys by the Ouse, that summer afternoon, long ago. Both of us unaware that only a year later we would leave York together for London, man and wife, happy to start our family, the great adventure of our lives. I always got on with her father and brother Thomas, despite deep disagreements about politics. Maybe because of them: they loved a hot debate. Her mother proved a different kind of woman to my own. I soon learned from whom Gladys inherited her affectionate heart. Then came our children, three daughters to delight and vex us, each quite different and loved in different ways, followed by the inevitable grandchildren.

Most of all, it is Gladys I choose to remember. Though she died last year of cancer, quite suddenly, I still feel her presence beside me. I must do so until my time comes to join her. I always used to call her Glad, not Gladys, because that was how she made me feel. Though her education as a girl had been poor, she spent a lifetime making up for it. She was always brighter than me, more curious; always better informed. And when there were setbacks – we had our share of those – she carried our family through them with grace.

So you see, we did take our walk together by the river of this world. We did. And every moment meant more than we understood.

Life is very like a film, a succession of frames passing until the spool runs out. You now know the people behind the credits from this old man's youth. It's all here like in a script, set out in black and white. The other actors' versions of my story would be entirely different, of course. Thank goodness. Thank goodness for the gift of being uniquely human and gifted with free will to write our own script, until the lights come on when the credits roll, in the greatest show on earth.

The END

Acknowledgements

Behind every story are lifetimes of stories, and *The Electric* is no different.

I first met William Lea when I was in my late twenties in the mid-1990s. Bill was sixty years older than me, a widower living in a sheltered flat in West London. He was blind apart from a tiny sliver of peripheral vision. I had volunteered for a visitor scheme with the idea of going round once a week to offer some company and support. The volunteer co-ordinator warned me Bill had already 'got through' two other 'lady visitors': she hoped he would get on better with a man.

Her choice was wise. We hit it off from the start. Over several years we graduated from beers in his front room to the local pub and even to Proms concerts. Bill had a particular passion for music, arising from his career as a professional violinist. First, in silent cinemas and then, after the advent of the talkies, leading the band in a transatlantic liner sailing between Glasgow and New York. Finally, as musical director for civic orchestras all over Britain.

After such a diverse and long life, Bill had no end of stories. A born raconteur, he could talk for hours, and through him I learned about the lost art of the cinema musician. An interest that sparked years of research into how silent films were brought to life by a forgotten army of musicians.

This book is therefore dedicated to Bill. If I could thank him for all he taught me about resilience, generosity and humour when my own dreams were at their lowest ebb, I would – and clink a glass with him, as we so often did.

There are many other people to thank for *The Electric*.

First, the incredibly generous strangers – experts in the music of the silent cinema – I discovered through social media and websites. Neil Brand, in particular, one of the UK's leading silent cinema accompanists and film composers, maintains a wonderful website at *neilbrand.com*. Likewise, many thanks to Dr Chris O'Rourke from Lincoln University for information on the nature of early picture houses.

Closer to home, I would like to thank early readers of the novel who encouraged me to press on: Sara Bowland, Jane Collins, Richard Gray and Bob Horne.

A special thank you to Rose Drew, Alan Gillott and Caitlin Brown of Stairwell Books for their enthusiasm and creativity in publishing *The Electric*.

Finally, my thanks, as always to my wife, Ruth. Not just for her sharp eye with a draft, but for supporting my writing in incalculable ways over the decades.

Other novels, novellas and short story collections available from Stairwell Books

Needleham	Terry Simpson
The Keepers	Pauline Kirk
A Business of Ferrets	Alwyn Bathan
Shadow Cat Summer	Rebecca Smith
Shadows of Fathers	Simon Cullerton
Blackbird's Song	Katy Turton
Eboracvm the Fortess	Graham Clews
The Warder	Susie Williamson
The Great Billy Butlin Race	Robin Richards
Mistress	Lorraine White
Life Lessons by Libby	Libby and Laura Engel-Sahr
Waters of Time	Pauline Kirk
The Tao of Revolution	Chris Taylor
The Water Bailiff's Daughter	Yvonne Hendrie
O Man of Clay	Eliza Mood
Eboracvm: the Village	Graham Clews
Sammy Blue Eyes	Frank Beill
Margaret Clitherow	John and Wendy Rayne-Davis
Serpent Child	Pat Riley
Rocket Boy	John Wheatcroft
Virginia	Alan Smith
Looking for Githa	Patricia Riley
On Suicide Bridge	Tom Dixon
Something I Need to Tell You	William Thirsk-Gaskill
Poetic Justice	P J Quinn
Return of the Mantra	Susie Williamson
The Martyrdoms at Clifford's Tower 1190 and 1537	John Rayne-Davis
The Go-To Guy	Neal Hardin
Abernathy	Claire Patel-Campbell
Tyrants Rex	Clint Wastling
A Shadow in My Life	Rita Jerram
Rapeseed	Alwyn Marriage
Thinking of You Always	Lewis Hill
Know Thyself	Lance Clarke
How to be a Man	Alan Smith
Here in the Cull Valley	John Wheatcroft
Tales from a Prairie Journal	Rita Jerram
Border 7	Pauline Kirk
Homelands	Shaunna Harper
The Geology of Desire	Clint Wastling

For further information please contact rose@stairwellbooks.com

www.stairwellbooks.co.uk
@stairwellbooks

Lightning Source UK Ltd.
Milton Keynes UK
UKHW010506161022
410543UK00004B/140